"Will you read me a story, Daddy?"
Emily asked.

Daddy. It was the first time she'd called him that, and the feeling that flooded Devin stunned him. Like a fist to the solar plexus. He'd used the word himself in his thoughts, but somehow, hearing it from her made it more real, more special.

Devin opened his arms and Emily climbed up onto his lap, settling her head just under his chin. She smelled like her peach-scented bubble bath, all warm and fragrant. He gazed into green eyes as familiar as his own. The shadows of fatigue were gone from her cheeks, the sadness had disappeared from her eyes and she no longer woke during the night, crying for her mother. She also had the sweetest smile, he decided, as he opened the book.

Of course she would. She was his daughter.

Dear Reader,

It's going to be a wonderful year! After all, we're celebrating Silhouette's 20th anniversary of bringing you compelling, emotional, contemporary romances month after month.

January's fabulous lineup starts with beloved author Diana Palmer, who returns to Special Edition with *Matt Caldwell: Texas Tycoon*. In the latest installment of her wildly popular LONG, TALL TEXANS series, temperatures rise and the stakes are high when a rugged tycoon meets his match in an innocent beauty—who is also his feisty employee.

Bestselling author Susan Mallery continues the next round of the series PRESCRIPTION: MARRIAGE with *Their Little Princess*. In this heart-tugging story, baby doctor Kelly Hall gives a suddenly single dad lessons in parenting—and learns all about romance!

Reader favorite Pamela Toth launches Special Edition's newest series, SO MANY BABIES—in which babies and romance abound in the Buttonwood Baby Clinic. In *The Baby Legacy*, a sperm-bank mix-up brings two unlikely parents together temporarily—or perhaps forever....

In Peggy Webb's passionate story, *Summer Hawk*, two Native Americans put aside their differences when they unite to battle a medical crisis and find that love cures all. Rounding off the month is veteran author Pat Warren's poignant, must-read secret baby story, *Daddy by Surprise*, and Jean Brashear's *Lonesome No More*, in which a reclusive hero finds healing for his heart when he offers a single mom and her young son a haven from harm.

I hope you enjoy these six unforgettable romances and help us celebrate Silhouette's 20th anniversary all year long!

Best,

Karen Taylor Richman
Senior Editor

Please address questions and book requests to:
Silhouette Reader Service
U.S.: 3010 Walden Have., P.O. Box 1325, Buffalo, NY 14269
Canadian: P.O. Box 609, Fort Erie, Ont. L2A 5X3

PAT WARREN
DADDY BY SURPRISE

Silhouette®

SPECIAL EDITION®

Published by Silhouette Books

America's Publisher of Contemporary Romance

This book is dedicated to Perry and Ginny Huellmantel,
old friends and traveling companions, with affection

 SILHOUETTE BOOKS

ISBN 0-373-24301-4

DADDY BY SURPRISE

Copyright © 2000 by Pat Warren

Visit us at www.romance.net

Printed in U.S.A.

Books by Pat Warren

PAT WARREN,

mother of four, lives in Arizona with her travel agent husband and a lazy white cat. She's a former newspaper columnist whose lifetime dream was to become a novelist. A strong romantic streak, a sense of humor and a keen interest in developing relationships led her to try romance novels, with which she feels very much at home.

Chapter One

If there was one thing Molly Shipman hated it was arriving anywhere late. The kitchen clock indicated that she had exactly seven minutes to get to her appointment with Della Bailey, her friend, Trisha's, mother and the owner of a roomy duplex on a quiet residential street in south Scottsdale. She'd gotten up at six just so she wouldn't have to rush. Of course, if she hadn't dripped orange juice on her blouse, necessitating a change, or broken a nail opening the coffee can, she'd have had time to spare. As it was, she had to fly.

Stuffing the last bite of toast in her mouth, she grabbed her large canvas bag before racing down the outside stairs of her apartment building. She unlocked the door of her eight-year-old Honda and got in, wondering why she ever bothered to lock it. Nobody but the truly desperate would steal old battered Bessie.

Sending up a silent prayer, Molly turned the key in

the ignition and breathed a sigh of relief when the tired
old engine wheezed into life. Just two more paychecks
and she'd have enough saved to take old Bess in for a
much-needed tune-up.

Whipping out of the parking lot, she turned onto
Thomas and headed east. If only this rental would turn
out to be perfect, or nearly perfect, Molly mused. According to Trisha, who waitressed alongside Molly at
the Pan Handle Café, the recently vacated house with
an upper and a lower apartment had just had a face-lift
consisting of fresh paint and new carpeting. Mrs. Bailey, who lived next door and used the income from
several such homes to supplement her Social Security,
always kept up her properties.

The mid-April sun was already quite warm as Molly
made a right turn, her mind racing. Since learning that
her apartment building was converting to condos, she'd
given notice and been searching for a place not too far
from her job because old Bess couldn't be counted on
for long daily trips. Good rentals at reasonable rates
were hard to find and the lower unit sounded ideal. She
was sick of the three flights of stairs she'd had to climb
several times a day for the past three years. Molly
hoped no one else had spotted the For Rent sign and
beaten her to the punch. Reminders of the early bird
getting the worm buzzed through her anxious thoughts.

A quick glance at her watch told Molly she was only
a few minutes late as she swung onto Cactus Lane. As
she completed the turn, a noisy Harley came zooming
around the bend behind her. The driver wasn't wearing
a helmet, she noticed in the rearview mirror, his dark
hair shifting in a soft morning breeze.

Slowing, she turned into the drive of number 9430
where, thankfully, the sign was still in the lawn. The

two-story stucco house with its southwestern style, red-tiled roof was set back from the street leaving room for a small lawn and several old cottonwood trees that provided much-needed shade. Mrs. Bailey was waiting on the porch and raised her hand in a wave. Molly turned off the engine and got out. But before she could take a step, the Harley pulled in alongside the Honda, blocking her path.

Unhurriedly, the rider dismounted and engaged his kickstand. Arizona sunshine reflected in his mirrored sunglasses before he took them off, tucking one stem inside the opening of his white knit shirt. Molly found herself staring into the greenest eyes she'd ever seen.

He didn't look like her idea of a biker, she thought, dressed conservatively as he was in clean jeans and very white Nikes. His square chin—sporting a deep dimple—looked as if it had been carved from granite, hinting at a stubborn streak. His gaze was every bit as measuring as hers. An unexpected sensual pull lasted mere seconds yet took her completely by surprise. Why was this man following her? Molly wondered, her pulse slightly erratic.

"Do I know you?" she asked, though she doubted very much she'd have forgotten this man.

His smile softened his hard image, his teeth gleaming white against his tan face. "I haven't had the pleasure," he answered, holding out his hand. "Devin Gray."

From the corner of her eye, Molly noticed Mrs. Bailey shuffling her feet impatiently. But she could hardly ignore the man's offer to shake hands. "Molly Shipman," she said, noticing that her fingers barely touched his skin before her hand was engulfed by his. Oddly fascinated, she stared at the contrasts, pale to tan, small to large, soft to hard.

He was the first to break away as he nodded toward the house. "I'm here about the rental. You, too?"

Molly swallowed around a dry throat and took a step back. "Yes." Did she want to share a house with a ruggedly handsome biker? she wondered. However, she might have no choice in the matter, she realized as he fell in step beside her on the walk to the porch.

"Hello, dear," Mrs. Bailey greeted Molly.

"It's good to see you," she told the older woman, then stood aside as the newcomer introduced himself.

Della Bailey patted her short hair, which was dyed a becoming ash blond, and smiled at both young people. "I hate to rush you two, but I'm being picked up shortly by a friend. We're going to the Indian reservation casino to play bingo."

Molly knew Mrs. Bailey since she often came into the café to visit her daughter. She also knew that the widow had two passions: bingo and kids. A retired schoolteacher, she baby-sat several neighborhood children after school.

"We wouldn't want to hold you up," Devin said, opening the screen door for the short little woman to lead the way into the lower apartment. He watched Molly Shipman walk past, her eyes avoiding his. She seemed a little nervous and he wondered why.

"As you can see, this unit's unfurnished," Della began, showing them through a good-sized living room, one large bedroom and an old-fashioned kitchen with wooden cupboards. The smell of fresh paint was evident.

Not bad, Molly thought, checking out the living room with its tiny corner fireplace. She'd have to get rid of the heavy drapes, get something light and airy. She strolled on, admiring the cozy window seat in the bedroom, the bright blue carpeting, the sunny kitchen where her plants would thrive. Yes, it would do nicely. Best of all, no stairs to climb. As soon as Trisha had told her about the place, she'd hoped she'd like the lower. "I have my own furniture," she said, opening the refrigerator, pleased at how spotless it was. When she looked up, she noticed that Devin Gray was studying her far more than the apartment, which brought a frown to her face. Was this man going to be a problem?

Devin could see by her expressive face that Molly Shipman was already moving in mentally. "Is the upper furnished?" he asked as Mrs. Bailey checked her watch. He had a few things, but he'd moved too often to drag along a houseful of furniture.

"Yes, and it has its own entrance and stairs in the back." She led the way onto the back porch and pointed to a door at the far end. "That's the laundry room. You'd have to share." She started up the stairs. "The upper's rooms are a bit smaller, but there're two bedrooms. I believe you said you needed the extra room." Devin followed her.

She'd already decided she wanted the lower, but it wouldn't hurt to look at both, Molly thought as she trailed after them. Her gaze naturally fell on Devin Gray's broad muscular back, the way the faded denim fit over impressive buns and long, long legs. Quite a package, her feminine side couldn't help registering. But not for you, her practical brain reminded her.

Along with the usual appliances, the kitchen contained a small oak table with two chairs and checkered linoleum that looked newly installed. An archway opened into a square living room with a couch and pole lamp along one wall. A short hallway led to two small bedrooms and a bath. A double bed, dresser and nightstand were in the largest room, but the other was empty except for a studio bed.

"I suppose I should say this unit's semifurnished," Della said as Devin examined the second bedroom. "You mentioned you work from home. Is this large enough for what you had in mind?" she asked, peering at him through her new bifocals that she still evidently hadn't gotten used to.

"It's fine." Devin turned from the window. "Is that pool in the lot next door yours?" She'd told him on the phone that she lived one house over. "It's not exactly the ocean I'm used to in California, but it sure looks inviting."

Della smiled. "Use of it comes with each rental. I keep the gate locked so no children will wander in, but give all my tenants a key."

Just what he needed, Devin thought. His job consisted of putting the seat of his pants on the seat of the chair for hour after hour. Without regular exercise, not only would his muscles cramp up, but he'd start getting wide in the beam. "That's great," he told Mrs. Bailey.

He'd been staying at a motel since arriving last weekend. Last night, he'd driven around this neighborhood and found it quiet with a minimum of distractions. No basketball hoops or garages or kids playing in the street. There were also several restaurants within a few blocks for nights he didn't feel like cooking, which were many.

The apartment was only temporary, of course, a year at the most. But for now, it suited his needs perfectly. "I'd like to take the upper." He took out his wallet and started counting out bills, then handed her a folded sheet of paper. "And here are the references I mentioned."

In the doorway, Molly felt a frown form. Devin Gray wasn't someone she'd choose to have live above her. He didn't look like someone who worked indoors. She'd wager he'd once been a California surfer from his tan and mention of the ocean. Carefree and seductive, she assumed from the looks he'd been throwing her way. Pretty successful at it, too, she imagined from that killer smile. He was too big, too masculine, too self-assured.

If the apartment wasn't ideally located and priced right, she'd walk away. However, she'd handle it. Mr. Charm would soon learn she wasn't the least interested. She'd been fending off men like him for over three years. Trisha had once said Molly had turned rejection into an art form. Molly took that as a compliment.

"I'd like to take the lower, Mrs. Bailey," Molly said, reaching into her canvas bag for her checkbook. "First and last month's rent all right?"

"That would be fine." Della strolled to the kitchen, pleased that her vacancies were no more. "Maybe I'll see more of my daughter with you practically next door, Molly," she said with a laugh. "She works too hard."

Molly was aware that, like so many single mothers, Trisha needed every cent she could scrape together to support herself and her eight-year-old son, Danny, even though the two of them lived rent-free in one of Della's houses several blocks over. The boy's father sent support checks only when the ponies were running well. Still, Trisha had that great kid, which was more than Molly had wound up with from her disastrous marriage.

But she wasn't going to dwell on that today. Ripping out the check, she handed it to Mrs. Bailey. "I'll definitely have Trisha and Danny over as soon as I get settled. I can move some boxes in tonight and the rest tomorrow, if that's all right."

Della held out a small ring with two keys on it. "It's yours, honey." She turned and took the money from the tall man as well and handed him his keys. "I'll check out your references and if everything's okay, I'll have your lease ready tomorrow. Oh, wait. You said you'd prefer to rent month-to-month, right?"

"Yes. That's why I've paid you for three months in advance, the first two and the last month's deposit."

"That's fine." They walked out onto the porch overlooking the fenced backyard.

Molly's gaze took in the grassy area with a clothesline stretched between two poles and a small shed at the back. "I'd like to plant a garden at the far end, if you wouldn't mind. Maybe some flowers. I've lived on the third floor of an apartment building for three years and I've really missed having a yard."

"You're welcome to garden, if you like," Della said, heading for the stairs.

"One more thing," Devin said, aware that his new landlady was anxious to get going. "I forgot to mention that I have a dog, a German shepherd, yard trained. Naturally, I'll pick up after him, even cut the grass. King's a good watchdog, as well. Hope that's okay?"

"I like dogs," Della said, "as long as they're well behaved." She heard a car pull into her driveway next door and her friend's horn honking. "You two can work things out between you about sharing the yard. Molly, I'll have your lease ready for you to sign tomorrow. Trash pickup's Friday and cans are in the back shed. I've got to run. See you later." One hand adjusting her glasses, the other on the railing, Della made her way down the stairs.

Devin turned to Molly Shipman and saw she was frowning. Again. Much as she had been throughout their tour. He wondered what was bothering her.

A dog, Molly thought. A *big* dog. She liked animals well enough, though she preferred smaller breeds. "German shepherds are large and sort of scary. I have a Brownie troop, eight six-year-old girls. We meet once a week at my home and do projects." Her sister had talked her into being a leader awhile back and Molly had to admit she enjoyed working with the girls. But she couldn't afford to be sued by a parent over a dog bite. "I'd hoped to be able to use the yard for some meetings."

Once a week? Just what he needed, Devin thought. He knew from long experience that kids were noisy, accident prone and could create messes in minutes. There went his nice quiet neighborhood. However the apartment was just right and he was tired of looking. He tried a reassuring tone. "King's good with kids. He's friendly, even gentle. But I'll keep him inside with me on the days you need the yard for your projects." As for the garden, he didn't add that King would probably eat the petunias and dig up her vegetables.

What could she say in the face of such a reasonable attitude? Truth be known, it wasn't the dog that had Molly concerned, but rather his owner. The way those green eyes looked at her, looked *into* her, as if trying to read her thoughts. She'd just have to avoid him, that's all. With her work schedule and outside projects, that wouldn't be so difficult.

"All right, I'll hold you to that." Another glance at her watch had her digging out her keys. Hank Thompson, the café's owner, frowned on his people being late. "Well, I guess I'll see you around then." She flashed a brief, distracted smile and skipped down the stairs, heading for her car.

Devin leaned back against the porch railing and watched her. Did he really want to live practically on top of such an attractive woman? Molly Shipman, with that head of shiny blond hair, eyes the blue-green of the sea on a cloudless summer day and a body even her plain white blouse and black slacks couldn't disguise would be an unwelcome distraction.

He needed the place he lived and worked in to be a quiet haven with no diversions or temptations. Molly wasn't overtly tempting, but he'd always been drawn more to the subtle than the obvious. Her staid costume and offhand manner had him more interested than if she'd been wearing something skintight and acting flirtatious. Or was his interest centered in the fact that he'd been single-minded about his work for so long, to the detriment of his social life?

Straightening, Devin breathed deeply and could still smell Molly's scent, a light fragrance that suited her perfectly. In those big blue eyes, he'd spotted a keen intelligence, a definite wariness and something else. Something shadowy where a vague sadness lingered. It would be challenging to see if he could discover more.

Perhaps having an attractive woman one deck below wouldn't be so bad, after all. He could ask her up for dinner, conversation, a little touchy-feely tension reliever. Maybe he could…

Annoyed with his thoughts, Devin ran a hand

through his hair and frowned. He was here to work, not play. His deadline was a mere three months from now. He'd best keep that in mind.

He locked the door and left the porch.

Molly arrived at the Pan Handle Café and noticed from the big clock above the counter that she had five minutes to spare. She caught Trisha's eye and made a circle with her thumb and forefinger, indicating she'd gotten the rental. Trisha winked her acknowledgement before lowering the heavy tray and turning to serve her customers.

Molly waved at Hank at the cash register, greeted the short-order cook by name and walked on past the ladies' room to the back locker area. The air-conditioning was set on high, but with all the heat from the kitchen, it was fairly warm inside most of the time. Quickly, she stashed her bag and fixed herself a tall iced tea with lemon. It was too hot for coffee some mornings. She sipped it slowly, glad that the breakfast rush hour was tapering off.

She was aware that many people looked down on waitressing, but as far as Molly was concerned, it was honest work that she enjoyed and was good at, and the tips weren't bad. The Pan Handle was located in a small strip mall that bordered an enclave of older, well-kept homes peopled mostly by young families and year-round retirees who kept the ten booths along the windows, the six counter stools and the eight tables filled almost constantly. Word-of-mouth also brought tourists to the café with its down-home cooking and reasonable prices. And then there were the truckers who'd first discovered Hank's place. Molly enjoyed the diverse clientele.

Of course, that didn't mean she intended to spend
the rest of her life waitressing. The people she worked
with were aware that she was taking night classes, but
only Hank knew that she'd attended the University of
Arizona on a full scholarship and quit in her senior year
before getting her degree. Foolishly starry-eyed, she'd
rushed headlong into marriage. Four years later, divorced and on her own with no job skills to speak of
despite years of schooling, she'd faced a frightening
reality check. Although she'd had a variety of part-time
jobs for spending money during her college days, she
was poorly qualified for a steady full-time position.

After many long days of job hunting and being
turned down mostly for a lack of experience, she'd
stopped in at the Pan Handle for a cold drink and spotted the Help Wanted sign. Her smile shaky, she'd told
Hank that she'd never waitressed, but she was a quick
study and she badly needed a job. He'd hired her on
the spot, earning a permanent place on her grateful list.

Of course, Molly worked hard and earned every cent
she made. In three years, she was only two courses shy
of enough accounting credits to take the state CPA
exam. Dreams of her own company, her own business,
kept her going through all the hours on her feet serving
others and the late evenings she did typing, charging
by the page. When that day came, she'd set up her
office, hire a staff, eventually get a reliable car and
maybe even a small house of her own.

Molly Shipman had vowed she'd never be beholden
to anyone for anything ever again.

"So, you moving in soon?" Trisha asked, joining
her after turning in two orders.

"I've got the weekend off." She squeezed her
friend's hand. "Thanks for telling me about your

mom's vacancy. It's perfect. Another hour and it would've been snatched up." As she'd driven away from the duplex, a young couple had stopped their car, eyeing the sign Mrs. Bailey hadn't bothered to remove and taking down the phone number. "I owe you."

"I'll settle for a cold drink. It's been a madhouse in here since six." Trisha bent to rub her sore calves.

Molly poured the drink, adding two sugars for energy the way Trisha preferred her tea. "Tell Danny the living room has a cable TV hookup for when he stays over." A tall, slim brunette, Trisha was outgoing and dated a lot, often leaving her son with Molly evenings when her mother was unable to keep him. Molly had taught Danny to play chess and now he was beating her regularly.

"Will do. He'll be thrilled." Trisha took a long swallow, then left to check on her orders.

Time she got to work. Setting aside her glass, Molly put on a bright smile and walked to the front to greet an older couple who were regulars.

Hank's gaze slid to Molly Shipman and his face relaxed. Of his three full-time waitresses, it was Molly who pleased him most. He enjoyed just looking at her. He watched now as she delivered an order to an older couple, then went to pour coffee all around for three truckers in a front booth. He saw their eyes wander over her slender frame, frankly admiring, boldly appraising. She laughed at something one of them said, then politely dodged their comments and one wandering hand as she wrote up their order. Little did they realize that no matter what they said or did, Molly wasn't buying.

Unlike Trisha who flirted outrageously and dated frequently, in three years, Hank had never seen one cus-

tomer get to first base with Molly. Oh, she was friendly
to everyone, some more than others, but there it ended.
She always went home alone and her phone number
was unlisted. Hank didn't know the story of her marriage or the reason for her divorce, but he figured she
had to have had a rough time. Never once did she speak
of those years. Divorced himself, he understood, but at
nearly fifty, it wasn't so surprising that he didn't want
another go around. But Molly was only twenty-eight,
too young to want to be alone.

If only he was a little younger, Hank thought uncharacteristically dreamy. Then the scowl returned and
he called himself a fool. What would a lovely young
woman want with a slightly pudgy guy with thinning
hair and a bad hip? He'd better keep such thoughts to
himself if he wanted to keep Molly as a friend and an
employee.

Molly stepped up to the service counter and raised
a questioning brow. "You okay, Hank?" she asked,
wondering at his grimace as she handed him her order
slip. Hank was usually easygoing.

"Hector's going to be late," he complained, blaming
his mood on that.

"Oh. If you need me to stay longer…"

That was Molly, always willing to help out, but he
couldn't let her do that. "Nah, we'll manage. I hear
you're moving."

"Yes, tomorrow."

"I'll get my nephew to help. We'll go to your place
with the truck. Is seven good?"

He'd known she'd been looking and had offered to
help her move in some time ago. Still she hesitated,
hating to accept favors and remembering that Hank had
a bad hip. "Listen, Hank, you don't have to…"

"That's right, I don't. I *want* to. Seven?"

She gave him a grateful smile. "If you're sure."

"Positive."

"Then thanks." The bell over the door rang out. Molly swung around and waited for the new arrivals to seat themselves before going over with menus.

Carefully placing the last box in Bessie's trunk, Molly closed the lid and paused to gather her shower-damp hair into a ponytail. Only April and already the daily highs were in the eighties, quickly approaching ninety, with four or five more months of summer ahead. You had to love heat to live in Arizona, she thought, settling behind the wheel. Fortunately, she did. She'd liked the weather in Colorado, too. She'd left for other more important reasons.

The car was loaded—trunk, backseat and even the passenger side—with boxes and bags containing nearly everything from her cupboards. If she could get her new kitchen in order tonight, she'd be ahead of the game, leaving tomorrow free to figure out furniture placement. Not that she had that much, just the neces-sities and a few luxuries that she'd managed to pur-chase over the last three years. But at least it was all hers.

She'd left her ex's house without any of the lovely wedding gifts that her mother and sister had insisted were half hers. She'd taken not a plate nor pot nor pan from the kitchen, not a favorite photo or designer suit or piece of jewelry. Only her own things, though not the expensive clothes and jewelry Lee had gifted her with. She'd wanted no reminders of him or his mar-velous family.

Even with no tangible evidence of her four-year marriage in the small apartment she'd moved into, it had been many months before she'd been able to sleep through the night without waking and remembering. Many long weeks when Lee's hurtful words kept replaying in her head like a broken record spewing out a litany of her shortcomings. Endless days when she'd had to force herself to quit hiding and leave her small sanctuary to look for work. Though Lee had never laid a hand on her, she'd felt beaten up and beaten down.

But that was then and this was now, Molly thought, starting up old Bessie and moving out into traffic. She was beginning a new chapter in her life, a new place to live and, hopefully in about a year, more meaningful work that would lead to a bright future. She'd read somewhere that you can handle anything as long as you know one day it'll end. That thought kept her going.

The sky over the McDowell Mountains was streaked with orange and purple in preparation for one of Arizona's spectacular sunsets. Tonight Molly scarcely noticed as she flipped on the radio and heard a bluesy voice sing about moving on. She laughed out loud. Yes, that's exactly what she was doing, and it felt good.

She was humming along when she turned into her new driveway and saw that her neighbor's Harley was parked alongside the backyard fence. And there, guarding the gate, his black eyes on her and his ears on alert, was the biggest German shepherd she'd ever seen.

Slowly, Molly got out of her car, wondering if he could jump that fence, wondering how fast she could run after a long day on her feet. He was beautiful, she couldn't help thinking, but dangerous-looking. His coat was mostly tan with black markings and he hadn't moved a scant inch, just stood watching her. Drawing in a deep breath, Molly decided she'd best make friends with him if they were to share a yard. Determined not to show any fear, she walked closer.

"Better let me introduce you," Devin said, coming down the back stairs. "If you're with me, King knows you're okay."

"Fine," Molly said, never taking her eyes from the dog.

Devin paused. "You know much about dogs?"

"I've never owned one, if that's what you mean."

He walked over to where she'd stopped. "Some dogs, especially trained guard dogs, consider eye contact to be an act of aggression."

"Oh." Molly's eyes shifted to his face. "I didn't know that."

"Many people don't. Even a smile can be a problem because when dogs go on the attack, they bare their teeth. So they sometimes mistake a smile where teeth are showing as a challenge."

"I see." She glanced over at the dog whose stance seemed more relaxed since Devin's arrival. She avoided his eyes. "I thought you said he was friendly, even gentle."

"He is, once he gets to know you. Let me take you over and he'll know you're a friend."

Molly walked with him, her gaze fixed on the fence rather than the animal she didn't want to give the wrong signals to. At the gate, she felt Devin stop and move close behind her. He took her hand in his, then stretched toward the big dog.

"Hey, King," Devin said in a firm voice. "Meet Molly, our new neighbor." He drew Molly's hand closer to King, allowing the dog to get familiar with her scent.

A scent that seemed oddly familiar to him already.

She'd changed into denim shorts and a loose-fitting black shirt. Her bare legs were long and shapely. Devin felt his pulse stumble.

Molly's breath backed up in her throat, whether from nervousness about the dog or because the man she'd met mere hours ago was all but wrapped around her. Her head only came to his chin. He was so tall, exuding a sense of power, yet making her feel oddly protected.

She watched the big animal sniff her hand, glance up at her, then lick his owner's hand once with his pink tongue. After a moment, he touched his wet nose to Molly's thumb. "Does this mean we're friends?" she asked, wondering if everyone who came to visit her would have to go through this ritual before being accepted.

"I think he likes you," Devin said, his voice a little husky. His face was almost in her hair, as he drew in a deep breath. He could smell shampoo and bath powder. "Did you just shower?"

The question surprised her. "Wouldn't you, after eight hours slinging hash, so to speak? First thing I do after every shift is strip and shower." Molly's eyes grew round as her words echoed in her head. Why on earth did she blurt out every thought so graphically?

Devin's fertile imagination pictured the shower scene perfectly. He glanced down at her small hand resting in his. He found himself not wanting to let go of her.

Molly felt her fingers grow damp with nerves. It had been years since she'd allowed a man to get this close. "How long must we stand here like this?" Molly asked, looking over her shoulder at him, a smile appearing at the absurdity of the situation.

"Two hours, three at the most." He grinned, squeezed her hand and reluctantly let go.

"Well, that was fun," Molly said to cover her embarrassment, "but I've got boxes to unpack."

"I'll help you," he offered, walking with her to the car.

"Thanks, but I can manage just fine."

Stubborn, independent and beautiful, Devin decided. She'd soon learn he could be stubborn, too. As soon as she opened the trunk, he lifted out what he guessed was the heaviest box.

"I told you…"

"Yeah, I know. Look, you've put in an eight-hour day, right? Mrs. Bailey tells me you're a waitress and I know that's hard work. I've done my share of slinging hash for tips and minimum wage. There are no strings attached if I haul in a few boxes for you, honest." Holding the heavy container, he waited while she studied his face. He could almost see the wheels turning while she tried to figure out whether or not to believe him.

Molly didn't want to set a precedent on the first day sharing this house with him, allowing him to think she was some helpless female who'd be ever so grateful for his heavy-handed help. She'd let him, this time, but she'd set some ground rules.

"What else did Mrs. Bailey tell you about me?" she asked, picking up a second box and heading for the back door. Maybe she'd have to have a little chat with her landlady about being less than pleased at being Topic A with her other tenants. Molly hadn't been crazy about living in the large three-story apartment complex she was vacating, but at least a person could remain anonymous there if she wished. And she definitely wished.

Devin waited until she unlocked the door, then followed her into the kitchen and set the box on the counter where she indicated. "Not much, just that you waitressed at the Pan Handle with her daughter. Is the food good there?"

He was pretty adept at controlling the conversation, she decided. "Since I eat more than half my meals there, I must think so."

"I'll have to try it sometime," Devin answered, following her back out to the car.

Molly waited until every box, bundle and bag was inside her new kitchen before turning to him. "Thanks. I appreciate your help." She turned aside and began measuring shelf paper she'd brought along, obviously dismissing him.

"Where do you want to stack these canned goods?" he asked, poking around in a sack.

He was either obtuse or being deliberately annoying. Molly stopped and drew in a deep, calming breath. She checked her watch, then looked up at him. "Look, I've been on the move since six this morning and it's nearly eight. It's been a long day and I really want to get this done tonight. So, if you don't mind..."

"It'll go much faster if we do it together. I moved my stuff in earlier and it takes forever if you work alone." Devin wasn't sure why he wanted to help her. Maybe it was because he was a nice guy. Or maybe it was because she looked dead on her feet and he knew how that felt. More likely it was because she attracted him and it had been a long while since anyone had.

Scissors in hand, Molly studied him. He wore a V-neck black T-shirt and tan shorts, a generous sprinkling of dark hair visible on his muscular legs and what she could see of his chest. She'd never been especially drawn to obviously virile-looking men. Why then did this one interest her despite her usual reluctance? "Are you always this insistent?"

Grinning, he shrugged. "Sometimes even more so."

Damn but he had a dynamite smile. He was wearing her down and she was too tired to argue. "Just my luck." She indicated the long cupboard at the far end. "Cans in there, if you insist."

Chalk up one for our side, Devin thought as he opened the pantry cupboard. "Any particular order? Want them alphabetized or arranged by category, like fruits one side, vegetables opposite?"

Though he had his back to her, Molly sent him an incredulous look. "You've got to be kidding? Do you honestly do that in your kitchen?"

Still smiling, he began unpacking cans. "Yeah, but it's real easy at my place. I have two cans of soup and one box of microwave popcorn." He studied the can he held. "Spaghetti sauce. Funny, I'd have bet you made your own sauce from scratch." His mother always had, even while raising six kids and working full-time.

Carefully, Molly stretched to fit the shelf paper she'd cut in place. "Fast and easy, that's my style. Actually, I've never mastered the fine art of cooking. Growing up, my mom cooked, then at college, our landlady was a terrific cook." And when she'd married Lee, he'd tasted one or two of her efforts and hired a cook, but she decided not to mention that. "Today, with all the shortcuts available, you can eat really well and not know how to do much besides read the labels."

He glanced over, taking in those incredibly long,

sleek legs. "Yeah, but I thought all women knew how to cook, like it was in the genes or something."

"Sorry to explode that little myth."

Devin finished emptying one sack and went searching for another from where they were stacked on the floor while Molly went to work on the second shelf.

"Where in California are you from?" she asked. All right, so she was a little curious about him.

"The L.A. area." He unloaded boxes of crackers, pancake mix, pasta. "How about you? Are you a native? It seems everyone I talk to in Arizona was born somewhere else."

"Not me. Born and raised in Phoenix."

"Never lived anywhere else?" He found that hard to believe. She didn't look small-town and, by Los Angeles standards, Phoenix was almost backwoods.

"I lived in Tucson during my college years. And, for a while, in Colorado."

He caught the change in her tone at the mention of Colorado, the reluctance. "Not a happy time?"

Her head swiveled to him. He was too quick, a man who actually listened, not just to words but to voice inflections. It was unnerving. "No, it wasn't."

Molly was grateful that he apparently decided to let that alone. They worked in silence for awhile, until she finished papering the shelves and bent to retrieve the dishes she'd carefully wrapped last night. She stretched to reach the top shelf while her sore muscles protested, but she ignored them, as usual. When there was work to be done, Molly just did it.

She'd almost forgotten he was there when he spoke up. "Are you just off a divorce?"

Surprise and irritation warred for dominance in her blue eyes. "What makes you ask that?"

Devin shrugged. "You're skittish, kind of secretive, touchy. And you have a sad expression around your eyes when you think no one's watching you."

Stopping with a dinner platter in her hand, Molly frowned. "What are you, a psychiatrist?"

He had the decency to look sheepish. "Worse. I'm a writer."

"Figures. Well, save your psychoanalysis for your characters."

"I'm right then. You've just gone through a bad divorce."

"Your vibes are a little off. It's been three years."

"Whoa! Three years and you're still so testy. Must have been bad."

Molly had had enough. "Let's turn the tables here. What about you? Are you married? Have you ever been? Divorced? Children? How is it that you're probably at least thirty and still renting furnished apartments? Bad relationships or just bad judgment? And how do you enjoy the third degree?" Letting out a whoosh of air, she ran out of steam. Turning aside and brushing back a lock of hair that had come loose from her ponytail, she set the platter on the counter with unsteady hands. "Oh, Lord. I'm sorry. I have no right to go on the attack. I hardly know you. I must be really tired." One hand braced on the counter, she stood with her eyes downcast.

He stepped in front of her. "It's all right. I goaded you and I deserved your tirade. I apologize. Occupational hazard. I have this insatiable need to know everything about everyone I meet. Gets me into a lot of trouble, as you can see."

She still hadn't looked up, so he went on. "To answer your questions, I'm not married, never have been, and no children. I'm thirty-three and I left California mostly because I have this big, overwhelming family and I need a quiet place so I can write without interruptions. I've had a few relationships, one in particular that lasted quite awhile, but when she realized I meant what I said when I told her I didn't want the house, the picket fence or the two-point-five children she had in mind, we parted quite amiably. Bad judgment? Yeah, I'm guilty of that occasionally, but who isn't?''

"Certainly not me," she said so softly he had to move closer to hear the words.

Devin dared to reach up and touch her chin, forcing her to face him. "I'm sorry if I was out of line, Molly. Don't be angry, please." The word fragile came to mind. He hadn't figured under all that bright energy that she'd be fragile.

His eyes were the color of jade tonight in the glare of the overhead kitchen light. So deep a green they were almost black. Maybe she was being taken in, but they also seemed sincere. "I'm not angry, just tired. Let's forget it."

Turning to gaze about the kitchen, Molly saw that only two boxes of dishes remained unpacked on the floor. "I think it's time to call it a night. I'll get to the rest tomorrow." She walked over and picked up her canvas handbag, then snapped off the overhead light.

Standing in the moonlight on the back porch, she locked the door, then made a mistake. She looked up at him again and their eyes collided and held. Molly saw far more than she wanted to see in those green depths.

Slowly, Devin trailed a fingertip along the silk of her cheek and saw the pulse in her throat leap. "You're going to be a distraction I don't need, Molly Shipman.''

"No, I'm not. I don't want to get involved with you, with anyone. I want you to ignore me as I plan to ignore you.'' She stepped away and didn't look back. "Good night.''

Walking to her car, Molly wondered if she had the fortitude to stick to her guns.

Chapter Two

Devin turned off his computer with a nod of satisfaction and leaned back. It was working just fine, thank goodness. His computer was the only item he'd carried up the stairs and into his spare room with the same care he might have shown delicate bone china, if he had any. In a way, computers were just as fragile. Unexpected jarrings or, God forbid, a near-drop and all that intricate wiring inside could cause the loss of a great deal of important data. Whole files could be erased or be extremely difficult to retrieve.

With all the many moves in his travels, fortunately he'd never had a problem. But he'd heard horror stories about systems crashing and motherboards that needed replacing after relocation. So he babied his equipment as if his livelihood depended on each and every component part. Because it did.

Stepping back, Devin gazed around his new office.

The computer desk was in place along with his lucky chair, a somewhat beat-up old leather swivel that he'd sat in to pound out his first fiction pieces back when he was writing short stories on an ancient portable Smith-Corona. He had a sleek electric typewriter now as backup on the long table that also held his printer, copier and fax machine. Amazing the machinery a person had to have to write today. He'd read that Ernest Hemingway had carted an old portable Underwood all over Europe and done fairly well on it. But this was the nineties.

Devin strolled over to his bookcase filled to overflowing with reference material, books dating back to his college days and a shelf of well-read paperbacks he couldn't seem to give up. With a sense of awe that was still very present in him, he reached to the top shelf and picked up his first published book, *Murder at Oak Creek Canyon.* Never had he seen anything more beautiful than his name above the title or his words and thoughts inside.

For as far back as he could recall, Devin Gray had wanted to write. And he had—essays, a journal, stories, even some very bad poetry—for his eyes only. Then, as a student at the University of Southern California, he'd met a professor who'd recognized his talent and encouraged him. In the beginning, he'd written short stories, nine his first year after graduation as he'd traveled all over the southwest, working all sorts of odd jobs to pay for rent and food. After two years, they'd finally begun selling. The income wasn't much but the euphoria of seeing his name in print kept him going.

Devin lovingly ran his hands over the dust jacket. He'd kept moving, traveling, learning, researching. A hundred short stories later, he decided to try a novel.

His love of the west combined with his fascination with mysteries led him to concentrate on western mysteries, which only a handful of authors were writing at the time.

He'd hired an agent who'd begun submitting his work to various publishers. It had taken three years—three long, hard years—before his first book sold. The following year, he'd published the second just as the first was published in paperback. Now, at long last, he was on his way, contracted for two more for more money than he'd dreamed possible.

Replacing the book alongside his second novel, Devin anchored them between two brass owl bookends, gifts from his father. He strolled into his living room, stopping to look out the large double windows. He could see Camelback Mountain in the near distance, serene as always under a clear, sunny sky. He'd visited many parts of Arizona in his travels, and fallen in love with the redrock country he used as the backdrop for some of his books.

Recently, when he'd decided it was time to leave the hustle and bustle of Los Angeles for a variety of reasons, he'd picked Scottsdale on the eastern border of Phoenix. Because it was small enough, western yet hardly provincial, classy yet homey. And it was only an hour's flight to visit his family if he got the urge.

Here he could live quietly with a minimum of interruptions and only an occasional pang of guilt for not being at the beck and call of his huge clan. Devin loved his parents and five siblings and their spouses and his eleven nieces and nephews. But there was total bedlam when all the Grays got together, which was often enough to distract him big-time. They all seemed to thrive on chaos where he preferred quiet solitude. He'd decided to rent for a while and see if he liked the area well enough to build his dream house here. Already Scottsdale felt like home.

The almost constant sun rose early these days, and he'd been up with it, arranging his television set across from another old favorite, a stretch-back leather lounger. He'd hooked up his stereo in his bedroom and unpacked a few family pictures he set out in every apartment he'd ever occupied. Devin took a moment to study one framed photo of the entire clan taken at his parents' anniversary party last year. There was no denying the Grays, for they all resembled their father with his black hair, green eyes and that prominent cleft in a square chin.

His mother was a lovely woman, but not one of her six offspring had inherited her blond hair, fair skin and blue eyes. Yet she'd been the guiding force of the family, working long hours alongside her husband at the family hardware store, making sure it succeeded, then grew from one store to two, then three and finally six. She'd run the household of six children strictly, relying heavily on the help of her eldest, Devin. She'd piled a lot of responsibility on him at an early age and he'd come through, always there for household chores, baby-sitting, often discipline. Even attending college, he'd lived at home because the family had needed him. Perhaps that was why he'd escaped into travel soon after graduation.

It had felt good, being on his own. Yet even on his travels, he'd been constantly called home for this emergency or that disaster where his help was needed. When he'd settled down in an apartment clear across town, they'd taken to inviting him over or dropping in constantly, hanging on the guilt if he begged off. He'd felt hounded, smothered. He'd simply had to get away.

At the moment, he didn't even have a phone, though they'd promised him service Monday. He'd put in an address change at the post office, but he was going to guard that information for awhile. He wouldn't put it past several members of his family to come charging over to check out his new digs. An unmarried son, no matter what age, was always fair game.

Through the window, he saw Molly's Honda turn into the drive followed by a truck stacked high with furniture. Molly pulled up close to the back door, then quickly jumped out and walked over to the two men getting out of the pickup. One was tall and thin, young enough to still be in his teens, wearing a baseball cap backward. The other was middle-aged and balding with the start of a pot belly. Quickly the three of them began unloading furniture.

Should he go down and offer to help? Devin wondered. Last night, he'd helped her in the kitchen because he was curious about her more than anything else. She'd made it perfectly clear that she didn't want his assistance, as she probably would again if he went down. If solitude was what he wanted, if noninvolvement was what he'd decided on, if being left alone to do his work was his primary goal, then he'd best stay away. After all, she had two guys to give her a hand.

Who were they? he wondered idly. People she'd hired? Relatives? Friends? Surely Molly wasn't romantically involved with either. He watched as the teenager's eyes followed her as she reached into the truck and hauled out a lamp. Devin couldn't blame the kid. She was wearing another loose cotton shirt over jeans and white canvas shoes. Her face was free of makeup and her hair was pulled back and anchored with some sort of plastic gizmo. She looked about sixteen. Devin saw her smile at the boy before walking away and noticed the teenager's face redden. Poor kid had a crush on her.

Stepping back, Devin decided he could spend his hours more gainfully than watching his neighbor move in. He walked into his office, pulled out his chair and stared at the computer. From somewhere below, he heard a laugh drift up. Female, smoky, mellow.

What the hell! They'd finish faster with another pair of hands. He started for the stairs.

Devin saw that the two guys were in the pickup untying a dresser before unloading it. "Hi. I thought you could use a hand."

The kid wearing the baseball cap turned toward him. "Uh, yeah, sure, I guess." He glanced over at his uncle.

Hank glanced at the newcomer. "We can handle it, but thanks."

Real friendly, Devin thought. "I'm a neighbor," he said by way of explanation.

"Uh-huh." Hank concentrated on untying a snagged knot, obviously hoping the man would go away.

Annoyed, Devin picked up a kitchen chair that was standing alongside the truck and carried it onto the porch. The screen door had been taken off the hinges and placed off to the side. Giving a quick warning knock on the doorjamb, he walked in and spotted Molly in the kitchen. He strolled closer and saw she was setting up a small bowl that held an assortment of colorful stones, a hunk of fern and a blue fish nervously swimming around. "Hey, there," he said, not wanting to startle her.

Wiping off the bowl, she looked up. "Hey, yourself. Meet Jo-Jo, my beta fighting fish. My niece named him."

Devin set the chair down and leaned over for a closer look. "He doesn't look very scary like a fighter should."

"He would if you were another fish. These little guys are so mean you can't put more than one in a bowl or they'll kill each other." She scooted the bowl into the far corner of the kitchen counter and stood admiring him.

"So you got him for protection, eh?"

She smiled at that. "Actually, I got him because I wanted something alive in the house…" She waved toward the other side of the room. "…other than my plants."

She did have plants, Devin thought, gazing at two hanging baskets, a tall ficus in a red pot and several small containers along the two windowsills containing African violets. "They must keep you busy watering and trimming." He didn't have a plant or a fish at his place. Only his dog who right this minute was whining in the fenced yard wanting to inspect the men unloading the truck.

Devin set the chair he'd carried in next to a white pine table, noticing in the sunlight that poured in through the windows that she had a sprinkling of freckles across her nose, something he hadn't seen last night. They made her look even younger. "I came down to see if you needed another pair of hands."

"Molly," came a gruff voice from the open front doorway, "you wanna come show us where you want this dresser?" The burly older man was sweating profusely and staring at Devin none too friendly-like.

"Sure, Hank." She hurried ahead of the men, moving into the bedroom and pointing to the wall where she'd decided her dresser would go. Stepping aside, she waited until they'd set down the heavy piece, Hank grunting with the effort. "That's perfect. Thanks."

Wiping his broad forehead with a soggy handkerchief, Hank made his way back to the living room. "We're going back for the living room stuff. You coming, Molly, or are you staying here?" His eyes shifted to Devin as if reluctant to leave her here with him.

"If you don't need me, I think I'll stay and make up the bed and put things away." She noticed Devin standing in the archway. "Devin, this is Hank Thompson, the owner of the Pan Handle, and this is his nephew, Jerry. They volunteered to move me. Hank, this is…"

"Yeah, I know, your upstairs neighbor. We met."

Wondering why this guy was so curt with him, Devin decided to give it one more shot. "You sure I can't help? I'd be glad to go along." He tried a smile. "I've got a strong back."

"We've got things under control. Be back soon, Molly." Stuffing his kerchief into his back pocket, Hank followed his nephew outside.

Frowning, Molly watched them get into the truck. "That was a little rude," she commented softly, wondering why her boss was being so unfriendly. "Hank's usually not like that."

"Maybe we were enemies in another life."

"He's a little protective of his girls, as he calls the three waitresses who work for him." Molly checked several boxes on the floor, searching for the one filled with linens.

Or maybe good old Hank had designs on Molly himself and wanted to issue a warning. "Is he married?"

"Divorced. The Pan Handle seems to attract divorced people. Every one of us except Hector, the evening shift cook." Hoisting the box, she headed for the bedroom.

Curiosity had Devin following her. "Do you and Hank...you know...date?" The man surely was acting territorial. Of course, it was none of his business.

Molly removed the mattress pad from the box and tossed it onto the bed before raising her eyes to Devin's face. Studying him, she recognized that unmistakable male-female interest in his eyes that she'd become aware of last night on the back porch, and wondered what to do about it. She didn't want to be as rude as Hank, but that sort of thing could become a problem, living so close as they would be. And it had absolutely nowhere to go. Perhaps it would be kinder to lay it all out for him once and for all.

"No. I don't date Hank. He's a good friend and old enough to be my father. I don't date anyone else, either, for that matter." She waited for the disbelief, the inevitable questions. She'd been down this road before.

Moving to the opposite side of the bed, Devin automatically grabbed one end of the mattress pad and began pulling it into place. "You don't date *anyone?* I guess your ex really did a number on you."

Intent on making him see, Molly adjusted her side of the pad to fit. "Actually, my decision has little to do with him." Which wasn't exactly true, but close enough. "I simply don't have time. My work at the café, including quite a bit of overtime some weeks, keeps me very busy. I take night classes on Tuesdays and Thursdays at Arizona State, except the summer session. During tax season, I work part-time for a CPA. With all that, I scarcely have time to get in six hours of sleep, much less a date.'' She reached for the pale-peach fitted bottom sheet, wondering why she was bothering to explain herself to this stranger.

Maybe because he was so damn persistent.

Grabbing his side of the sheet, Devin bent to maneuver it into the upper corner. ''C'mon, Molly. Everyone needs a little R-and-R now and again. Haven't you heard about all work and no play making Jack—or Jill—very dull?''

Why was it that men thought that their mere presence in a woman's life would change dull to unbearably exciting? ''I take time for myself. I have friends, two in particular, former college roommates, and Trisha. I go shopping with my mother, have an occasional dinner out with my sister, take my niece to the movies. Oh, and sometimes I baby-sit Trisha's little boy when she goes out. I watch television, read, garden. I think my life's pretty full.'' She sent him a challenging look.

He didn't let her down. ''Were you always so reclusive, content with work, family, friends and TV? Don't you get lonely for a one-on-one with a man? You probably dated a lot before your marriage. You had to have. I mean, a woman like you...''

Molly's head jerked up from securing her corner. ''What do you mean, a woman like me?''

Devin straightened, wondering why she was so defensive. ''I mean a woman who's very attractive and obviously intelligent. Why would you choose to spend all your free time with your mother, old college friends and a couple of kids?''

She *had* dated a lot in college and some after she'd

first walked away from Lee. The problem was that by the second date, indeed if they'd waited that long, they'd been all hands and pressure and a wet, seeking mouth. So she'd stopped dating, stopped hoping there was someone out there who could care for her for all the right reasons, a mature man who was his own person. One who could love a flawed woman with a trampled heart.

After three years, she'd about convinced herself that no such man existed, and she didn't want the other kind.

"It's just easier, that's all." She picked up the top sheet and shook it out, then realized what she was doing. She was making up her bed with a near stranger, an intimate act if there ever was one.

Molly drew in a deep breath. "Listen, I can do this myself. Don't you have some work to do?" Maybe rude was all he understood.

He'd watched the play of emotions revealed so clearly on her transparent face. "You really have a great deal of trouble accepting help, don't you?"

Their conversation was exasperating her. "When I need help, truly need it, I'll ask. But I've been making beds alone for years. Don't you have a book you need to write, or is this part of your research?"

He smiled at that. "Are you worried you'll wind up in one of my books?"

"Not really." She began spreading out the top sheet. "My life is too dull to interest anyone."

Despite her admonitions, he pitched in on his side of the bed. "I doubt that, not if someone were to dig deep enough. Readers like to read about people's good points and bad. Genuine people, warts and all."

"I have as many warts as a pondful of frogs."

"Toads."

"What?" She reached for two pillows, then their cases.

"Toads have warts, not frogs."

"I stand corrected, since you're the writer. Did you major in English or journalism or American Literature? How does one become a writer?" All right, so he was interesting to talk with. And, Molly had to admit, she had few adult conversations that didn't center around a menu.

"I majored in Business Administration at my father's insistence since he was paying the tab. But I minored in English and took all the lit courses I could squeeze in." He stuffed the fluffy pillow into the case, struggling to get it to fit. "As to how someone becomes a writer, I think it's something some people just *have* to do because they have these stories in their head they need to get out. And because they're unable to fathom holding down a structured job, day after day, doing the same thing over and over. Like my parents did. Or rather still do."

"What do they do?"

"They're in hardware. Own and operate six stores in the L.A. area. They've worked twelve-hour days seven days a week as long as I can remember."

"So it's the long hours you want to avoid and the monotony?"

"Not even that." He caught his half of the light-weight cotton blanket she spilled onto the bed. "Apparently they love what they do. Different strokes for different folks, as they say. I like to set my own hours. Sometimes I write half the night and sleep all day. Some weeks I work every day, other weeks only three days. Depends on how the book's going and how close my deadline is. I like the freedom of making my own choices without punching a time clock." Finished, he straightened, wondering if in stating his preferences, he'd offended her since waitressing was as structured as working in a hardware store.

Stopping to gaze out the window, Molly sighed. "I understand perfectly and I couldn't agree more."

Devin walked over to her side of the bed. "Tell me why."

As Molly turned to face him, they both heard the toot-toot of Hank's truck horn. "I've got to go."

He touched her arm. "Later, maybe?"

"Maybe." She walked around him, needing to go outside. Hank wasn't in the best of moods and she didn't want to upset him. She also didn't want to reveal any more about herself right now. Devin Gray seemed able to knock aside her usual defenses and get her to talk about herself far more than usual.

Interesting, Devin thought as he walked toward the back door. He decided to go back upstairs so old Hank wouldn't get his nose any further out of joint. Besides, he'd discovered that he and Molly Shipman had more in common than he'd thought.

Worth pursuing, he decided as he poured himself a cold drink in his kitchen. Definitely worth pursuing.

It was two o'clock by the time the last of her things had been brought over and unloaded. A grateful Molly opened two cold drinks and handed them to her helpers. "You can't know how much I appreciate all you've both done, guys."

"No thanks necessary," Hank answered for both of them before tilting his head back for a long swallow.

Molly couldn't help noticing how her employer's

mood had brightened after he became aware that Devin
had left. She still couldn't figure out why Hank had
been borderline rude. Walking out to the truck with the
two of them, she decided there was no point in bringing
up Devin's name.

She smiled at Hank. "Now I've got the rest of today
and all day tomorrow to put everything away so I'll be
ready for the early shift on Monday."

Jerry moved closer to the fence enclosing the pool.
"You get to use this?"

"Yes, it's part of the rent. I'm sure Mrs. Bailey
wouldn't mind if you wanted to take a swim, Jerry,"
she offered. "You, too, Hank. I know you're both hot
and tired."

"Nah, we don't have time," Hank said, as he
drained the soda can.

Molly watched a disappointed Jerry stroll back. She
reached up to give him a quick hug. "Maybe some
other time, then." She saw the blush he couldn't prevent before he turned away.

Hank's narrowed gaze was on the upper apartment.
"He give you any trouble, anything at all, you let me
know, you hear?"

Molly almost smiled, but she knew that would hurt
his feelings. Not only protective but almost fatherly. If
her father had stuck around long enough, maybe he'd
have felt the same way. "Why would you think Devin
would give me trouble?" she asked quietly.

"I don't trust him. He's got shifty eyes."

She knew he meant well, but at twenty-eight, Molly
didn't think she needed quite so much protection. Nevertheless, she owed Hank a lot. Stepping close, she put
her arms around him and pressed her cheek to his.
"Thanks, for everything."

"Yeah, sure." Somewhat embarrassed, he climbed behind the wheel.

Molly watched them drive off, then hurried back inside. She still had a lot to do to make that small apartment into a home.

From his upstairs window, Devin stood looking down. He'd seen Hank glare up at his place, guessing he'd then issued a warning to Molly about him. Over what, he couldn't imagine. Apparently it hadn't bothered her for she'd given Hank a big fat hug.

Stepping back, he stuck his hands in his pockets, annoyed with himself. Why should he care who Molly Shipman hugged? To be fair, she'd hugged the kid, too. She'd stiffened each time he'd touched her yesterday, but she hugged these two freely. Because she knew them well, he decided.

Maybe he'd get to know her well, too. He wouldn't mind taking her in his arms, holding her close, feeling her heart beat against his. No denying it, she intrigued him. A man couldn't spend every spare minute working. He'd operate on the reward system, he decided. He wouldn't allow himself to check on Molly until he'd finished the chapter that was halfway completed. No guilt that way.

Whistling, he went back to his office.

Sunday morning just before ten, after putting in three less-than-fruitful hours on his novel that suddenly wasn't going all that well, Devin decided to ride his Harley to the nearby strip mall and pick up the *L.A. Times.* He felt nostalgic about his hometown newspaper.

Jogging down the steps, he decided he'd pick up

some bagels and coffee to see if he could tempt Molly with some breakfast. He'd be willing to bet she was so busy settling in that she'd forgotten to eat.

Leaning over the fence, he rubbed King's head briefly, not feeling guilty about leaving him behind since he'd taken the dog on a half-hour run around six. As he unlocked his Harley, he saw a vintage blue Cadillac drive up, its horn honking away.

Two women got out, one on the chubby side and dark-haired, the other older and very blond, artificially so most likely, Devin thought. A curly-headed girl of five or six climbed out of the back and squealed Molly's name. Molly stepped off the porch, looking surprised. "Samantha!" she cried.

The child hugged her aunt happily. "Mom says you've got cable TV now. Does that mean Disney, Aunt Molly?"

"You bet it does, sweetheart." Molly smiled down at her pug-nosed niece.

"She probably hasn't had time to get someone to hook it up yet, Sam," the girl's mother said.

"I hooked it up myself," Molly informed her sister, then moved to take a large pan from her mother. "What's all this, Mom?"

Gloria Shipman withdrew a box from the back seat before answering. "It's roast chicken and vegetables. I just know you won't take the time to eat right." She held up the box. "And chocolate chip cookies."

"Mmm," Sam murmured. "We're having a welcome-to-your-new-home party, Aunt Molly."

"What a terrific idea." Although she still had a long list of things that needed doing, Molly smiled her welcome. It was so seldom that the four of them got to-

gether, mostly due to her busy schedule. "Let's go inside. I've got coffee made."

Though he felt a little overwhelmed by four females
all at one time, Devin couldn't very well retrace his
steps and sneak upstairs, nor could he continue to stand
there staring. As unobtrusively as possible, he walked
his Harley down the drive, giving a wide berth to the
new arrivals.

But he wasn't fast enough to escape the notice of an
inquisitive little girl. "Wow, a motorcycle!" Samantha
abandoned Molly and ran over. "Is it yours? Will you
take me for a ride?"

"Sam!" The child's mother hurried over to clamp
her hands on her daughter's shoulder. "What have I
told you time and again about talking to strangers?"

Looking more mischievous than repentant, Sam was
ready with an excuse. "He's not really a stranger if
he's in Molly's yard, is he?"

Aware of her precocious niece's friendliness, Molly
went over, still carrying the pan her mother brought.
"Actually, he's not, Lucy. He's my neighbor, just
moved in upstairs." Quickly, she introduced her family.

Devin acknowledged each of them, noting that
Molly didn't resemble any of the three. Her sister and
niece had dark hair and eyes, as did her mother despite
the obvious fact that Gloria Shipman dyed her short
hair even blonder than Molly's. Both women were several inches shorter and full-figured whereas Molly
could be described as tall and willowy. She must take
after her father, he decided.

"It's good to know you'll be living here with my
daughter," Gloria Shipman said, her approving gaze
roaming his tall frame. "Not that this is a bad neigh-

borhood, but a woman alone can't be too careful.'' Her smile was just short of flirtatious.

She can't help herself, Molly thought, for the umpteenth time. An attractive woman in her youth, Gloria still turned on the charm for every man she met, young or old, tall or short, rich or poor. She basked in the glow of attention from men as much as Molly turned from it.

Molly sent an apologetic look to Devin, but she needn't have bothered. He'd read Gloria like a book.

"I agree, Mrs. Shipman. I'll certainly keep an eye on your daughter.'' He turned his attention to Sam whose wide eyes were checking out the chrome of his Harley. "It's not safe for someone as young and pretty as you to ride one of these without a helmet, and I don't have one small enough to fit you. Maybe one day, we'll pick one up. Okay?''

"You mean it? Great.'' Sam's mind raced with possibilities. "Is that your dog?'' she asked next, spotting King who was pacing along the fence.

"Yeah, but I'd rather you didn't go over to him until I take you to meet him, and I don't have time right now. Is that all right?''

Reluctantly, Sam nodded. "Okay.''

Molly had to hand it to Devin. He'd appeased the daughter without upsetting the mother. His people skills, which hadn't charmed Hank, were more in evidence today.

Her head cocked, Molly's sister Lucy had been studying the man with the Harley. "Did Molly say your name is Devin Gray? Are you the Devin Gray who wrote *Murder at Oak Creek Canyon?* You are, aren't you? I recognize you from the picture on the back of the dust cover.''

Devin seemed embarrassed. "I guess you caught me."

Lucy's round face moved into a big smile as she turned to her sister. "I'll bet you didn't even know that this man's famous?"

Molly was taken aback. Devin had told her he was a writer, yet she hadn't even bothered to ask what he'd written. She sent him her second apologetic look in as many minutes. "Lucy works at a bookstore in the mall." She felt she had to say more, to explain. "I don't have much time to read fiction."

"You should find the time to read this one," Lucy insisted. "It takes place here in Arizona, up in Sedona." Her smile beamed at Devin. "You've got a second one just out, something about the Grand Canyon, right?"

"Yes. *Death at the Grand Canyon.*"

"My, my," Gloria murmured. "A celebrity in our midst."

"A very minor one, I assure you." It was the first time he'd been recognized with the exception of book signings, Devin realized, and the attention made him oddly uncomfortable. Molly's sister probably wouldn't have recognized him if she didn't work in a bookstore. He'd rather people concentrated on searching out his books rather than the author.

"I'll have to get you to autograph a copy for me," Lucy went on.

"Any time." Devin cleared his throat. "Well, nice to have met you all." He nodded to Molly, winked at Sam, then climbed on his Harley.

All four of them watched him ride off, his dark hair whipping about in a strong morning breeze.

Gloria was the first to speak as she turned to her

oldest daughter. "Molly, you didn't know he was a famous writer?"

She shrugged. "He'd told me he was a writer, but I didn't ask what he wrote."

Lucy exchanged a knowing glance with their mother. "Of course you didn't. I'm surprised you knew his name, as cautious as you are."

Molly felt she had to defend herself as she led the way into her apartment. "I only met him two days ago."

"Leave her alone, Lucy," Gloria admonished. "Now that Molly knows he's an important writer, besides being quite a hunk, she'll warm up to him."

Whether he'd written *War and Peace* or drove a garbage truck, Molly knew she had no intention of warming up to Devin Gray. Not wanting to have this same old discussion again, knowing full well that both her mother and sister were critical of her hands-off-men policy, she decided to bring a little levity into play. "Mom! A hunk! I can't believe you said that." Holding the roasting pan on one arm, she slipped the other around her mother and hugged her. "There may be snow on the roof, but there's still fire in the heart, eh?"

"Well, I'm not dead nor am I blind. He's a very attractive man, Molly. And he probably makes a pile of money. You could do worse." She stepped through the door Molly held open.

"You saw him for five minutes and you think I should set my cap for him?" She loved her mother, but her constant nagging that she should find a good man to take care of her rather than work so hard got on Molly's nerves. She'd had a so-called good man, and where had it gotten her?

"Who said anything about permanence?" Lucy

asked with a grin. "You don't have to marry him to have a little fun with him. I'm going to have to get his books. I wonder if he's a sexy writer."

Molly set the roasting pan down on the kitchen counter. "So, you haven't read his books?"

"Not yet, but I intend to. I'll bring them over after I finish so you can read them, too."

Molly wasn't altogether sure she wanted to read what Devin Gray had written. It would indicate more interest in him than she was willing to admit to.

Determined to put her neighbor out of her mind, she took Sam's hand. "How about the grand tour, which should take all of five minutes? The apartment's not real big, but it's sunny and clean and close to work."

"I think it's charming," Gloria commented, leading the way.

By four that afternoon, Devin had had it. He had a crick in his neck and his shoulders ached. He'd been at the computer since he'd returned with The *Times*, leaving it to read later. On his ride, he'd worked out one of his plot problems, an old habit of his, and he'd gone to work immediately after returning. Finally, he was back on track.

Rolling his shoulders, he saved his material and shut off the computer. His rumbling stomach reminded him he hadn't put anything in it lately except several cups of coffee. In the kitchen, he opened the refrigerator and examined its pitiful contents. It looked very much like he'd be having canned soup and a glass of milk again. He really had to go grocery shopping tomorrow.

As he grabbed an apple from the bowl on the table, he heard King give out several playful barks. The German shepherd was three years old and not much of a barker. Chewing, Devin sauntered out onto his back porch. He couldn't have been more surprised at the sight that greeted his eyes.

Molly was hanging sheets on the clothesline with King trailing her every step. Devin could hear her talking to him, though he couldn't make out what she was saying. He saw her reach to take the stick from King's mouth, then throw it across the yard before bending to her clothes basket for a pillowcase.

The big dog raced across the grass, picked up the stick and hurried back to her. Smiling down at him, she petted his large head, then reached to secure the pillowcase. Devin could swear he saw King move close to Molly and nuzzle up against her bare legs. How had she managed to win his dog over in a couple of short days?

She was wearing a long yellow top that came nearly to the hem of her white shorts. She had incredibly long and very shapely legs. Definitely a distraction, one that got his juices flowing every time he looked at her. Watching her bend down to hug King's head, Devin felt a foolish flash of jealousy. How far gone was he that he was beginning to envy a dog? he wondered.

As Molly gathered up her basket and spare clothespins, Devin went down the stairs and met her at the gate. "Don't you ever let up, take a break, maybe sit down and relax? I hear you moving around down there constantly. I would imagine you're exhausted." She didn't look exhausted, just a little warm. The temperature had to be over ninety.

"Not really. I needed to get settled in since I have early shift tomorrow morning." He was wearing a black T-shirt over gray knit shorts and hadn't bothered to shave. The word *hunk* that her mother had used floated back to her. Yeah, it fit. "I hope I'm not making so much noise I'm disturbing you." The house had to be at least thirty years old with a few squeaky floors and air vents that allowed some sounds to travel between the two units. "I wouldn't want to keep you from writing the great American novel."

He saw her mouth twitch and realized she was teasing him. "Not to worry. My books will never become required reading in school. Purely escape stuff. And you're not disturbing me."

"Good." He seemed genuinely modest, had seemed uncomfortable at Lucy's comments. She liked that about him. She felt King's wet nose at her back through the cyclone fencing, turned and smiled before raising a hand to acknowledge him.

"I see you made friends with King."

"Yes. He's quite the sweetheart when you get to know him."

Devin glanced over at the pool, shimmering in the late afternoon sun. "I was just thinking of cooling off with a swim. Want to join me?"

Molly had no trouble picturing that hard, masculine body in a swimsuit. "Thanks, but I've still got some things to do." Carrying her basket, she walked off. "Have a good swim."

Damned if he wouldn't, Devin thought. It would have been nice to have company, but he'd go alone. He needed the exercise.

Molly stood at her kitchen window, gazing out through the gauzy curtains she'd brought over from her former apartment, watching Devin do laps in the pool. He was big and looked very strong with not an ounce of fat on him. She'd been counting and was up to twenty. Finally, he eased out and brushed his wet hair back with both hands as water dripped from the dark curls on his chest and legs. He turned to straighten a lounge chair while Molly admired the smooth skin of his back, the muscles rippling as he moved. He sat down in the chair and leaned back, closing his eyes and letting the hot sun dry him.

Her hands trembled ever so slightly as she wondered what it would feel like to run her fingers over those broad shoulders, to examine that deep cleft in his chin. It had been so long since she'd touched a man, or allowed one to touch her. That brief moment when he'd first introduced her to his dog, the nearness of his big body close to hers, the way his hand had lingered on hers, had awakened a dormant need. She would deny it if asked, often denied it even to herself, yet there were times like now that she longed for that strong male touch that was like no other. A man who could make her want and need and ache.

Like she was aching now.

Four years she'd been married to Lee Summers, and there had been some good times at the beginning. He'd been very attractive, too, and very aware of it. Yet she'd learned the hard way that even strong, attractive men have their weaknesses. Lee's had killed any feelings she'd had for him.

Gazing now at Devin Gray, she could easily see his attraction, his strengths. And she couldn't help wondering what his weaknesses were.

Chapter Three

Monday morning, with one eye on the clock, Molly grabbed a box of cereal and her canvas bag before heading out the door. Settling behind the wheel, she inserted the key and turned it. A few chugging sounds, then nothing.

"Ah, c'mon, Bessie," she coaxed. "I can't be late today after Hank gave me the whole weekend off." Usually she had to work either Saturday or Sunday. More gently, she tried again, knowing that sometimes when the car hadn't been driven in a couple of days, old Bess took her sweet time. However, not even a gasp on the second try. The menacing red light on the dash flashed on.

"Damn!" she muttered under her breath before getting out and propping up the hood. Leaning under, Molly made a quick assessment and moaned out loud. "Not today!"

"Having a problem?" asked a deep, masculine voice at her elbow.

Recognizing the voice's owner, Molly didn't even look up. "You could say that."

"I take it she won't start. Want me to take a look?" Devin offered. Although she looked cute in her neat white blouse and black slacks, trying not to get dirty as she stared into the innards of the Honda, he could all but see steam rising from her in frustration.

"I know what's wrong," Molly muttered in exasperation.

"You do?" Most women he'd run across knew zip about car engines. "What is it then?"

"The alternator." Molly removed her blond head from beneath the hood. "I knew it was on its last legs, but I'd hoped it would hold out another few paydays." There went her carefully planned budget. Ken at the auto repair service had warned her, but she'd stubbornly held out.

Not convinced she knew an alternator from a radiator, Devin persisted. "Mind if I try anyhow?"

"Suit yourself," Molly said, wondering whom she could call to beg a ride from.

Devin got behind the wheel and gave the key a couple of useless tries, then noticed the red warning light. He got back out. "Could be your starter, or maybe a broken belt. But more likely your alternator."

"Yes, I know."

Puzzled, he studied her. "How do you know so much about cars? Your dad teach you? Maybe a boyfriend?"

Molly shot him a withering glance. "I took a night course in auto mechanics. Much more reliable." She checked her watch. "Of all days…"

"Listen, it'll probably have to be towed in to be fixed. That may take awhile. I can give you a ride to work, if you don't mind riding double on a Harley." Hands on his hips, he stood watching her. Daring her.

He thought he had her, that she'd sooner walk than ride a motorcycle, Molly thought. He was wrong. She smiled at him. "Thanks. I'd love to." She grabbed her bag and box of cereal before following him to his bike.

"What's with the cereal?" he asked over his shoulder.

"Breakfast." To demonstrate, she stuck her hand in, came out with a fistful of Cheerios which she proceeded to eat. "Fast, efficient and good for you."

"Uh-huh." He bent to undo his lock. "Ever ridden one of these?"

Her gaze swept over the huge black-and-chrome machine, but her expression didn't change. "Not recently. Once, in college, I rode double on a Kawasaki." She'd done it on a dare and found it fun after her initial fright. She'd done a lot of dumb things in college.

"Well, then, you're an old hand." Devin saw the hesitation in her eyes and wondered if she'd woven a story to impress him. One thing he felt was true about Molly Shipman even on short acquaintance was that her independent streak wouldn't allow her to back down from a challenge.

"Hold on a minute." Quickly, he ran up to his apartment and was back in short order carrying a white helmet. "You need to put this on."

"You don't wear one," she commented. It was only a couple of miles to the café and that stupid thing would really mess up her hair.

"You're right and I should. If you want to ride with me, however, you'll put this on." It was one thing to

risk his own neck and quite another to endanger someone else's. He didn't wait for any more arguments but
unfastened the strap and slipped the helmet over her
head.

The backs of his fingers touched the silk of her hair
as he tucked in loose strands. Yes, just as soft as he'd
imagined. While she stood perfectly still, he fastened
the chin strap in place. Her eyes stayed on his face,
making him wonder what she was thinking. He took
her bag and cereal box, placing them in the leather tote
attached to the back of his bike. "There, all set."

Devin shoved up the kickstand and mounted, scooting forward on the generous seat. "Okay, climb on
behind me."

Molly hesitated for just a moment, wondering if
she'd made a mistake accepting this ride. Probably
Trisha could have come over for her by now and they'd
be on their way. Taking Devin up on his offer meant
she owed him now, and she hated that feeling. However, it was a little late for second thoughts.

Pulling up her pantlegs ever so slightly, she swung
a leg over and behind him. The slope of the seat had
her scooting right up against his hard body. She felt
her pulse take a wild leap as she stared at the back of
his head. "Now what?"

Devin pointed out the metal footrests on each side
and bent to guide one shoe in place to demonstrate.
"Now put your arms around my waist and hang on."

The roar of the engine as it caught was loud in her
ears. There was no turning back now. Molly slipped
her arms around his broad back, her hands coming to
rest at his sides which caused her torso to slide even
closer. She felt the heat rise in her face.

"Not like that." Devin took her hands and pulled

them as far to the front of him as they would reach. "Like that. If you don't hang on real tight, you'll fly off if we hit a bump." Which wasn't exactly so, but sounded good. "I'm your only anchor so stay close."

Sprawled across the back of him, Molly couldn't imagine getting much closer. Beneath her hands, she could feel his ribcage under the thin cotton shirt he wore. Her breasts were flattened against his back, her head turned to the side and pressed to him. This was definitely not how she remembered her last ride in her college days.

Fighting a grin she couldn't see anyway, Devin started the Harley down the drive as he raised his feet. She'd all but disappeared against his back so that he couldn't see her in his rearview mirrors. But he could feel her.

Despite the thrumming of the bike, he could feel her heart rapidly beating against his back, could feel the soft flesh of her breasts as they pressed through the thin material of her blouse. He could feel her small, capable hands gripping his shirt in front as if holding on to a lifeline. And he could feel her warm breath as she exhaled in short puffs, revealing her anxiety.

"You okay?" Devin shouted, glancing over his shoulder as he swung onto Thomas Road.

'Fine,'' Molly answered, her voice quavery. The huge machine seemed to hum with a life of its own, causing her body to tremble in rhythm with it. Or was it the nearness of the man plastered to her in a close-ness she never would have permitted off the cycle? She drew in a deep breath and smelled soap and the clean scent of man. She felt her heart gallop even faster.

Unbidden, Molly felt her senses stir and come alive. Here she was, curled around a very masculine form after vowing she'd never again put herself in that position. And worse yet, her traitorous body was enjoying the ride far more than her cautious mind. Swallowing hard, she closed her eyes.

Would they never get there? Molly wondered.

Devin wondered if he dared take a circuitous route, whether or not she'd notice. He found himself not wanting to stop, let her off and watch her walk away. Despite all his protests to the contrary, his constant affirmations that work had to come first, he had to admit that he was losing the battle. Not until recently did he realize how very much he'd missed the closeness of a woman.

Boiling it down even further, the nearness of *this* woman. For there was something about Molly that had him thinking soft thoughts, daydreaming, planning seductions. He wanted to sneak past all the barriers she'd put up since her divorce. He wanted to know more about her so he could figure how best to approach her. He wanted her to willingly and knowingly put her arms around him, not just because she didn't want to fall off his bike. Now that he'd had the pleasure of being close to her, he wanted more.

However, he'd have to put those thoughts aside, he decided as he spotted the Pan Handle up ahead. Slowing, he swung into the nearly empty parking lot and brought the Harley to a stop near the side windows.

The vibration of the powerful machine still had her body throbbing, Molly realized as she opened her eyes. She wasn't altogether certain her legs would support her. Watching Devin get off looking steady as a rock unnerved her. She prayed she wouldn't embarrass herself by crumbling to the ground.

Devin offered her a hand and saw that hers was

trembling as she gripped his fingers. "Just swing your leg over," he gently instructed. He watched her do as requested, then ease her full weight onto both legs, still a bit shaky. "So, was this ride the same as your first?"

Molly concentrated on unfastening the helmet, avoiding his eyes. "Pretty much." If you don't count the fact that the first ride had taken place when she'd been eighteen, not twenty-eight, and she'd ridden with a boy while there was no mistaking that Devin was a man.

Fluffing out her hair with her hands that had finally steadied, she managed a smile. "Thanks for getting me here in one piece."

Devin retrieved her bag and box of cereal. "You want me to call someone about your car?"

"No, thanks. I have a mechanic I use all the time. He has my car at his shop more than I have her on the road. I should get him on retainer." She smiled because if she didn't, she just might cry. She was pouring more money into old Bess than into groceries.

He searched for something to say to keep her with him just a little longer. "Maybe you should consider trading your Honda in for a Harley. I could give you some buying tips."

This time Molly laughed. "I think not." She checked her watch, then glanced up at the café's windows. To her shocked surprise, both Trisha and Hank were leaning over a booth staring out at her.

Devin followed her gaze and noticed them, too. "You're not late, are you?"

"No. I think they're just surprised to see me arriving on a motorcycle." She settled her purse strap on her shoulder and hugged her cereal box to her chest. "Again, thanks. I'll see you later."

"Right." He watched her walk away, then called her name and waited for her to turn around. "You'll need a ride home. My phone's supposed to be put in today. I could call you."

"I'll catch a ride from one of the girls, but thanks." She seemed always to be thanking him. It was getting tiresome. "You'd better get back to the great American novel."

He smiled at her. "Yeah, I guess so." His eyes following her, he climbed back on, but he didn't drive off until she'd gone inside. Only then did he most reluctantly leave.

Only two booths and one counter stool were occupied as Molly strolled in. Hank was back in the kitchen, but Trisha came charging over, a curious look in her eyes. "All right, give. Who is he?"

"A neighbor," Molly answered as she pawed through her purse looking for her small address book. "My car wouldn't start. The alternator, I think. I have to give Ken a quick call."

But Trisha's thoughts were elsewhere. "Never mind your car or Ken. Where exactly does this gorgeous hunk of a neighbor live?"

There was that word hunk again. "In the upstairs unit of your mother's house." Finding the black book, she thumbed through searching for the mechanic's phone number.

"Well, well. Things are looking up, eh?" Trisha's smile was all-knowing. "The two of you seemed mighty chummy. What's he like?"

Lord, if she told Trisha that Devin was a famous writer she'd never let up. Frowning, she walked to the wall phone in back. "Chummy? I was merely thanking him for the ride." Glancing at the card, she quickly dialed the service station, hoping Ken wasn't too backed up. She needed her car. While it rang, she turned back to Trisha. "Do you think you could give me a lift home tonight?"

"If it means you'll introduce me to your sexy neighbor, I sure will." With a wink, she went back to work.

Molly had scarcely finished her call when Hank appeared at her elbow. Thinking he was wondering why she wasn't up front, she looked apologetic. "I had to arrange for my car to be towed. Sorry if I'm late clocking in." Which she didn't think she was since the Harley had gotten her here much faster than Bessie could have.

"Why didn't you call me if you needed a ride?" he asked, sounding hurt.

She almost sighed. This big-brother concern of Hank's was getting on her nerves. "I was going to, but then Devin was right there, offering a ride, so I thought that would be faster."

"Motorcycles are dangerous, you know. And that guy, I don't know." Hank smoothed his thinning hair with one thick hand. "How come you trust him so quickly when you hardly know him?"

Molly clamped down on her temper because she knew Hank meant well. But she had to set him straight. "Hank, I accepted a ride from him, not a marriage proposal. I've been on my own for quite awhile now and I've done all right. Please, stop hovering over me." That said, she deliberately walked around him and to the front, grabbed two menus and walked over to a young couple who'd just sat down. She didn't want to hurt Hank, but enough was enough.

His book was going well, Devin thought as he left his office, surprised to discover that it was nearly eleven at night and he'd worked way past dinner. Perusing the contents of his refrigerator, he saw plenty to eat since he'd gone shopping that morning. But it was too late for a big meal. Instead, he grabbed a banana and sauntered out onto his back porch.

It was a beautiful evening, a half moon high in a cloudless sky, the heat of the day cooled down to a reasonable eighty. He watched King patrolling along the fence line, pleased again that he'd rented a place with a yard. Although Devin usually kept him inside the apartment during the hottest part of the day, he knew that the big shepherd was happiest in his own domain.

Early each morning, they'd go for a run together, then Devin would swim his laps before settling down to work. It was a good routine for both of them. As soon as the sun set, Devin shut off the air and opened his windows and doors. He much preferred fresh air over artificial coolness. Of course, in another few weeks, the hot Arizona summer would force him to leave the air on full-time.

But for now, he breathed in the fragrant scent of a nearby jasmine shrub and ate his banana. Mrs. Bailey's house on the other side of the swimming pool was dark, indicating she'd already gone to bed. It was fairly quiet except for the occasional cricket's song and another sound he couldn't immediately identify.

Leaning on the railing, he listened with his head cocked. It was a tap-tapping noise, coming from below. Stepping to the stairs, he decided it was coming from Molly's place, drifting through her open screen door. It resembled typing, but why would a waitress be typing so late at night? She'd mentioned night classes, but she'd said she skipped the summer session. She'd also said she worked part-time for a CPA, but only during tax season which had ended a week ago.

Devin finished his banana, tossed the peel into the trash container and walked down, his nosiness getting the better of him. A soft glow from the kitchen light fell on her back porch. Standing in shadow, he saw her seated at her table, a pile of papers on either side of a typewriter that looked older than his ancient Smith-Corona. Curiouser and curiouser.

Devin gave a quick knock, then tried the door and, finding it open, walked in.

Eyes widening, Molly looked up. "Oh! You startled me."

"You should lock your doors, you know. This is a good neighborhood, but break-ins happen all over. This guy at the supermarket was telling me someone broke into his place just two blocks over."

"You're right, I should," Molly agreed, somewhat distracted.

He stepped closer, pulled out the chair opposite hers and folded his lanky frame into it. "You're awfully busy for such a late hour."

Sighing, Molly sat back, reaching to rub the tense muscles of her neck. "Why don't you come in and sit down?" she said, staring into his eyes pointedly since he'd already done just that.

He had the sensitivity to look chagrined, but only a little. "I was out back and heard the typing." He stared at the pile of papers, trying to read upside down. "Don't tell me you're writing the great American novel, too?" Nearly everyone he met said they either were writing or planned on writing one day.

Molly shook her head, knowing she might as well

tell him since persistence was his middle name. "I do typing for the junior college, theme papers for the students, tests and class plans for the teachers. And I do forms for a couple of insurance companies that farm out their work."

Leaning forward, Devin frowned. "Does that pay well? I mean, you've already put in a full day at the café. I should think you'd want some time to yourself."

She did, but leisure time would have to wait. There were bills to be paid, goals to be reached. Molly riffled through the stack to her right. "Pay well? At a dollar a page, what do you think?"

He raised an impressed eyebrow, guessing the number of pages to be seventy-five or eighty. "I see." But he didn't, not really. She worked two, no, three jobs plus took classes. What was she aiming for? "Are you saving to take a trip around the world?"

"That's a good one." Molly rose and went to the fridge. "Would you like something cold to drink?" She might as well offer him something since he wasn't going to be polite and go away.

"Whatever you're having would be fine."

"Just water." She saw him nod so she took out two small bottled waters and handed him one.

Devin watched her throat as she swallowed thirstily. Again, she wore no makeup, her hair loose around her face. So young to be so intense. He sat back, a perplexed frown on his face. "Didn't you say you went to college? I can't help wondering why an educated woman would prefer waiting on tables and typing half the night for extra money. There's nothing wrong with waitressing, but surely you could get a better-paying job and not have to work so hard."

Carefully, she set her water bottle down and raised her eyes to his. "You sure ask a lot of questions."

"Questions bring about information and suddenly, we're communicating. Besides, I told you. Occupational hazard. If I'm out of line, you can send me back upstairs."

"Oh, you're out of line, all right. But we might as well get this over with because I have a feeling you'll just keep asking." She noticed that he didn't bother to deny it. She certainly owed him no explanations, nor would she tell him everything about her life. Just enough to satisfy his curiosity so he'd stop pestering her.

"Yes, I went to college, but basically I wasted my educational opportunity. I took classes I wanted to take instead of subjects that would qualify me for good jobs. Classical languages, architectural ruins, playwriting. I had the counselors tearing out their hair. Your father was right to insist you take business administration in case your English Lit classes didn't pay off. But there was no one to guide me so I frittered away those years having a good time. And I'm paying for that self-indulgent miscalculation now."

"Your parents didn't give you any direction?"

Molly paused, wondering if she should go into this. Well, why not? "My father walked away from us when I was six and Lucy only three. We never saw him again. My mother had married young and had absolutely no marketable skills. She's also kind of fragile, the sort of person who needs taking care of rather than one who takes care of others. She's a dear person and I love her, but she has trouble coping."

Devin had been with Molly's mother for a matter of minutes and, except for the fact that she dyed her hair and wore clothes a bit too youthful for her age, he hadn't had time to form much of an opinion.

"Apparently, she tried several jobs and got fired from them all. So her only answer was to depend on 'the kindness of strangers,' as Blanche DeBois said." She watched him, waiting for a response.

Something was expected of him, Devin gathered. "By strangers, you mean men." He did not pose it as a question.

"Yes. You can see why I don't tell this to people easily. My mother's a good person and she coped in the best way she knew how."

"Molly, I'm not judging her. People do what they have to do."

"That's right. So Lucy and I had a series of *uncles*. I have to give my mother some credit, here. She didn't drink or go out and leave us alone. I'm not certain to this day where she found these guys, but they moved in with us, first one and after him, another. And another. They all had jobs, paid the bills, and never abused either her or us. In return, I assume they were compensated by the pleasure of my mother's company. I know each one shared her room for a time, but it was never overt, scarcely even noticeable. Gloria always saw to it that my sister and I were clean, well fed, went to school, and so on. Then one day we'd come home and Uncle Fred or Tom or whoever was gone and in a week or so, another uncle would move in."

Devin sat back wearing a half smile. "Interesting."

"We didn't exactly lead normal lives, but it wasn't all bad, either. At any rate, I always got good marks— even skipped the fifth grade—and wound up with a full scholarship to the University of Arizona which, as I've mentioned, I wasted. Lucy married right after high school graduation, telling us she was madly in love. They had Samantha that same year. Bob Raynor was a nice enough guy, except he loved the bottle more than his family. He died in a head-on collision when Sam was two, his blood alcohol level twice the legal limit.''

Devin leaned forward, propping his elbows on the table. ''This is all very interesting, but I don't see what it's got to do with why you're working twenty hours out of twenty-four.''

''I'm coming to that. As my mother got older, the men she could interest became fewer. So, when she's between *uncles,* I help her out. And as you may have guessed, Lucy's husband had no insurance and she earns far less at the bookstore than I do at the café. Sam's got a periodontal condition, brought on by a fall on cement when she was four and that's fairly expensive. So I help out with that. Now you know it all.''

Not by a long shot. He studied her for several moments, then smiled. ''I think you left out quite a bit. What about your marriage?''

A frown of annoyance passed over her features. ''We're definitely not going into my marriage. Suffice it to say that I married a man I met in my senior year in college, stayed with him four years, then left and filed for divorce.'' Deliberately, she put on a smile, needing to end this discussion on a high note. ''But things will be improving soon. A couple more accounting courses and I'll have my degree. Then I'll quit the café and go to work for Bud Grant, the tax man I do part-time work for now. Two years' experience working full-time with him and I'll be able to take my CPA exam and get my certificate so I can open up my own place.''

She sighed wearily, stretching her arms high over her head. "That's the plan and that's why I put in all these extra hours now. I have a goal and this time, nothing's going to stop me." Like her ill-advised marriage had.

"You sound as if someone messed up your plans once before." He saw a shadow move across her face and knew he'd hit a nerve.

"That happened a long while ago." Just about the time she'd come to her senses and begun thinking about her future, Lee had come charging into her life on his big white horse. Only what he'd offered had been only an illusion.

"Quite a story. I admire you for all you do for your family." Devin felt a familiar guilt wash over him. He'd walked away from his overly demanding family, yet it still bothered him occasionally. Like now when he saw someone who worked three jobs to get ahead and still managed to help her family. Then again, he'd been there for them all through his teens and much of his twenties, hadn't he?

Realizing she was too tired to type any more tonight, Molly began straightening her paper stacks. "I don't do all that much, really. Besides, if you care about people, that's what you do, help out if you can." Absorbed in cleaning up, she didn't notice his troubled look. "As you know, it's not such a sacrifice. My sister's had it rough and Sam's a little angel. And my mother's such a sweetheart. She does such thoughtful things, like bringing over my dinner on Sunday and crocheting sweaters for me." Molly chuckled. "She's a terrible cook, even worse than me, and the sweaters are so godawful that I never wear them, but she means well."

He saw the love on her face, the affection, and it touched him. "I hesitate to ask, but does your mother have a current *uncle* in her life?"

Molly leaned against the kitchen counter, crossing her arms over her chest and smiling. "As a matter of fact, she does. Doug Draper is a used-car salesman who dyes his hair this improbable shade of red, chain-smokes and brings my mother a bunch of violets every payday. He doesn't make much money, but he makes her happy."

Devin rose, nearly bumping his head on the hanging basket filled with healthy green ferns, and walked over to her. He saw her dark-blue eyes grow wary as he stepped closer. "Did anyone ever tell you you're really something?"

"Sure. Twice a day." She eased back from him as he tried to invade her space. "Look, it's nearly midnight and..." She felt his hands take hold of her arms, uncross them and drape them over his shoulders. "What are we doing here?" she asked softly.

"Communicating." His hands settled at her waist and his mouth settled on hers. It was a slow brushing of lips, a savoring taste, the most gentle of kisses. And then he released her, stepping back because what he really wanted to do was pull her closer and bury himself within her. "Good night, Molly."

She watched him go, heard his footsteps on the stairs going up, then his door close. She let out a shaky breath, then ran her tongue along her lips. And tasted him.

If, since meeting Devin Gray, she'd have imagined kissing him, it hadn't been like that. If she'd imagined such a kiss, she'd have undoubtedly thought it would have quite a kick, but never would she have dreamed it would have the power to touch her so deeply. Yet, if she'd have allowed herself to dream, it might have been of just such a soft, tender kiss.

How had he guessed she was a sucker for tenderness?

Chapter Four

Molly straightened from weeding around the delicate new growth in the shaded area alongside the backyard shed. Pulling off her gardening gloves, she surveyed her fledgling vegetable patch with a satisfied smile. Not bad for a low-budget beginning.

The four tomato plants were staked in the back row, the radishes and green onions labeled, but it was too soon to see any results there. And the front space, reserved for leaf lettuce, was coming along beautifully, the tender shoots pushing through, seeking sunlight.

It wasn't a large garden, and the yield would be small, but it felt good to work in the fragrant earth again, something she'd loved all her life. One day she'd mentioned her passion for gardening to one of her regular customers, Charley Jablinski, never realizing he owned a small nursery until he offered to help her get started. She'd stopped by his place and he'd given her the tomato plants, seeds and a bag of topsoil at what she was certain were bargain prices.

Strolling to the back fence, Molly gazed affectionately at her blossoming flowers, again courtesy of Charley. She had hardy marigolds in a cluster, proud snapdragons standing like colorful sentinels and a patch of pink-and-white petunias. The purple alyssum she'd planted as a border looked a little droopy, but they'd catch hold and spread. Just gazing at her garden made Molly feel good.

Fortunately there was almost day-long shade back here from the large palo verde and the cottonwood tree on the side or the hot May sun would fry these poor plants, Molly thought as she turned on the hose and filled the tin sprinkling can she'd found in the shed. Just a drop more water here and there and she'd quit.

As she bent to pick up the can, she had the uneasy feeling she wasn't alone. Glancing toward the house, she saw Devin on his back porch leaning over the railing quietly watching her, his dog beside him. He was not a man easily ignored. She gave him a brief wave before turning back to her garden. It seemed every time she was out in the yard planting or watering or weeding, he was there, in that exact spot, watching her with those sea-green eyes. He rarely came down, didn't actually bother her, yet he was there, as if waiting for something.

She hadn't spent any time with him since that brief kiss in her kitchen over a week ago. Yet he was constantly turning up everywhere she went.

He'd taken to eating at least one meal almost daily at the Pan Handle, nearly always managing to seat himself at her station. He was unfailingly polite, not overly chatty, just quietly watchful. His presence at the café

never failed to bring a frown to Hank's face and to fill
Trisha with questions. Once the overzealous waitress
had deliberately directed him to her station so she could
wait on him herself to satisfy her curiosity, though it
hadn't. Her questions had continued. Molly had decided the less said about Devin to her co-workers, the
better.

There was more. She'd run into him twice in the
laundry unit that they shared at the far end of the back
porch. Another time at the supermarket. She'd even
been stopped at a light and Devin had pulled up alongside, smiling at her. Hard to miss that Harley.

They had to be coincidences, Molly decided as she
sprinkled her budding lettuce shoots. He certainly
didn't have time to follow her around. She knew he
worked long hours because no matter how late she
came home from the café even when she closed up,
the light was on in the room he'd turned into an office.
Sometimes she heard him pacing late, around midnight.
Back and forth in the small confines of his apartment.
Once she'd heard him slam out the door, jump on his
Harley and roar off, not coming back for over an hour.
But he'd taken the steps two at a time when he'd returned, seemingly eager, as if he'd worked out a story
problem during his ride.

Finished, Molly put the gardening tools back in the
shed and stuffed the weeds into a trash bag, wondering
if she'd have some time later to start Devin's book.
Lucy had brought it over one day, telling her how wonderful a mystery it was and how she hadn't guessed
the murderer till the very end, which Lucy considered
to be the mark of a really good writer. Molly couldn't
help wondering how much of the man would be revealed through his writing.

She'd never known an author before, had no idea if the stories they wrote exposed their personalities and inner feelings, or if they were just works of imagination, pure fiction. To her surprise, she was nosy enough to find out for herself.

Turning, she saw that Devin and King had gone back inside and was relieved she didn't have to talk with him. On the one hand, she wanted to know more about him. Simple curiosity, she told herself. On the other hand, she was wary of getting too close, of becoming interested in him. She already knew Devin Gray was a man who could excite her, who could make her feel things she'd sworn off feeling. If what Lucy had learned in her bookstore was true, that he'd only scratched the surface of the popularity he'd soon achieve as a writer, then he would surely be out of her league in no time. He'd likely be moving on, to a bigger house, maybe a lavish spread around Camelback Mountain. She'd already been down that road, a poor girl involved with a rich man. If something had nowhere to go, why pursue it? And if someone was off-limits, why waste time thinking about him? she chided herself. Besides, hadn't she sworn off men for all time? Always she came back to that shaky vow.

Stopping in the laundry room off the back porch, Molly took a load of towels out of the dryer and threw the next load in. She had a lot to do, but it felt good to be home tonight after working double shifts for two days because Dixie, the third waitress, had been home with some dental problem.

Hefting the clothes basket, she turned to leave and almost bumped into Devin leaning against the door-jamb. Startled, she stepped back.

"I knocked."

In the warm, damp enclosure, she smelled fresh aftershave and wondered if he'd just put it on for her, then chided herself for being silly. "I couldn't hear you from the noise of the washer. I'll get out of your way." But he didn't move. She raised her eyes to his face.

"I'm not doing laundry right now." Without asking, he took the basket from her, checking out its contents. "You sure use a lot of towels."

Molly led the way to her kitchen, wondering what was on his mind. "Those aren't mine. Mrs. Bailey sprained her ankle so I'm doing a couple of loads for her." As soon as he set the basket on a chair, she began folding towels.

Now she was doing the neighbor's laundry. Next thing she'd be driving the school bus and working in women's shelters. In her spare time. Which, since he'd been watching her from a safe distance for over a week, she had absolutely none of that he could see. He'd stayed a safe distance away because, although it had been a mere gentle brushing of lips, he'd thought of that kiss and of her far more than was good for his peace of mind.

He'd gathered she'd been working overtime since she was gone for something like twelve hours at a time and when he rode by the Pan Handle, her car was always in the lot. Evenings, he could hear her typing until the wee hours. She'd mentioned that she needed money for her mother, her sister and niece and for car repairs. The woman did nothing but eat, sleep and work, not much of the two formers and way too much of the latter.

"I see you've got your car back," he commented, making small talk as he studied her.

Oh, yes, old Bess was back. After a rebuilt alternator

and several hoses and labor, amounting to over two hundred dollars, her car was back. At least the extra hours she'd put in had enabled her to pay cash. "Yes. Bessie's a clunker, but she's *my* clunker."

He picked up a faded pink towel and began copying her folding ritual. "I finished my chapter early and I was wondering if you'd like to go out with me. You know, have some dinner somewhere."

The invitation had Molly sorely tempted. How long had it been since she'd dressed up and gone into a nice restaurant, let someone wait on her, be spoiled a little? Too long. During the years of her marriage, she and Lee had eaten out a lot. But more than just her eating habits had changed since then.

She was thoughtful so long that Devin wondered if she was trying to think of a polite way to turn him down. It was only six, not terribly late, but maybe she wasn't hungry. "Or have you already had dinner at the café?"

"Actually, I haven't." She finished the last towel and placed it on top of the others before indicating the pot on the stove. "I've got spaghetti sauce heating. I was just going to have a bowl of pasta, then get to my typing. I've missed the last two evenings and I'm getting behind."

He'd smelled the tempting aroma as soon as he'd walked in. But with all her varied activities, he'd figured she was making a cauldron of sauce for the homeless. "All right." Nobody could say he wasn't a good sport. "How about tomorrow night, then?" A persistent good sport. He'd keep asking until she ran out of excuses.

"Mmm, I'd like that, but tomorrow I've got Samantha's Brownie troop coming over. We're rehearsing our

Fourth of July skit that several troops are putting on for the parents.'' She saw the disappointment in his eyes and felt bad. ''Maybe you'd like to help out. We can always use another adult. There're only eight six-year-olds.''

Only eight. Eight little girls—giggly, silly, messy. ''I think I'll pass. I'm not very good with kids.'' Maybe she was giving him the brush-off and he was too dense to see it. Then again, maybe she was doing him a favor.

Molly went to the stove to stir her sauce, coming to a decision. Not that she owed him anything, but he *had* asked her out and looked so little-boy-hurt when she couldn't go. ''Why don't you have some pasta with me tonight? It's meatless, but I added some mushrooms and it's pretty good. I could make a salad, heat some garlic bread.''

Devin didn't bother to hide his smile. ''If you're sure you have enough.''

She indicated the large simmering pot. ''I always seem to overdo.''

''Great. Why don't I go upstairs and get a bottle of wine?''

''None for me, thanks. I've got to keep a clear head for my typing tonight.''

''One glass couldn't hurt. I'll be right back.'' Ignoring her protests, he hurried upstairs.

Getting another pot out to boil water, Molly wondered if she'd just made a large mistake. Out in her garden, she'd convinced herself that staying away from Devin was the best plan. Yet in his company a matter of minutes and she'd invited him to dinner. What had happened to her firm resolve?

''You have *five* brothers and sisters? Wow, that's hard to imagine.'' Molly forked a bite of salad. ''Your poor mother.''

"My mother is a very organized woman. She perfected an almost military approach back when we were all kids. My dad needed her in the store, often from early morning till evening, so she ran the house like a field operation. She used to make out the week's menu on Saturday and grocery shopped with that in mind. She posted menus, daily chores and everyone's schedule on the kitchen bulletin board. We all knew what we had to do and we did it or there was hell to pay when she got home."

"You must have had a housekeeper, someone to supervise six children in her absence." Slowly, Molly swirled pasta on the tines of her fork.

"You're looking at him." Devin reached for more warm bread. "You know, this sauce is really good. I'll bet even I could make this. What brand do you use?"

"Paul Newman's. I figure if it's good enough for Joanne Woodward, it's good enough for me." Her thoughts returned to their conversation, her curiosity aroused. "What do you mean, you were the housekeeper?"

"Housekeeper, chief cook and bottle washer, babysitter, homework supervisor, disciplinarian—you name it." Devin scooped another delicious bite. He hadn't realized how hungry he was.

"Did the other kids resent you for being in charge?"

"Not really. We all had our list of chores, only mine was the longest because I'm the oldest."

"But that was such a lot of responsibility for you. How much older were you than the others?"

"Let's see, I'm three years older than Donna, five older than my brother, Dale, seven older than the twins, David and Donald, and nine years older than the baby, Diane."

Molly raised a surprised brow. "Your names all start with *D?*"

"Yes, and my parents are Dan and Dottie Gray." He watched the corners of her mouth twitch. "Go ahead and laugh. Everyone does. Kind of corny, eh?"

"Oh, I don't know. I think it's kind of cute."

"It used to cause me to stutter. I'd say, hey, Don, I mean, Dave, no, Dale. I got so I wanted everyone to wear big name tags."

She saw he was smiling. "You're making that up."

He smiled back at her. "Some of it, maybe."

"You didn't mind spending all your spare time taking care of your brothers and sisters? I mean, you couldn't take part in sports or band, or just hang out with your friends much."

The last thing he wanted was for her to feel sorry for him. "I found time. I played some football in high school. Overall, they were pretty good kids."

Molly was having trouble understanding a mother thrusting so much responsibility on a child. "Surely your mother was around some days. I mean, kids get sick, have to be taken to the doctor or dentist."

"Emergencies only. See, my folks started out with this small hardware store, then expanded it. Then opened another and another. More stores meant more hours to work. Even though they had managers and a staff, they had to oversee everyone. Mom used to tell us not to call her unless it was *really* important, like someone was bleeding."

Molly frowned at him. "You're kidding." Her mother, while a little ditzy, had always been around and always softhearted. Maybe she'd been luckier than most, Molly thought.

Devin took a sip of wine, noticing that although she'd allowed him to pour her a glass, she'd scarcely touched it. "I can understand why, in a way. With six kids, if she'd let us, one would be phoning every few minutes with burning questions like could they go play next door or could they have a soda. It made more sense for her to tell me how to handle their questions and leave her free to help Dad build his little hardware empire."

Molly thought she heard a hint of resentment in his voice, even now after all these years, and wondered if he was aware of it. Not that she blamed him. His parents had robbed him of his childhood. "You must have been a very dependable boy."

He was tired of talking about himself. Finishing, he sat back and wiped his mouth. "This was a great meal." Or maybe it was the company.

But Molly was thinking about all he'd said and left unsaid. "Is all that the reason you don't want to join me and the Brownie troop tomorrow?"

He shrugged. "I guess so. I've put in my time with kids, you know. Did you baby-sit any when you were a teenager?"

"Every chance I got." She'd always loved children, had wanted lots of them. But the fates had envisioned another scenario for her.

"You enjoyed it, eh? Well, you might not have if you'd have had to do it every day, including weekends."

She kept her eyes on his. "All that turned you off children, is that it?"

"Nah. I like kids, as long as they belong to someone else." He smiled, but it seemed forced.

Molly wondered if his parents knew how their single-minded rush to success had affected their oldest son. "Is that when you started writing, to escape?"

She surprised him by being astute enough to spot something he'd only recently figured out himself. A woman who could read between the lines that well could be dangerous. Perhaps he should choose his words more wisely. "Pretty transparent, am I?"

"No, not at all. But I remember as a teenager, when my mother and one of our *uncles* would be on the couch talking and laughing, sort of lost in their private world, I'd go outside and work in the garden or go for a bike ride or take my sister to the library. I think I was probably jealous that I was left out, that she was involved in something I couldn't participate in, so I had to find my own activity, something to do so I wouldn't feel lonely." Again, she captured his eyes and held them. "I thought maybe you felt that way, too."

"Pretty much." His voice was soft and low. She'd described his lost and solitary feeling perfectly. Only she hadn't touched on another aspect. "As a kid, did you ever feel trapped, as if you'd never be able to do what *you* wanted to do when you wanted to do it?"

Molly leaned back thoughtfully. "I think every teenager does to some extent, because so many things are denied them until they're older, and they have to listen to that authority figure. That's why I grabbed that scholarship when it was offered. It was a way out even though I hadn't a clue what I wanted to study."

He nodded his understanding. "I guess we all have our own way of coping." Deciding that things were getting way too serious, Devin straightened and put on a smile. "But hey, we survived and it wasn't all that terrible, right?"

"Right." She glanced at the clock and saw that it was heading toward eight. Where had the evening gone? She still had about four hours of typing to do. Rising, she carried her plate to the sink. "This has been nice." She almost always ate alone, even at the café.

Devin followed with his. "You wash and I'll dry, okay?"

"No, really. I can handle these few dishes." Going on tiptoe, she reached into the high cupboard for a leftover dish for the remaining sauce. She grabbed it and turned, then realized he'd come up alongside her and was very close. Her breath backed up in her throat as her feet flattened on the floor.

Molly had a flash of *déjà vu.* Who'd have thought to be on guard in their own kitchen?

Devin watched her eyes darken, saw a flicker of nerves pass over her face as his hands took hold of her arms. "Molly, I…"

The ringing of the phone shattered the quiet.

"Let it go," Devin whispered, one hand reaching up to stroke her cheek.

"I…I can't." What if her mother had taken ill or Samantha had gotten hurt? With a look of apology, Molly went to answer it.

Annoyed at someone's timing, Devin turned aside.

"I understand…no, really, it's okay…uh-huh, I know. I'll be there in fifteen minutes." She hung up, then turned to explain. "That was Hank. He just got word that a busload of tourists will be at the café shortly, about thirty people wanting dinner, and he's one waitress short. I have to go." Hurriedly, she scooped sauce into the dish, needing to refrigerate it before she left.

Both irritated and frustrated, Devin just stared at her. "You're going back to work this late?"

Surprised that he should care one way or the other, she frowned. "The café doesn't close till ten. Hank needs me."

"What if you hadn't been home when he called? He'd have muddled through somehow." Devin knew he had no business criticizing her actions, but he couldn't seem to help himself.

"But I *was* home," Molly told him, as if that explained it all.

He let out a ragged sigh. "Do you ever turn down anyone who asks for your help? There's your mother, your sister, your niece, your neighbor, your boss. Who else? There must be more."

Carefully, she set down the container and turned to him, feeling her temper rise. "Look, I'm not real crazy about someone trying to tell me how to run my life. My mother's tried, so has my sister and even Hank. I've told them all to back off, as I'm telling you now. Maybe you got used to telling people what to do while you were helping raise your siblings, but I don't need some self-important writer-type pointing out the error of my ways. I've been managing quite well on my own for some time. Now, if you'll excuse me." She turned back to spooning sauce, furious that her hands were shaking.

He'd certainly handled that well, Devin thought. "I'm sorry. I told you, I have this habit of asking questions." Which didn't excuse a thing. She didn't look up or respond. "Thanks for dinner." He left, wonder-

ing if he should slink out on his belly like the lowdown
snake she probably thought he was.

Molly slammed the sauce container into the fridge
and marched in to change into her uniform, unsure
whether she was angry with Devin or herself for giving
him enough information that he felt he had the right to
judge her.

The giggling and laughter and noise drew Devin out
onto his back porch. It was four the next afternoon and
it seemed as if the entire backyard was filled with little
people. Molly, her hair in a ponytail that matched several of the little girls' hairdos, looked very much like
them, only taller.

He'd kept King inside and could hear the big dog at
the screen door snuffling his disapproval of strange little people invading his territory. As Devin watched,
Molly tried to organize the kids into three loosely
formed groups, labeling one as the chorus, another as
the actors and the third as dancers. It took her a while,
but finally they settled down and haphazardly followed
her directions.

The skit had something to do with Uncle Sam, that
much Devin was able to discern. Other than that, he
could make out very little over the chattering and
squeals of delight. Molly would never have lasted at
his mother's house. Not firm enough, serious enough,
strict enough. But there was no mistaking that the girls
were having fun. Perhaps that was the purpose, after
all. Fun hadn't been a high priority at *Casa Gray*.

He went inside where he could watch through the
window without being observed himself. He'd been in
the backyard with King when Molly had come home
from the café, but she'd sailed in her front door without

even a glance toward them. Still annoyed because of last night, he supposed.

He didn't want her to think he was spying on her, yet he was. Just trying to figure out what made her tick, he told himself. Because he was a writer, someone who studied people. She obviously loved children, loved doing for others. She should be married with a houseful of kids. He wondered why she wasn't, what had gone wrong in her marriage. Perhaps she'd divorced her ex-husband because, like Devin, he hadn't wanted any rugrats, much less a houseful.

One of the Brownies fell down, scraping her knee on a stone and making a fuss. Devin watched Molly take care of the small wound, wiping the child's eyes, hugging her close. He hoped for Molly's sake that one day someone would come along who'd want what she so obviously wanted, children of her own. He certainly wasn't that man, as much as he was attracted to Molly. Why couldn't she just relax and have fun with him until her special someone came along?

Maybe he was barking up the wrong tree, Devin thought as he poured himself a glass of juice. Maybe he should ignore Molly, quit worrying about her working such long hours and being taken advantage of by everyone she knows. He should just concentrate on finishing his book and keep his mind uncluttered.

Sipping slowly, he heard a loud, off-key version of "Yankee Doodle" being sung with childish enthusiasm. Despite his need to disassociate himself, he couldn't help but smile as he went back to work.

"Hey, King! How are you, boy?" Molly let herself into the fenced yard, barely able to squeeze past the eager dog. Crouching down, she hugged his big head, talking softly to him. "Are you glad it's cooler tonight? I'll bet you are." She stroked his sleek neck.

He really was a beautiful animal and far more gentle than she'd have guessed when she'd first met him. However, a delivery man had wandered over to the fence recently when she'd been out back and she'd seen King bare his teeth and growl from deep in his throat. The poor guy had run off, probably certain the big shepherd would jump the fence and go after him.

"You're alone too much out here, aren't you?" she went on. "I know you get lonely." She glanced up at Devin's place where lights were on already though it was only seven in the evening. She'd seen him earlier watching her with the Brownie troop. He hadn't lingered on the porch long. Perhaps he'd figured out she was still greatly annoyed with him.

"He's got a hell of a nerve taking charge of the world, telling everyone what to do, doesn't he, King?" She scratched behind his ears. "You think he'll ever learn? No, me either." Straightening, she went over to the hose and unwound it.

Even though her garden was shaded much of the day, the heat dried out plants quickly. Today, she'd purchased a sprinkler that she decided to set up so they'd get a nightly soaking without her having to water them individually. Dragging the hose over, she narrowed her eyes, trying to estimate where to set the sprinkler so it would maximize the spray. King followed her around as she surveyed the yard.

"You've been such a good boy to leave my flowers and plants alone." He perked up his ears at her tone, aware she was praising him. "Just keep up the good work."

Her back to the house, she swung the hose about,

lining it up. She just about had it in position when King brushed past her, giving a short bark, one that sounded like a welcome. Turning, she saw Devin come up behind her.

"I've come to apologize. I seem to keep stepping out of line with you. I don't mean to and I'm sorry."

She searched his face, decided he meant it. "Apology accepted." She bent down to screw the nozzle onto the sprinkler head.

He squatted alongside her. "Can I help you with that?"

"Thanks, but I can manage." Her tone was still cool.

"You're still angry. Look, I know what you do or don't do is none of my business. I've got this terrible habit of probing into other people's lives. I'm trying to kick it."

Her hands busy, she didn't look up. "Let's not blame your criticism of me on your occupation. You weren't asking questions. You were telling me how I should run my life. There's a world of difference between curiosity and dictatorship."

He winced. "Ouch! That hurt. I was that bad?"

Molly gave the connection a final turn, then rose. "I'm afraid you were."

"All right. King is my witness. I swear I'll turn over a new leaf. No more critical comments. Cross my heart and hope to die."

She watched him make the sign of the cross over his heart, his expression in the early twilight serious though his eyes were smiling. "Okay, let's forget it."

Whew! He didn't want to go through that again, so he'd better not give voice to his thoughts so readily, Devin decided. For reasons he didn't want to go into too deeply, he hated having Molly mad at him. "Now can I help you with that?"

"I can handle it, honestly I can." He was overdoing the *mea culpa,* Molly thought as she set down the sprinkler at her chosen spot. She had no desire to have him make amends.

At the spigot, she turned on the water and watched it spurt out of the sprinkler holes as King hustled out of its path. It was the kind that weaved back and forth, covering a lot of territory. "King may not want to be out here when this is going."

"He'll stay out of the way once he figures it out." Devin stood, admiring her long, bare legs as she hurried over to shift the sprinkler a fraction to the right while the spray was shooting in the opposite direction. She was wearing white shorts and a V-necked yellow T-shirt, her feet bare. Her face was screwed up as she concentrated. Because his hands ached to touch her skin again, to take up where the ringing phone had interrupted them last night, he shoved his fists into the pockets of his shorts.

Just one more adjustment, Molly decided as she dashed over again, hurrying to avoid the undulating spray. King chose that moment to run after her, but he miscalculated and got caught in a loop of the hose. As the big dog tried to pull free of the entanglement, he pulled the hose taut, trapping Molly's foot. Down she went, her bare feet slipping out from under her in the wet grass. Of course now, the sprinkler swung about, liberally sprinkling both dog and woman.

Devin couldn't help himself. He laughed.

King was the first to recover, running off, shaking himself vigorously. Devin went to Molly to help untangle her foot. But the hose was stubborn and before he could free her, the sprinkler seesawed back, flooding him, too. He closed his eyes against the force of the spray as Molly's laughter rang out.

Soaking wet, they struggled to their feet, both giggling now. Devin walked Molly out of reach of the spray as she brushed her wet hair off her face. He shook his head, much as King had shaken his body, spraying them both again. Smiling, they stood there looking into each other's eyes.

Devin was quite suddenly aware that her wet T-shirt clung to her curves like a second skin, made more prominent when a shiver took her. Noticing, Molly tried to lessen the impact by plucking at the material of her shirt, but her actions only emphasized her near-transparent state. She felt heat move into her face as she looked up at Devin and watched his smile slip and his eyes darken with desire.

Stunned at the intensity she saw there, she took a careful step back. "Wait, Devin, I..."

"No. We've waited long enough." His arms slid around her and his mouth captured hers. Crushing her closer, he drank from her the way he'd been longing to. When he heard a soft sound come from deep inside her that hinted at pleasure, he deepened the kiss.

The sweet, hot taste of him spread through Molly, warming her blood. She forgot the chill of being soaking wet through and through, forgot she was still a little angry with him, forgot her resolution not to get too close. She knew only that strong arms were holding her tightly, that a vibrant heart was thudding next to her own, that needs she'd denied for years were suddenly reawakening.

Devin couldn't remember how long it had been since he'd kissed a woman, but he knew without a doubt that it had been one hell of a long time since a woman had kissed him back like this. Her hands that had been caught between their bodies traveled up over his shoulders and finally tangled in his hair. Her mouth moved against his, soft and bold and beautiful. Her slender body molded to his, straining to be closer, just as he was. She was all he'd dreamed of and more.

Her heated blood was racing and Molly wanted the feeling to never end. She yearned to be touched, to be cherished, to be loved. Yet when his hands skimmed down her back then lower, pressing her against himself in a way that left no doubt as to his state of readiness, something clicked in her mind and she broke the kiss. It was one thing to want and quite another to give in to that swift desire. Mindless loving was for the very young or the very stupid, and she was neither.

Easing back from him, Molly ran a less than steady hand through her damp hair.

Having trouble catching his breath, Devin rubbed the back of his neck. It had been some time since he'd had to put on the brakes quite so hastily. He had to say something. He just wasn't sure what.

"I suppose now you're upset with me again."

"No. I'm upset with me. I saw that coming. I could have stopped you."

"Why didn't you?"

She took her time answering. "Because I wanted to know what it would feel like to kiss you, to *really* kiss you."

"And now that you have?"

Molly swallowed around a dry throat. "I know what they mean when they say it's best to let sleeping dogs lie."

He appreciated her honesty. "I didn't have to kiss

you to know I wanted you. You've been on my mind since we moved in together.''

That didn't quite describe their living arrangement, but she was in no mood to nitpick. She also avoided his eyes since he would probably see that she wanted him just as much. ''The difference between children and adults is that adults know they can't have everything they want.'' She walked over to the spigot and turned off the water. There'd been quite enough sprinkling for one night.

Devin wasn't about to let her walk away on that remark. He touched her arm, turned her to face him. ''Are you saying that you want me, too?''

''I could hardly deny that with a straight face after that kiss, now, could I? But you're playing a game here, Devin. Get acquainted, get close, get into bed. I don't play those games. However, I'm sure you'll have no trouble finding any number of women who'll gladly play with you.'' She turned, needing to escape to her safe little apartment.

''But it's you I want.''

He'd said it so quietly, so confidently. But she couldn't take him seriously. ''You'll get over it. We hardly know each other. It's not as if this is love at first sight.''

He grabbed her arm, pulled her wet body close to his and took possession of her mouth. This kiss was long and thorough, stealing the breath from her, leaving her stunned and shaken.

Devin stared into eyes hazy with arousal. ''Tell me you feel that way when any man kisses you.''

''I...no man has kissed me in...well, a long time.'' But she knew it had never been like that, not ever.

That surprised him. ''Then what's to stop us, Molly?

You're single and free. So am I. Why not enjoy one another?''

Why not, indeed? He'd left out one small thing: feelings and the complications they caused. "I can't afford to get involved with you, Devin." Though she'd known him only a short time, she knew instinctively that he could break her heart. It was still cracked from her last encounter three years ago. One more fracture and she might never be whole again.

"I don't see why not. If you think it's too soon, all right. Let's get to know one another better. Let me take you to dinner tomorrow. We can…"

"I'm going to Tucson tomorrow." She took in a deep breath, trying to calm her racing heart. "It's my day off and I've got a long-standing date." She watched his face cloud over and almost smiled. "With my two college roommates and our landlady from our university days. Maggie Davis, a wonderful woman. She'll be sixty-four tomorrow. The four of us meet every year for lunch on her birthday."

"All right then, the next evening." Patience, he told himself.

Odd how once a man makes up his mind he wants a woman, he expects her to drop her life and fall in line. Lee had persisted the same way. "I can't plan that far ahead, Devin. I have to work and I can't afford to get behind in my typing and…"

He leaned down to her, touching his lips to hers in a kiss that was quick and amazingly tender, yet had the power to send her pulse throbbing all over again. "That's so you think of me in Tucson." He let her go, whistled for his dog and left the yard, bounding up the stairs.

Molly stood staring after them, thinking she finally knew how it probably felt to be in a hurricane.

Chapter Five

Laura Marshall stretched out her legs in the passenger seat of Molly's Honda and glanced over at her friend behind the wheel. "I don't know about you, but that's the most fun I've had since our last reunion luncheon a year ago."

Molly couldn't have agreed more. "Me, too. I wish we could have stayed for the whole weekend, especially since this is the tenth anniversary of the year we all met. But, unfortunately, I can't take any more time off right now." They'd lingered for more than three hours at Gentle Ben's, a favorite restaurant near the U of A campus.

"That's all right. I've got a client coming in for a consult tonight." Laura's Studio of Interior Design was finally out of the red ink. "Can you even remember ten years ago when we were scared and giggly little freshmen?"

"Barely."

"Maggie really looks good, doesn't she?"

"She sure does. How come that woman has more energy at sixty-four than I do at twenty-eight?" Molly's fondness for Maggie Davis, the widow who'd converted her home into a rooming house for University of Arizona students after her husband died, was shared by her other two roommates. The three-and-a-half years she'd spent living on Maggie's second floor were the happiest Molly could remember. Not only had Maggie been like a surrogate mother to all of them, but Laura Marshall and Tate Monroe had remained her closest friends even though the three of them now lived miles apart.

"Don't complain to me," Laura commented, being a year older than Molly. "I'm on the fast track to thirty, which means I can no longer blame my mistakes on youthful ignorance."

"Speaking of that, I'd like to ask you something."

"Go right ahead. You're one of two people I have no secrets from." Laura brushed back her shoulder-length black hair, her blue eyes behind sunglasses gazing out the windshield at the late afternoon traffic.

"Do you regret marrying Marc Abbott so soon after graduation?" An all-American-boy type, Marc had gone to work for Marshall Realty owned by Laura's father. He'd been a man on the rise who'd wooed and won the boss's daughter and everyone had thought they'd live happily ever after. But they'd divorced after only a year and a half.

"You know what they say about hindsight. I think I was in love with the idea of marriage. Marc was so charming that I didn't stop to think that I didn't love him." There was more, but Laura wasn't going to go into all that just now. She turned to Molly. "But Marc never hurt me as badly as Lee hurt you."

Molly's hands tightened on the wheel just a fraction before she caught herself and forced her fingers to relax.

"Do you ever hear from Lee?"

"No, and I don't care to." Lee had remarried and they'd since had a son. "I saw his picture in the paper recently. His dad put him in charge of their new store." Her ex-in-laws owned a chain of furniture stores throughout the southwest and Lee, as an only child, was moving up the company ladder, with a nudge from Daddy, no doubt.

Molly turned onto the expressway ramp leading to Phoenix, hoping old Bess wouldn't act up at least until she could drop Laura at the restaurant where she was meeting an attorney friend who'd driven her down while he took a deposition. Needing to change the focus of their conversation, she zeroed in on their absent roommate. "Tate looked a little tired, don't you think?"

Tate Monroe, the third roommate to share Maggie Davis's home, had gotten pregnant in her senior year by a man who'd later become quite powerful. He'd walked away from Tate before learning of her pregnancy, marrying instead a woman who could help his career. Maggie and Tate's two roommates had helped deliver her baby one rainy night right in her room at Maggie's, a night none of them would ever forget.

After Josh was born, Tate had sworn both Molly and Laura to secrecy as to the identity of the boy's father, wanting only to forget him. But, to this day, Tate lived in fear that he might return and try to claim her son.

"Surely Josh's father won't bother Tate after all this

time.'' Molly's voice didn't sound convincing even to her own ears.

"You can never tell. I think that's why Tate looks so pale and nervous. Now that she's moved back in with Maggie, at least she's got some help with Josh. And let's face it, if that bastard wants to find her, he will no matter where she goes.'' Laura realized she sounded cynical.

Molly was terribly afraid that Laura was right. Tate had been the pretty one. Beautiful, actually, with thick auburn hair, green eyes and a terrific figure. Laura had been the rich one and Molly the smart one. The three of them had clicked from day one. And here they were, ten years later, neither one gloriously happy as they'd been so certain they would be with the naïveté of youth.

"Why do you suppose not one of us has been lucky in the love department?'' Laura asked, not really expecting an answer.

"Beats me,'' Molly said, passing a station wagon stuffed with half a dozen kids and a laughing couple in the front. Glancing at the happy family unit she felt a pang of envy so strong it was almost physical. Maybe she shouldn't have had that glass of wine, though she'd followed it with a big lunch. Wine usually made her sentimental. Or, God forbid, maudlin.

"Say,'' Laura interrupted her thoughts, "I've been meaning to ask. Who was that tall, dark and handsome fellow leaving your drive on a Harley when we drove up? Not bad.''

No, not bad at all. And he kisses like there's no tomorrow. "He lives in the apartment above mine. He's a writer. Devin Gray. Have you heard of him?''

"No, but then, I'm way behind on my reading. What does he write?"

"Western mysteries. Lucy says he's really good."

Laura's antenna began receiving signals. She turned to study her former roommate.

Molly felt eyes on her and shot Laura a quick glance. "What?"

"Is there something you're not telling me? Are you and the Harley man developing plots together?"

Molly frowned. "Hardly. I've only known him a few weeks."

"And he's never asked you out?" Molly had certainly had her pick of men during their college days.

"He has, but I've turned him down."

"Why, for heaven's sake? Does he kill cats for kicks or have an ex-wife who's a sharpshooter? What?"

Laughing, Molly shook her head. "He has no perversions that I know of. But you know how I feel. I can't get involved, not until I've reached my goal— financial independence. And maybe not even then. Laura, it's simply not worth it."

"Who said anything about getting involved? As we just mentioned, we're not getting any younger. Tell me, do you like him? Is he fun? Does he excite you?"

Molly let herself remember that long sensual kiss in the backyard last night and felt the memory warm her. "Yes, I like him, but I think all he wants is a fling. He's renting on a month-to-month basis, not even a year's lease. Once this book he's working on is finished, he'll go somewhere else."

"So what's wrong with a fling? If he's handsome, fun and can show you a good time, I say go for it. We only go around once, you know."

Molly sent her another searching glance. "That

doesn't sound like you, Laura.'' Of the three of them, Laura had been the most serious.

Laura sighed heavily. "Yeah, well, time has a way of changing us. I've been alone since my divorce, and there are days I'd give a lot for a nice guy around the house. Don't get me wrong, I like my life. But it gets damn lonely sometimes. Trouble is, there aren't enough of the right kind of guys around, and who wants the other kind?''

"Amen to that. Still, I keep thinking that even if I got to know Devin better, if he learned about me, *all* about me, there's a good chance he wouldn't want me. I'm not sure I could handle a second rejection over the same problem. It's easier to just avoid the whole situation.'' Although Devin had told her he didn't want children, she felt certain he'd change his mind someday.

"That's a bunch of bull.'' Laura crossed her long legs with some difficulty. "Damn Lee Summers for what he did to you.''

"Not all of what happened was his fault. He had himself checked out, as you know. I'm to blame for not being able to give the heir apparent a son.''

"If a man loves a woman, that shouldn't... couldn't...''

"Matter. You're right, I suppose. Apparently Lee didn't love me enough, so it mattered.''

"Because he's not man enough, that loser, to stand up to Daddy.''

Molly felt hot tears at the back of her eyes as she reached over to squeeze her friend's hand. "I love you, too, babe.''

Laura squeezed back. "Men! Who needs them, right?''

Blinking rapidly, Molly tried a crooked smile. "Right.''

* * *

"Tell the truth, did you think of me yesterday?"
Devin asked Molly the moment she stepped out of the
car after work the next day. Even though her feet hurt,
she almost smiled at the boyish look on his face. He
didn't kiss like a boy, but sometimes he reminded her
of one.

"Not even once," she said, slamming the door and
moving toward the back porch.

But he saw her lips twitch then give it up and break
into a big smile. He stopped her with a hand on her
arm. "Aha! Your face gives you away."

"All right, I thought of you. Once when for a minute
my car wouldn't start. I wished you'd been there to get
it going."

His eyes as green as the shirt he was wearing narrowed. "You're lying. You know more about what's
under old Bessie's hood than I do. C'mon. 'Fess up."

In her entire life, Molly had never met anyone more
persistent. She decided to turn the tables on him.
"What about you? Did you think of me?"

He gave her his slow, secretive smile. "Only all day.
I was writing a love scene and picturing you in it."

Heat moved into her face instantly and she almost
dropped her keys. "You what? I thought you wrote
mysteries."

Devin laughed. "I do and there are no love scenes.
Had you going there for a minute, eh?"

She gave him a playful punch on his arm. "Stop
that! Honestly." She circled past him and went up the
porch steps.

He trailed after her. "I'm glad you had the early shift
today. Why don't we go for a ride, take a picnic lunch
and…"

Just then, an older model Chevrolet wheezed into the drive, Lucy behind the wheel and her daughter, Samantha, waving a greeting.

"That's why I can't go," Molly told Devin.

"Brownies again?"

"No. My sister has a doctor's appointment so I'm watching Sam. I promised I'd take her to the park. They live in an apartment and she doesn't have a yard." Molly left the porch. "Hi, guys."

Lucy gazed at Devin through her open window, a big smile on her face. "I read your first book. It was great."

He walked over to thank her. "Glad you liked it."

"I didn't guess the ending. You're very good."

Devin smiled. "Always nice to hear." He saw Sam get out and give her aunt a big hug. Molly was doing it again, helping someone out after she'd worked all day rather than take some time for herself. But he knew better than to comment on how he felt about her compulsive volunteering.

"Hi!" Samantha called out to Devin, skipping over. "Did you get a small helmet so I can ride on the motorcycle with you?"

He'd forgotten that kids never forget what you say. "Not yet, but I'm working on it."

"Sam, you're way too young to ride on that big cycle," Lucy said emphatically, letting both her daughter and Devin know she wouldn't permit such a thing.

Devin winked at Lucy. "Not to worry." He turned back to Sam, trying to cheer her up. "I hear your aunt's taking you to the park. Maybe I'll tag along." Did those words come out of his mouth? Devin wondered, nearly panicking. He looked over at Molly who was staring at him as surprised as he. "Well, why not?" he asked her, amazed at the lengths a man will go to to be with a woman he wants.

"You're coming with us?" Sam beamed, always pleased to have a man along since men in her life were rare. "Great!"

Molly's blue eyes were dubious. "Yeah, great."

Lucy looked from one to the other and decided to stay out of it. "Will you drop her back home, Moll?" she asked her sister. "I should be back by four, five at the latest."

"Sure. Don't worry. She'll be fine." But she kept looking at Devin whose face was carefully blank. So he wanted to go to the park, eh? Fine. She'd show him the park, all right.

She slipped an arm around her niece as Lucy drove off. "Come in with me while I change, okay?" She glanced at Devin. "We'll be ready in ten minutes."

"Terrific." He sat down on the porch steps, wondering whatever made him volunteer to go to the park. He used to go quite often in California when his brothers and sisters were young. They'd bicycle over, have a picnic lunch, play baseball. But he'd been a kid then, too. It wasn't exactly the way he'd pictured his first date with Molly, but he'd show her he was adaptable.

Devin leaned back on the park bench, licking the last of his chocolate ice cream cone. Alongside him, Molly was working on her strawberry cone more slowly, as relaxed as he'd ever seen her. Down at the edge of the man-made pond, Sam, who'd finished her cone first, happily fed bread chunks Devin had purchased at the food stand to the ducks who lived there. The full-grown ones quacked their appreciation while the baby ducks missed most throws, diving under and surfacing, then fluttering back for more while Sam giggled at their antics.

"It's a nice park," Devin commented. "A lot nicer than the one we used to visit in California."

Molly had to admit he'd been a good sport, even as Sam's boundless energy nearly wore him out. The six-year-old had him climbing boulders and catching her as she swooshed down the slide, then pushing her endlessly on the swings. Molly had hidden her smile as he'd folded his long legs into the small train that circled the perimeter of the park. A sucker for punishment, he'd even climbed on one of the horses on the merry-go-round next to Sam's, the two of them waving to Molly as she watched from a bench.

What was his game? Molly asked herself. Swallowing a soggy piece of cone, she studied him surreptitiously. He had on a black Henley shirt, the cotton stretched over his broad chest muscles, and tan carpenter's shorts with black boat shoes. His dark hair, rearranged by a summer breeze, had her remembering how she'd thrust her hands into its silky thickness and how his mouth had felt on hers. His sunglasses hung in the open V of his shirt, his green gaze on the child feeding the ducks. He looked perfectly relaxed.

Why had he invited himself along? At first, she'd thought he'd planned on being alone with her while Sam ran off to play on the monkey bars and swings. But he'd surprised her and willingly accompanied Sam on every ride, each climbing venture, all of it—while she'd watched from a distance. Was he trying to impress her? But if all he wanted was a fling, as she'd explained to Laura yesterday, why be nice to her niece? He could just as easily have waited for Molly to return to be alone with her. This new side of him puzzled her.

"Careful, don't get too close to the water," Devin called out to Sam who'd been scooting more and more forward. He had visions of her falling in and he'd be the logical one to jump into the murky water to pull her out.

"I thought you weren't nuts about kids," Molly finally said.

"I didn't say I didn't like children, just that I don't plan to have any of my own. Kids tie you down, change your life and require an enormous amount of work, if you raise them right. I've had a taste of that— a long taste—and it's not for me." Better she knew that up front, Devin thought. Not that he felt Molly was looking at him with any thoughts of permanence.

Molly stared ahead at the young girl who squealed in delight as one of the bolder ducks swam right up to her and grabbed the bread from her fingers. She felt the all-too-familiar pain squeeze her heart. She'd never have a daughter of her own like Sam or a son, either. Most of the time, she avoided thinking about children, but occasionally something would trigger a memory and the ache would return. She'd never understand someone like Devin who could have children and didn't want them.

She was quiet so long that Devin had to ask. "Did I say something to upset you? I was trying to be honest."

"No, of course not. You have a right to your feelings, whatever they are."

"But you don't agree with them?"

Suddenly, she didn't want the rest of her cone, scrunching it up in the napkin. "Devin, what's right for you may not be right for me, and vice versa."

"I guess so. We all get to choose what we want to do with our lives."

Only sometimes the choices are made for us, Molly thought. Rising, she tossed the napkin in a nearby trash can and looked at her watch. "It's nearly five. We'd better get Sam home."

Devin stood, realizing he'd discovered something today, and it was a little hard for him to admit. "Thanks for allowing me to include myself today. I had a good time. Sam's a real charmer." But he was still glad she was someone else's responsibility.

Molly searched his eyes, unable to zero in on him. He was a dichotomy, an enigma, a study in contradictions. Maybe one day she'd get a bead on him. "I'm glad you came along," she told him, and found she meant it.

"I probably shouldn't have given in to you," Molly said as she finished her iced tea. "I'm going to have to type into the wee hours after taking yesterday off and playing hooky again tonight." She smiled across the table at him. "But I'm glad I'm such a pushover."

Devin's brows shot up. "You, a pushover? You've got to be kidding. I've been trying to get you out and away from that house for three weeks." After dropping Sam off, he'd all but insisted she let him take her out. Since he was driving her car, he'd already been headed away from their neighborhood when she finally and most reluctantly agreed.

He'd driven her up to Carefree just north of Scottsdale, a small touristy community he'd read about but had never visited. The town boasted a dozen or more quaint shops on avenues with picturesque names like Ho Hum Drive and Easy Street, plus a large sundial clock in the square. They'd walked about, poked into several of the unique stores and finally had a terrific taco salad in a Mexican restaurant with outdoor seating.

Devin thought she looked relaxed wearing a navy knit shirt and white slacks. "You really ought to do this more often. Life's too short to become a slave to even a worthy goal like financial independence."

"People who say that usually have already achieved financial independence."

He leaned forward, needing to make his point. "I've been out of college eleven years, Molly, most of those spent in tiny one-room apartments, eating two meals a day because I couldn't afford three, driving a car held together with spit, glue and prayers, much worse than Bessie. It's only in the last eighteen months that I've made some serious money, and much of that's gone to pay off the many loans I'd taken out."

"I see you've paid your dues."

"I don't regret those years. They taught me a lot. But even at my poorest, when I had to bag groceries or flip burgers at a fast food joint because those were the only jobs available in whatever small town I was in, I always took time out to have a little fun. I'd go hiking up a mountain or drive up to a lake and swim or fish. Things I could do for very little money. You can go bonkers if all you focus on is work and more work."

She swirled the remaining ice cubes in her glass. "I suppose you're right." Looking up, she made the sign of the cross over her heart as he'd done a few days ago. "All right, I swear to have more fun."

"I'll hold you to that." He placed some bills on the check on the table, then held out his hand. "Ready to go?"

Molly placed her hand in his, felt the warmth, the comfort of his strong fingers enclosing hers. Maybe she was making a mistake, one part of her brain warned her, but this felt good.

The ride back was lovely with the sun setting over the mountains, streaking the sky with orange and pink, the clouds outlined in paintbrush strokes of purple. Old Bessie chugged south, keeping up with traffic.

Devin drove the same way he did everything, competently, almost lazily. He wouldn't start the engine until she'd agreed to lace her fingers through his as he rested their entwined hands on his right thigh. Molly hadn't felt so peaceful in a very long time. Comfortably relaxed, she leaned her head back and closed her eyes, not intending to sleep, just lightly dozing.

But she did drift off and, in what seemed moments later, she felt soft, warm lips on hers, teasing, tasting, tiny kisses coaxing her awake. Slowly, dreamlike, her eyes opened and she saw Devin's dark green gaze in the dim light of the interior of her car already parked in their drive. She didn't speak, just let her eyes caress the by now familiar planes of his face.

That fascinating indentation in his chin caught her attention. With exaggerated care, she stretched to touch her lips to that enticing dimple, her tongue tracing the contours. "I've been wanting to do that for some time," she told him.

Devin slid his arms around her. "I have a long list of things I've been wanting to do to you."

Her pulse beginning to pound, she kept her gaze steady on him. "Mmm, I'll just bet you do."

"Like this, for starters." He kissed her then, slowly, deeply, as if assuring her there was no hurry, no rush to the finish line. They could take their time, explore, experience. He waited until she made a soft sound deep in her throat and he felt her arms encircle him and tighten, then he slipped his tongue in. He felt a shiver take her just before she began to respond to the sensual mating.

She was a drumbeat in his head, Devin thought, a pulsing in his blood, a dream he didn't want to awaken from. Her small, strong hands traveled over his back, then slipped beneath his shirt to stroke his bare skin, setting him on fire.

Such gentleness, Molly thought. The kiss in the yard had been all flash and fire, swift needs and intense passion suddenly realized. But this was different. His lips brushed along hers, sipped from hers, flirted with hers. She'd never known such tenderness in a man's kiss, never dreamed this man would be so patient. The other kiss had overwhelmed her while this one lazily seduced her, and was therefore much more deadly.

She became aware of his hands shifting to the front, felt his fingertips trace the fullness of her breasts through her thin cotton blouse. The need to be touched, to be skin to skin with him had her arching her back, the hot, swift desire stunning her. She wasn't like this, Molly told herself. She'd never ever burned like this with the need to have a man's hands on her flesh. *This* man's hands.

A soft evening breeze drifted in through the car's open window and in the distance, a sudden sharp sound broke the silence. And the mood as Molly's eyes flew open and she eased back. "What was that?" she whispered.

A scream, followed by a dog's sharp bark, echoed through the thick night air. Devin catapulted from aroused to annoyed at the interruption to anxiety over what had to be a shriek of terror. Shoving open the driver's door, he heard another cry burst forth just as he got out, the sound followed by King's nervous barking from the yard. "It's coming from Mrs. Bailey's house."

Molly was already out and running, circumventing the fenced pool between the two houses, heading for their landlady's back door where a shaft of light beamed out onto the yard. She saw Devin easily overtake her just before she spotted a shadowy figure appear in that beam of light. "There!" she shouted. "Someone's there."

Devin sprinted over Mrs. Bailey's small bed of pansies, his eyes on the man who'd noticed them and had turned to run. But a stucco wall on the far side of the lot must have appeared too high for him to scale for he changed directions, retracing his steps along the back fence line.

"Go in and check on Mrs. Bailey," Devin yelled over his shoulder at Molly. "And call 9-1-1!"

He ran straight for the man who was carrying a sack and wearing a cap pulled low on his face. Devin saw that he was a good head shorter than himself, but built stocky and solid. If he'd had a gun, Devin felt certain he'd have flashed it by now. Then suddenly, the man paused and Devin saw the glint of a knife in his free hand. That more than evened the odds.

"Stay back or I'll use this," the man snarled, aware that he was trapped between the back wall and the pool fence. "Stay put and I won't hurt you."

Breathing hard from his adrenaline rush, Devin stood with his hands loose at his sides. He heard Mrs. Bailey's screen door open, then Molly's voice.

"Let him go, Devin, please," she pleaded.

Devin never figured himself to be a hero, nor did he wish to get hurt saving the few things the thief had in his sack. He looked so nondescript, so everyman, that if he let him go, the police would probably never find him. But if he'd hurt Mrs. Bailey, then he was more than merely a thief. "Go back inside," he yelled to Molly, never taking his eyes from the nervous man.

He waited, letting the intruder make the first move. The faint sound of a siren some distance away, which might not have even been on its way here, set the thief in motion. Knife held menacingly, he tried to rush past Devin.

When he felt the man was close enough, Devin dived for his legs in a flying tackle reminiscent of his high school football days, praying he wouldn't break any bones as he landed hard, taking the thief down with him.

But fear had the man recovering first as the siren sound seemed to be coming closer. He kicked out at Devin, bruising his shoulder before scrambling free. With supreme effort, Devin managed to grab his foot, holding on. When the thief couldn't shake him off, he bent down and slashed blindly with his knife. A sharp pain whipped through Devin's hand, but still he held on.

The siren became louder and the man more desperate. Jackknifing himself, the intruder raised his weapon again, aiming for Devin's middle. Fortunately, Devin saw the strike coming and rolled out of range, the man's shoe coming off in his hand. That gave the thief just enough time to regain his footing and take off.

Swearing to himself, Devin got to his feet and spotted the man already at the far corner. The last he saw of him was as he scrambled over a fence and disappeared from sight. Moments too late, a police car turned onto Cactus Lane, its searchlight scanning house numbers until they spotted the right one and swung into the driveway. Devin made his way over as the two officers jumped out, guns drawn.

He explained the situation, pointing to where he'd last seen the thief and holding up the shoe he'd managed to yank off him. It was then that he noticed blood trailing down his arm from the cut on his hand. When he heard Molly coming out, he held his hand down at his side. "Aren't you going after him?" Devin asked the officer already holstering his gun.

"Chances are he's half a mile from here by now, zigzagging from street to street, over fences, around yards. Probably pocketed the cap you said he had on, tossed the knife, maybe even stashed the stolen stuff. He's strolling down some street, looking like he's just some guy out for a walk. B-and-E guys are pretty shrewd."

Molly felt her temper rise. "Listen, he's missing a shoe, limping along. Shouldn't that look suspicious? Can't you radio other police cars to be on the lookout for him? Surely you're going to do *something* when he scared poor Mrs. Bailey half to death and stole from her."

"Is she hurt?" the older officer asked.

"Not physically," Molly replied.

The cops exchanged a look as if to say this was a useless call. "Did you get a good look at him?" the first officer asked Devin.

"Not so I'd recognize his face. About five-six, stocky build, dark pants and shirt, and you have his shoe."

"Uh-huh. You're describing half the men in town."

He took out a small notebook and pen. "We'll go in and see if the lady got a better look, get a list of what he took. Maybe, if he pawns the stuff, we'll get a line on him." He wrote down their names, the address next door, phone numbers, then the two officers started toward the back door. But the taller one turned back. "You'd better get that cut looked at," he told Devin.

Molly frowned. "You're hurt?" Why hadn't he let the man go? She moved around him, took his hand. "This looks deep. You'll need stitches."

It was hurting like hell, Devin had to admit. What bothered him the most was that the cut was in the meaty part of his thumb. He hoped it wouldn't prevent him from typing.

"When was your last tetanus shot?" Molly asked. "We don't know where that knife has been."

"I don't remember."

"Come on. I'll drive you to Emergency."

"What about Mrs. Bailey? Maybe you should stay with her. I can drive myself."

"I called Trisha and she's on her way over. She'll be fine. She's feeling a little foolish since she forgot to lock the back door." Molly guided him around to old Bessie. "However, it's a good thing we got home when we did. He didn't believe she doesn't have any money stashed away and was threatening her with a knife. If we hadn't heard that scream...well, who knows if he'd have hurt her."

She opened the car door, noticing that the wound was still bleeding heavily. "Sit down. I'm going to get a towel to wrap around that. He might have cut a small artery."

Damn, Devin thought, getting in. Just what he needed, to lose several days of work over a silly cut.

He leaned back, trying to think positive. Maybe Molly would hang around more, play nurse. Now that had definite possibilities.

It was nearly midnight when they finally were released from Emergency. There'd been a bad auto accident nearby and those victims had had first priority of the evening staff, naturally. By the time they'd put Devin in a cubicle and begun to clean the wound, he'd lost quite a bit of blood.

Molly had insisted on going in with him, over his protests. Nobody should be alone in a hospital situation, she believed. And the cut was quite deep, as the attending physician verified. They froze the thumb area, put in six small stitches and gave him a tetanus shot. By then his head was spinning, she could tell, though he'd sat stoically through the whole procedure, undoubtedly keeping a stiff upper lip for her benefit. Men! she thought.

The nurse had insisted he take a pain pill before releasing him with a small envelope of more pills in case the wound caused pain after the novocaine wore off, which she predicted it would. Molly drove home, noticing that Devin seemed pale. She took his arm and led him up the steps to the back porch.

"I want you to stay with me tonight, so I can keep an eye on you." Before he could protest, she opened her door and urged him into her kitchen. "I know it's not a life-threatening wound, but I'd just feel better." She saw his frown and went on. "Humor me, okay?"

He did feel a little weak and woozy, probably from that pain pill, which he never should have taken, Devin thought as he watched her turn down her bed for him. For weeks now, he'd been wanting to get her into bed and now here she was, about to tuck him in while he could scarcely keep his eyes open.

Too far gone to argue, he slipped out of his shoes, removed his shorts and shirt and lay down wearing only gray knit boxers. "Thanks," he whispered, his eyes already closing. Turning on his side, he was asleep in moments.

Molly pulled the sheet over him and adjusted the pillow. Then hands on her hips, she stood at the foot of the bed.

Look at that, will you? she thought. A handsome hunk in my bed and all he wants to do is sleep. Smiling, she left the room.

Chapter Six

Three o'clock in the morning was such a restless hour when you couldn't sleep, Molly thought. Heaven knows she'd tried, taking off her blouse and skirt, pulling on a comfortable blue football jersey that didn't quite reach her knees, curling up on the couch with a spare pillow and blanket. But she kept hearing sounds from the bedroom, then jumping up to check on Devin, only to find he hadn't moved. Her overactive imagination at work. Wearily, she'd resettled herself on the couch, only to punch and jab at the pillow all over again.

Finally, she gave up and went back to study him in the dim light trailing in from the open door of the bathroom across the hall. His dark hair was rumpled from his good hand impatiently plowing through it while they'd waited in Emergency. His face in sleep was relaxed, probably from the pain pill, yet there was that

aura of vibrancy about him that she'd noticed from the
beginning. Those compelling green eyes were closed
now, his dark lashes longer and thicker than they had
a right to be, resting on tan cheeks. There was a day's
growth of beard on those cheeks and on his strong dimpled chin, chasing away any traces of boyishness. He
should have look bedraggled and unappealing and out-
of-sorts.

He looked wonderful.

Carefully sitting down on the far side of the bed,
Molly wasn't sure if he would look great to everyone
or if only seen through her eyes. Because recently,
she'd come to know him and that changed how she
viewed him.

She'd found Devin Gray attractive from the beginning, which was reason enough to keep her distance
since getting involved was the last thing on her list of
priorities. She'd found his persistence, his constant
probing and questioning, annoying, yet he seemed genuinely interested in learning about her. Which in turn
had made her curious about him.

He hadn't had a carefree childhood, despite his family's obvious success. He'd worked hard to get where
he was through what had to be discouraging years waiting for his writing to take off. He loved his family,
even the parents who, in Molly's estimation, had
dumped way too much responsibility on his young
shoulders. He was good with kids, despite his protes-
tations that he had no interest in fatherhood. Already,
Sam adored him.

Then there was the selfless way he'd rushed to Mrs.
Bailey's rescue tonight, without regard to his own
safety. He hadn't gone after the thief to impress her,
but because he felt it was the right thing to do. He

could have just let the jerk get away, but he'd obviously felt a responsibility, this man who claimed he wanted no such obligations. There was that dichotomy thing again.

Giving in to an irresistible urge, Molly slowly stretched out alongside him, turning on her side facing him, cradling her head on one arm. With the other hand, she reached over to smooth the hair from his forehead. He didn't move.

Molly's gaze settled on his generous mouth that had worked such magic on hers in the car before Mrs. Bailey's scream had interrupted them. His hands had been on her breasts, awakening needs she'd purposely buried so long ago she'd almost forgotten their power. That tug of sensual desire that reminded her she was a woman. What would have happened, she couldn't help wondering, if that thief had picked another night to do his dirty work and there'd been no interruption? Would that white-hot need have carried them to his bed or hers?

No matter, for here he was, in her bed, asleep, enabling her to study him at will. Three in the morning was a time of truth, of setting evasions aside, Molly knew. There was no denying that she wanted him right where she had him, in her bed, only awake. How quickly she'd reached this stage, she thought with a frown. Yet hadn't she suspected from that night he'd first touched her in the kitchen that he'd somehow manage to break down her defenses?

Was it because he was special or because she was so very needy, something she'd denied even to herself? Probably both, she decided, if honesty was to count here. Just holding his hand warmed her, his touch on her cheek excited her, his kisses aroused her in a way she'd either forgotten or never known before.

Yet, if truth was the goal, she had to admit he was the wrong man to want. Already, she was halfway in love with him, meaning he could easily hurt her. By his own admission, he'd been traveling for years and would likely leave again. He was a young, healthy male who wanted a fling and nothing more, she was certain. He didn't want responsibilities, commitments, a future together. He'd told her he'd broken up with one woman already because she'd wanted more. Why should Molly be different?

She was different in that she wasn't looking for a man to spend her future with, either. She had plans, independent goals that she wanted to achieve on her own, beholden to no one. For years now, she'd held firm in her need to succeed, to not stray from the path she'd set for herself.

Until he'd touched her.

Molly let out a ragged sigh. So the ball was in her court. To give in to the passion he'd awakened in her so readily would mean temporary pleasure along with possible—no, probable, heartbreak. To pass on it, to discourage his advances knowing he wasn't for her, would leave her regretting what might have been.

Did she have the strength of character, the will-power, to do that? *What might have been.* Sad words. After all, as Laura had said, they weren't getting any younger. In the years she'd been alone, no man had interested her enough to matter.

But this one mattered. Probably too much.

She'd never had a fling, didn't know how to go about it. Was it acceptable for her to lie down with him like this, an obvious signal of her interest? Should she have waited until he'd recovered, then tell him she was open to suggestions? It seemed so calculated, to discuss a fling as casually as choosing a restaurant for dinner. Did singles do that these days?

Molly was aware that she had this terrible habit of overanalyzing everything. Why couldn't she just be the kind of woman who'd hop in a man's bed and enjoy him while she could, then send him on his way with no regrets?

Because her heart was involved. Because making love was not a casual thing to her.

Making love. Was that what she was seriously considering here?

Her gaze fell on his hand resting on the sheet at his side. Gently, she traced the tan skin, the long fingers, feeling his strength. There came a time in every woman's life, Molly thought, when she had to take a chance, risk her feelings, open herself up to possibilities. Regrets made very unsatisfactory bedfellows, she'd heard.

Tenderly laying her hand in his, she closed her eyes.

Later, Molly was to wonder what woke her. A sound, a movement, a vague dream? Her eyes opened slowly and her vision cleared, finally focusing in the dim light. She was gazing into dark-green eyes staring into hers as if he'd been studying her for some time.

She felt heat move into her face, caught having crawled into bed with a man uninvited. Her fingers were still twined with his, only he'd turned their clasped hands over, trapping hers. Peripherally she could see through the window that it was still dark outside, so she hadn't been asleep long. Her heart

picked up its rhythm as the minutes ticked by and still
his eyes stayed locked on hers.

Devin was the first to speak. "If I'd known all it
took to get you into bed was a small cut, I'd have
arranged it sooner."

Molly decided to let that comment go. She glanced
at his bandaged hand. "That cut isn't so small. Are
you in pain?"

"No," he lied, for the pain had awakened him. But
he'd forgotten it quickly enough when he'd realized
that Molly was asleep beside him. For a moment, he'd
thought he was dreaming. She looked so lovely, all that
blond hair spread out on the pale-peach pillow, the blue
jersey she wore barely skimming her slender thighs,
those long, silky legs. His body had reacted quickly,
predictably.

He reached over with his good hand and stroked the
backs of his fingers along the satin of her cheek.
"You're so beautiful." Silently, she watched him, her
eyes softening, her lips parting slightly. "I suppose you
hear that all the time."

"Constantly. Night and day." Her voice was low,
husky.

Devin closed the gap between them, touching his
lips to hers. Instantly, she opened to him, her mouth
moving under his, warm and welcoming. Just that fast,
his heart began to pound, his blood to heat. Scooting
closer, he deepened the kiss, encouraged by the soft
sounds she made in her throat, her obvious response.

Pulling back, Devin waited for her eyes to slowly
open and saw they were hazy with the beginnings of
passion. He smiled at her then, thinking that of all the
places in the universe, this was exactly where he
wanted to be. He didn't want to examine the whys and

wherefores, just wanted to be here with this woman enjoying the moment.

"Mmm," Molly whispered, "I don't know who taught you how to kiss, but she sure knew what she was doing."

"You're not so bad yourself. But then, I can only imagine that a woman as beautiful as you must have had a lot of practice."

She felt his arm slide around her, drawing her closer. "You'd be wrong. I haven't been kissed in…oh, over four years."

She'd told him she'd been divorced three years, which had to mean the last year of her marriage had been rocky. But no one since? "I can't believe that. No one?"

Her eyes held his. "There was no man I wanted, until now."

His heart skipped a beat hearing that, then did a happy little somersault. *Easy man,* he warned himself. *Don't get a swelled head over pillow talk.* But some things couldn't be ignored. "I can't get you out of my head," he confessed, still surprised himself. "When I'm working your face jumps on my computer screen. When I try to sleep, there you are, on my ceiling. That's never happened to me before."

She smiled, a soft feminine smile. "Poor baby." But the smile slipped when she saw he was serious. "Since we're playing True Confessions, I'll have to admit that the same thing is happening to me. I…I've even fantasized that you were here, in my bed. Believe me when I say that I've never done that before."

Her words had his body tightening. If she only knew where his fantasies had taken him. His hand shifted to encircle the nape of her neck as he touched his mouth to hers. The kiss began as soft and tender, but soon escalated into more. A flash of heat rippled through Devin as he leaned over her, pressing her into the mattress, unable to get close enough as his heated blood raced through his veins. Then, remembering that it was their first time, that he didn't want to frighten her, he gentled his touch, struggling for control.

Molly felt his hands tremble and realized he was nervous, too, which inexplicably relaxed her. Her arms encircled him, tracing the hard muscles of his back, glorying in the strength she found there. Her hands trailed to the waistband of his shorts and fidgeted there.

His mouth skimmed the long, slender line of her throat, then moved lower to press a kiss first to one breast, then the other. Through the thin cloth, he felt her grow fuller, reaching for his attention. Impatient with the material that separated them, he tugged at the hem of her jersey.

Molly was just as eager to be flesh to flesh with him, sitting up momentarily while he pulled the shirt off and tossed it aside. His eyes all but glowed as he saw she wore nothing beneath that small garment. His greedy mouth followed her down, his tongue circling each rigid peak before drawing deeply on her. Molly arched against him as waves of longing washed over her. A moan escaped from her parted lips as her restless body could no longer be still.

Though she'd denied every bit of it even to herself, oh, how she'd longed to be touched like this, to be held in strong arms again, to be kissed passionately. She could no longer deny how desperately she'd needed to feel like a woman again, a woman fiercely desired by a man.

Devin's breathing was ragged as his lips trailed

along her ribcage, causing her skin to quiver wherever
he touched. She was every man's dream, gloriously
responsive, unabashedly passionate. He felt her small
hands shove down his shorts and helped her by kicking
them aside. But he evaded those seeking fingers, wanting to send her soaring first.

His own needs swamped him, but he brutally pushed
them back, wanting to slow the pace. His mouth set
out on a new journey, tasting, sampling, nipping then
kissing, learning every inch of her. Her hands thrust
into his hair as his mouth streaked down her.

Now there was heat and fire and speed, then he saw
her eyes lose focus as her body tensed, then finally let
go. Thrilled at the power of her release, he held on as
waves buffeted her. When she drew in a deep breath
and began to relax, he sent her off the edge of the cliff
again, delighting in her soft cry.

But his own needs were clawing at him, screaming
for attention. With his last small vestige of control, he
waited until her breathing had slowed, her eyes open
and shining. "Do we need to worry about birth control?" he asked, wanting to protect her as well as himself.

A shadow passed over Molly's eyes for a fraction of
a second, then was gone just as quickly. "No," she
told him.

Only then did he position himself over her and slip
inside as if he'd been her lover for years.

Molly's hands tightened on his biceps as she adjusted to the size and feel of him. His rigid arms sup-
ported his weight as his eyes stayed locked with hers.
Then as she wrapped herself around him, he lowered
to her and began to move. He found her hands and
gripped them tightly while his mouth took hers in a

kiss that stole her breath away as he thrust long and hard and deep.

She didn't want it to end, wanted the sensations to go on and on, yet another part of her wanted desperately to reach the other side. With him, together as one. Sensations flooded her as Devin guided them both toward the summit. Breathing hard, she held on as he drove them both. When at last they tumbled over the edge together, Molly wasn't prepared for the beauty, for the wonder of it. Closing her eyes to hold in the feeling, she went limp in his arms.

Some time later, Molly felt him shift slightly, noticed a frown of pain creasing his forehead. "Did I hurt you?" she asked, concerned for his hand.

Devin's grin was unexpectedly sexy and smug. "I'm not sure. Why don't we do it again so I'll know?"

She swatted his shoulder playfully. "I meant your cut, silly."

Knowing full well what she'd meant, he decided the minor discomfort he felt from the sutures was worth every second of the pleasure he'd just experienced. But he might as well play up his infirmity so Molly could practice her nursing skills. "Oh, that. I think my doctor prescribed plenty of bedrest, with my nurse at my side in case I get delirious." He rolled to his side, taking her with him, settling her close against his cooling body.

"Delirious. Uh-huh."

"And he said it would heal faster if you'd kiss the boo-boo regularly and often."

"All right, give me your hand."

He tipped her chin up, his lips a breath away from hers. "Kisses travel," he whispered before touching his mouth to hers for a long, passionate kiss. Opening his eyes, he gazed into hers. "I think that one went all the way to the soles of my feet."

"Mine, too." Even her scalp tingled. But her thoughts returned to his stitched hand. "Are you sure you don't need another pain pill?"

"I'm fine," he said. "More than fine." He didn't want his mind fuzzy, wanted to be alert and awake for every moment of this. His hand began to roam over her shoulders, her bare back, inching lower as she lay against him. His body began to harden in response to her nearness.

Wrapped around him, Molly noticed and shifted to look at him. "I guess it's been a while for you, too."

"Yeah, but that's not the reason." His hand stroked a lock of hair from her face. "It's you. You're amazingly responsive. Your ex-husband was nuts to let you go."

The moment the words were out of his mouth, Devin wished he could pull them back as he felt her stiffen. "Sorry. Forget I said that. Chalk it up to my inexcusable nosiness."

Molly withdrew both physically and emotionally as she edged her head back on her pillow and pulled the sheet over them. Suddenly she felt too defenseless uncovered. "It's all right. I probably should have told you before this." She closed her eyes a moment, wishing she didn't have to say the next few words. "Lee didn't exactly let me go. He forced me out."

Devin wished he'd never begun this conversation, for he could see how difficult it was for her to talk about her ex-husband. "Listen, it's none of my business. You don't have to…"

"No." She shook her head, stopping him. "I want

to tell you." She took a moment to collect her thoughts. "I met Lee my last year of college at a U of A alumni football game. He was handsome and charming, seven years older than I, and he swept me off my feet. Four weeks after we met, I quit college and we got married quietly with just my roommates and two of his friends in attendance. After that was when the fun began."

"Your mother was upset that you didn't finish?" After all, Molly had had a full scholarship and was obviously smart. What mother would want her daughter to throw all that aside?

"No, my mother thought Lee was wonderful, the answer to her prayers for me. You see, I soon discovered that Lee Summers was filthy rich, the only son and heir to the Summers Furniture Store fortune, a three-generation family business. It was Lee's family who were less than thrilled, especially when they learned my new husband hadn't asked me to sign a prenuptial agreement."

"They thought you were after his money," Devin guessed.

"Yes." Molly scooted back against the headboard, sitting up and carefully tucking the sheet around herself. "The funny thing was that I hadn't even connected Lee with the furniture business. He'd told me he worked in his father's store and I hadn't questioned him further. When we showed up at the Summers house—more like a mansion, really—after a quickie honeymoon, I found out just how unwelcome I was. His father was cold to me and his mother cried. They took Lee into the study while I waited outside. I heard the words *gold digger* bandied about. So I got mad and trounced in there, took off the gold band Lee had given me, threw it at him and told him I'd get an annulment. Then I slammed out of there.''

"Good for you. Did Lee let you go just like that?'' Hadn't she said he'd forced her out?

"No, not that time. He stood up to his parents and came after me. It took a while, but they finally came around. They almost treated me halfway decent, until the first year went by and I still wasn't pregnant.''

"They wanted a male heir to carry on the family name, I imagine.'' Oddly enough, Devin had heard the same thing from his father at one time.

"Oh, yes. They gave us another year before the hints turned into demands. Then we started the rounds of doctors and it wasn't long before tests showed that Lee wasn't at fault. So it had to be me. Yet the doctors could come up with no medical reason why I couldn't get pregnant. They told us to just relax and it would happen. Only it didn't.''

"You could have adopted,'' Devin suggested.

She raised her brows in shock. "What, not have Summers blood flowing through the child? Not hardly. So we tried *in vitro* and that didn't get results. After three years of this, of fighting over this daily, our marriage was in deep trouble, as you can imagine.''

He could and his heart went out to her. Shifting closer, he took her hand. "Why in hell didn't Lee just tell his parents to butt out and let the two of you work things out in time? I mean, he'd stood up to them about the marriage.''

"I guess he'd run out of courage. Or maybe they threatened to disinherit him. Or perhaps he simply didn't love me enough. I don't know.'' She brushed a strand of hair from her cheek. "The last straw came when his father showed up one day when Lee was out and offered me a hundred thousand dollars if I'd divorce his son. I told him this was his lucky day, that I would move out by nightfall, file for divorce the next day and it wouldn't cost him a cent. He left the check, but I tore it up.''

''Maybe you should have taken it. You earned it, putting up with those people for four years. After all, twenty-five grand a year isn't much.'' Devin's voice was as scornful as his feelings for a family that would treat a young woman like that, but mostly for a man who wouldn't choose his wife over his parents.

''I didn't want a cent of their money. Their attorney gave mine a second check at the divorce hearing, but I wouldn't accept that one, either. Conscience money was all it was.'' Lacing her fingers with his, she looked into Devin's eyes. ''I don't know if you'll understand, but some things are more important than money. At least to me they are.''

He did understand and admired her greatly for it. ''You're really something, you know. I haven't met too many people who'd give up a sizable check to stand on principle.'' His thumb caressed her hand. ''Do you ever run into Lee around town?'' He'd noticed a Summers Furniture in a nearby mall he'd visited recently.

''No, but I heard he'd remarried and had a son.'' Oddly, she didn't sound bitter. ''Do you still have feelings for him—anger, hatred?''

''I was very angry at first, but I had to move past that anger. I had to let it go or it would eat me alive. I think I have, pretty much.'' She turned to him. ''So you see, that's why I wasn't concerned about birth control. I can't have children.''

That last was said with just a tinge of sadness, but Devin saw through her brave front to all the pain she still had. He'd chosen not to have children, but it was quite another thing to be unable to have them. He wanted to say something to let her know how he felt, but he wasn't sure he could find the right words.

He touched her face, his fingers trailing down her throat. "Molly, Lee Summers is a poorer man for having lost you. You have so much to offer. Don't judge all men by that bastard."

She blinked, struggling to hold back the tears threatening to fall after such an emotional confession. "Thank you. I try not to."

He took her in his arms then and kissed her, slowly, softly, thoroughly.

"Tell me something," Devin said when at last the kiss ended. "What made you decide to join me in this bed tonight?" He'd been wondering since she'd been holding him at bay all these weeks.

"I wanted to make love with you. Wasn't that obvious?"

"No, I mean what changed your mind, because you've been pulling back all this time, telling me you had all these goals and couldn't get involved? Don't get me wrong. I couldn't be happier, but I'm curious."

She shrugged, feeling a shade embarrassed. It wasn't easy, putting brand-new feelings into words. "I still have the same goals. That hasn't changed. But I guess I decided to stop denying myself all of life's little pleasures on the way to those goals."

"That's good enough for me." He bent to kiss her cheek, then kissed her eyes closed. "I can't tell you how much pleasure you give me. When I do this..." He trailed his lips along her throat, stopping to kiss the pulse pounding there. "And this." He lingered at the corners of her mouth as she shifted within his arms, becoming restless. "Tell me what you want and I'll do it."

"Hold me, touch me," she whispered, and reached to press her lips to his.

But Devin took over and the kiss was breathtaking and incredibly tender, rocking Molly to her very soul. Lust she could handle. Desire was familiar. But tenderness was her undoing.

Molly wound her arms around his neck and gave him her heart.

She awoke just before six and noticed the sun streaming in the window before turning to check on Devin. He was still asleep, carefully cradling his bandaged hand. Molly had a momentary pang of guilt, thinking she should have been more concerned over his cut and insisted he take another pain pill.

But she'd been too involved in making love with him. She smiled at that thought, remembering. Blushing. He was an incredible lover, one who seemed to genuinely enjoy a woman's body. Even in the glow of first love that she'd felt with Lee, she'd never experienced such pleasure.

Her body felt alive, tingling, energized. Getting up slowly, trying not to disturb him, she found her football jersey and slipped it on over her head. Padding into the kitchen barefoot, she shoved back her disheveled hair with both hands and put on some coffee. Then she glanced at the clock.

She was due at the café at eight, which meant she should jump in the shower and start getting ready. But she didn't move, her busy mind considering possibilities. In the three years she'd worked for Hank, she'd never taken a sick day or a personal day. What if she did now, if she stayed home and convinced Devlin to recuperate from his cut right here where she could tend to him? Kiss his boo-boo and other more interesting places. Would that be too much of a good thing too soon?

Nah, she'd better…wait! Hadn't she decided sometime in the middle of the night to stop denying herself so much? Hadn't she even told Devin why she'd changed her mind? She marched to the wall phone and dialed.

Hank answered on the second ring since he always went in early to bake biscuits and sweet rolls. Molly almost lost her courage when she heard his gruff voice. But she took a deep breath and plunged in, hoping he wasn't terribly understaffed this morning.

"I need to take a personal day, Hank," Molly told him, getting right to the point.

"Oh? Are you all right?" Concern softened his tone.

If he only knew how all right she was. "I'm fine. I just have some things I have to do." She was determined not to lie to him, but just skirt around the real reason. Instinctively she knew that Hank wouldn't approve of her spending the day with Devin.

"I see. Well, sure. I guess it's okay." There was reluctance in his voice, and curiosity. "I hope everything's all right. You're not sick, are you?"

"No, but a friend is and I need to help out." She'd told the truth without revealing too much. However, she didn't want to answer any more questions. "You're not shorthanded, are you?" Everyone had been in and feeling fine yesterday.

"No, we'll be okay." He paused as if groping for more information. "You'll be in tomorrow?"

"Yes, of course." She really couldn't afford to take

off more than one day. "Thanks, Hank." She hung up
and waited for the guilt to wash over her. To her surprise, she felt flushed with excitement at the thought
of an entire day to do with as she pleased.

Her euphoria didn't last long. Pouring coffee into
two mugs, Molly suddenly put down the pot as a new
thought registered. What if Devin woke up with plans
of his own that didn't include her? All he was interested in was a fling, she reminded herself. Perhaps
flings didn't carry over into the morning and day after.
She should have listened more carefully all those times
when Trisha regaled her with tales of the many flings
she'd had.

What was done was done. She'd have to play this
one by ear. If he seemed anxious to leave, she'd consider this a lesson learned. If he turned out to be
pleased by her decision to blow off work for a day, all
the better. Squaring her shoulders, she carried the mugs
into the bedroom.

He was sitting up examining his bandaged hand. He
glanced up and saw the coffee moments before he
smelled the welcome aroma. "Ah, you read my mind."
He took the mug she held out to him and sipped.
"Mmm, and she makes good coffee, too."

Molly sat down cross-legged on the bed, studying
him over the rim of her mug. Damned if he didn't look
just as appealing in the light of day as he had last night.
She watched him settle himself opposite her, oblivious
to his nakedness, greatly distracting her.

"I was wondering how I'm going to shower with
this bandage." The doctor had told Devin not to remove the dressing for three days, then return in a week
to have the stitches taken out.

"I can put plastic wrap around it, but you'll still

have to try to keep it out of the water as much as possible. My mother had surgery on her foot a while back and that's what she used to do.''

"Good idea." He drained his mug. "I guess I'd better get out of your hair. What time do you have to go to work?''

The moment of truth, Molly thought. "I called in and took a personal day off.'' She waited, her eyes on his face.

The significance dawned on him slowly as he realized she probably rarely took a day off. "Did you do that for me or because you have something you have to do?'' He thought he knew the answer, but he wanted to hear her say the words.

Her heart in her throat, she stepped across the line. "For you, if you want to spend the day with me.''

How many times he'd asked his mother to take the day off when he hadn't felt well, but she'd always gone in, telling him she was only a phone call away. His smile didn't quite make it as he felt an unexpected rush of feelings he couldn't quite put a name to. "I'm hardly gravely ill here, but thank you.'' His voice was oddly thick with emotion.

His reaction surprised her, the seriousness, the emotion in those compelling green eyes. "You're welcome.''

Devin took her mug and placed it along with his own on the nightstand. "Come here," he said, his voice husky. And he gathered her into his arms and into a kiss that made the room shift out of focus. Something was happening here and it was beginning to scare him just a little.

Easing back, he put on a mischievous smile, needing to lighten up. "Have you ever shared a shower?''

Thinking back, Molly realized she hadn't. Even in the first days of their marriage, Lee had never been particularly playful. "No, have you?"

"No. I think we should remedy that oversight. Besides, I remember my doctor saying my nurse should never leave my side while I'm recuperating."

"Is that right? I must have stepped out of the room when you and he had that conversation."

"Matter of fact, you had." Letting her up, he scooted off the bed. "I'll get the shower going while you get the plastic wrap."

Her footsteps light, Molly went into the kitchen and found herself humming. She couldn't recall being this happy in…well, in years. If she was headed for a crash, so be it. She would savor every moment of being with him until then.

In a matter of minutes, she had his hand thoroughly wrapped. Devin tested the water temperature, then stepped in, holding his other hand out to Molly who ducked under the spray.

"I'd better help you since you can only use one hand." She traded places with him and lathered up her big white bath sponge. He stood there obediently with his plastic-covered bandage held out to one side and waited.

Molly began with his shoulders, letting the suds slide down his torso as she shifted her attention to his chest. She couldn't help but linger over beautifully formed muscles sprinkled with dark hair. Quickly, she ran the sponge over both his arms and legs, avoiding other aspects of his body. Although she'd touched every part of him during the night, she felt oddly shy now.

"Here, you finish," she said, handing him the sponge.

"No, it's your turn," he said, pivoting her around so that her back was to him. Devin slid the soapy sponge over her soft shoulders, the tempting line of her back and along her ribs. Stepping nearer, he came up close behind her and slipped the sponge around to the front. After a moment, he dropped the sponge and slowly, sensuously slid his hand over her breasts and her flat stomach, arousing them both.

Molly's breath caught in her throat as his hand touched her intimately, almost causing her knees to buckle. She turned within the circle of his arm and grabbed on to him to keep from falling. After the night they'd shared, she hadn't thought she'd want him again so soon, so fiercely. But she did, oh, how she did.

Devin shook his wet hair from his eyes and pressed her back against the tile wall. It was a struggle, but he managed to lift her one-handed, wrap her legs around his waist and slip inside.

Molly wasn't sure if the moan that escaped from her was a welcome or a protest of fear over harming his injury. "Your hand," she reminded him.

But Devin's mind was elsewhere. "To hell with it." And he captured her mouth as he began to move.

Chapter Seven

In his office, Devin switched on his printer, tapped in a few computer key commands and sat back, waiting for Chapter Sixteen to print out. Absently, he rubbed his thumb in the area of the cut that was healing very well, the stitches removed a week ago. Now all he was left with was a thin reddish line and a fierce itching.

Fortunately, he'd been able to resume his work quickly since the injury was to his left thumb, the only finger never used in typing. Though there'd been some general pain and soreness that first week, he hadn't taken any more pain pills, hating the way the medication made him feel. Besides, Molly's intimate presence in his life kept him on a perpetual high.

Leaning farther back in his old chair, he clasped his hands behind his head, aware that his face had moved into a smile at the mere thought of her. He carefully avoided labeling his feelings for Molly Shipman, knew only that they were powerful. She made him feel good, in bed and out. Hell, she made him feel ten feet tall at times.

She was warm and loving and funny and bright and…and much more. She was so appreciative for the little things he did for her, like popping in after her shift, catching her stepping out of the shower, and massaging her aching feet. The first time he'd picked some wild desert flowers he'd run across riding his Harley and stuck them in a vase he'd found in her cupboard, then propped them in the center of her kitchen table with a corny note, she'd cried. Normally, he wasn't a romantic or even a sentimental guy, but she had him dreaming up things that would please her. So that she'd give him that wonderful smile. So that she'd move, warm and willing, into his arms.

The nights he spent with her in her bed or his had him wishing the daylight hours would hurry past.

But she had a temper, too. One night when he'd wanted to take her out, she'd adamantly refused, insisting that she had to finish her typing for the insurance company. Impulsively, he'd suggested she quit her evening job, that he'd give her a check each week to make up for the money she lost. He'd never seen eyes grow so frosty so quickly. No amount of apologizing could make her warm up. She hadn't talked to him or smiled in his direction for two days until he'd been ready to go down on his knees and beg.

The ringing phone interrupted his reminiscences. Recognizing the voice as belonging to his agent, Mark Hanson, Devin smiled. ''Hey, Mark, how goes the battle?''

''Not bad.'' Never one to disappoint, Mark asked the

question that he asked more often than any other. "How's the book coming?"

Devin almost laughed out loud at the man's predictability. "Great. More than halfway finished with the first draft."

"That's terrific. Since it's going so well, do you think you could take a little time out to attend a writer's conference in California? You could squeeze in a visit to your family."

Devin didn't take long to answer. "I don't think so. Not right now. But tell them I appreciate the offer." He talked with some member of his family every week so a visit wasn't a high priority. But the real reason he didn't want to leave just now was that he didn't want to be away from Molly, knowing she wouldn't go with him, busy as her schedule was. He could scarcely persuade her to take an afternoon off now and then.

"They want you to be keynote speaker, Devin. Good publicity." Mark never gave up easily. "It would only take three days, four at the outside."

"Thanks, but no thanks. I've got too much going on right now."

Mark paused, obviously thinking. "You've only been in Scottsdale five or six weeks. Your work's ahead of schedule, or so you've said. So what else is going on that takes up all your time?" Another pause. "Don't tell me, let me guess. A woman?"

Devin frowned, unwilling to discuss his personal life with his agent. But before he could reply, Mark answered his own questions.

"Nah, not you. I've never known a woman to throw you off course."

Devin decided to let that stand. "Anything else happening?"

Apparently Mark knew when to quit. "Not much. Do you want to send me your first couple of chapters? I'd like to see how it's hanging together."

Devin wasn't fond of sending out a book piecemeal, preferring to send the entire manuscript upon completion. But Mark's advice had been invaluable in the beginning, and the agent had stuck with him through the lean years. Besides, Devin was only on his third book and felt that he should be open to constructive suggestions. "Sure thing. I'll overnight it to you today."

"Great. Take care now." Mark hung up.

Devin picked up his first three chapters and decided to read through them before printing out a clean copy and going to FedEx.

Still in high spirits around six that evening after running several errands, Devin rode his motorcycle home and pulled into his drive, passing an unfamiliar car parked near the front porch. He knew that Molly was on the late shift tonight and wouldn't be arriving until after ten. Or had she gotten off early because old Bess had given out again and she'd had to get a loaner? he wondered as he dismounted and shoved the kickstand into place. He chained the Harley to the fence and flipped the lock into place, then patted King's big head before walking toward the front of the duplex.

He noticed two people on the porch, a child seated on the stairs clutching a raggedy stuffed animal and a tall woman who stepped down and walked toward him. She was slender with short brown hair, wearing some sort of uniform with blue skirt and jacket and a white blouse. She removed her sunglasses revealing dark eyes. There was something vaguely familiar about her, but he couldn't pinpoint where he might have seen her.

Since she was on Molly's porch, seemingly waiting for her, she was probably a friend.

"Hi, I'm Devin Gray," he said by way of greeting when she stopped several feet from him. "I live upstairs. Molly's not home yet. Can I help you?"

"My name's Marsha Wilkins," the woman said, studying his eyes. She stood there, as if waiting to see if her name rang a bell with him. "It's you I've come to see, Mr. Gray."

Devin frowned. "Should I know you?"

She gave a short, humorless laugh. "No, we've never met. But they say I look a lot like my sister, Sandy Wilkins." Again, there was that puzzling, watchful silence.

Of course, he knew Sandy Wilkins and could see the resemblance now. "Sure, I remember. We dated one summer when I lived in L.A. Has to be five or six years ago. How is Sandy?"

"She died about a month ago." There was a bitter edge to the woman's voice now.

Devin shifted his feet, studying Marsha Wilkins's face. Instead of sadness over a death in her family, he saw irritation and impatience. What, he wondered, was this woman doing here? "I'm sorry to hear that. Sandy and I had some good times together."

She gave him a sardonic smile. "I'm sure you did." Marsha removed a folded sheet of paper from her jacket pocket. "She asked me to give you this." She handed him the letter, then turned aside, shoving her hands in her jacket pockets and raising her head to look up at the sky.

Apparently he was expected to read Sandy's note now. Somewhat suspicious, yet oddly intrigued, Devin began to read.

Dear Devin,

I know this will come as a shock, but that can't
be helped. This letter will introduce to you Emily,
our daughter. She was six years old on February
1st. I chose not to tell you that I got pregnant that
summer seven years ago. Besides, by the time I
realized she was on the way, you were long gone,
pursuing your dreams. I didn't look for you because you'd told me you wanted nothing to do
with marriage or children. I knew that up front,
but something went wrong and I got pregnant anyway.

I worked hard to support myself and our little
girl. We were doing just fine until I developed
ovarian cancer a few months ago. The doctors
have tried but it's no use and I'm dying.

I had no intention of involving you in Emily's
life, but now I have no choice. I've contacted my
sister in the hope that she can locate you. Emily
is a sweet, intelligent, loving child.

Please do right by our daughter, Shakespeare.

Sandy

Shakespeare. It was the name Sandy had often called
him, referring to his prolific writing. But a daughter!
How could he be sure the child was his? Wasn't denial
everyone's first reaction when confronted with a shock-
ing dilemma?

Quickly, Devin read the letter again, then looked into
Marsha's impatient eyes. But before he could say anything, she went on the offensive.

"Don't you dare insult my sister's memory by denying that Emily is yours." Her voice was low, bitter.

"Are you so certain that's what I'm going to do?"

Although he'd thought just that, hadn't he? Yet how could this be? All his life, he'd been doubly careful about birth control, unwilling to be caught in just such a situation. Of course, he wasn't stupid; he knew that no birth control is a hundred percent safe.

Marsha had been watching a variety of emotions play across his expressive face. "I kind of thought you might. But when you see her, you'll know." Turning, she walked back to the porch.

Shaken but curious, Devin followed.

The child seemed small for six, he thought, though what did he know about kids these days? She was wearing sneakers, denim shorts and a red polo shirt. But it was the face that held his attention. Her eyes were bright green in color and her long lashes were spiked with tears ready to fall. Her curly black hair was long and as thick as his. Most telling of all, there was a deep dimple in her small chin which was quivering under his intense examination. She held a scruffy stuffed rabbit with one ear missing and a pillowcase that undoubtedly contained some of her little treasures.

Devin knew he could never deny that she was his.

"You can have DNA tests run, if you must, but I don't see how you can ignore the obvious." Marsha's voice had progressively hardened.

He tore his gaze from the child to look at the aunt. "That won't be necessary. Tell me, why are you so hostile toward me? I had no idea of this child's existence until now."

Blinking rapidly, Marsha frowned up at the sky. "Maybe because I was with Sandy when she died. She was in a lot of pain and her only thought was for her daughter. I tried everywhere to find you, but apparently you leave no forwarding addresses. I'm a flight attendant, you see, always on the go, rarely home. I've got this tiny apartment. The bottom line is that I can't raise a child. I was at my wit's end when I happened to pass a bookstore that was displaying your book in the front window. The owner told me you'd autographed there a while back and that you were planning on moving to Scottsdale.''

Through all this, Emily hadn't said a word, Devin realized. She just sat there looking up at the two adults, seemingly uninterested in her own fate. Or maybe she'd had so much happen to her lately with her mother's death and an aunt who obviously wanted to be rid of her that she'd closed down her feelings.

Devin cleared his throat and touched Marsha's elbow, guiding her back toward the car where Emily wouldn't overhear. ''I'm not quite sure what to do,'' he began. ''My place is small and…and I don't know the first thing about raising a child.'' He ran a shaky hand through his windblown hair.

''She's your responsibility so you'll think of something.'' Opening the rental car door, Marsha pulled out a small suitcase and placed it on the ground, then handed him a manila envelope. ''Her birth certificate's in here as well as her school papers and health records. Sandy did list you as the father so she has your name.''

Like a man sleepwalking, Devin took the envelope. He didn't much like Marsha from the little he'd seen of her, but he could sure use her help. ''I hope you're not leaving just yet. I mean, at least she's familiar with you. She doesn't know me at all. Can't you stay until I decide what to do?''

Marsha checked her watch. ''Sorry, but I've got to deadhead back to L.A. I'm working the redeye to the Big Apple leaving at midnight.'' Hurriedly, she walked back to Emily who'd scarcely moved, squatted down to say a few words, kissed her on the forehead and rushed back to the car.

The woman was all heart. She was clearly the complete opposite of her gentle sister. "Look, this isn't fair, coming here out of the blue like this." He hated the fact that he sounded almost whiny. "Not fair to Emily to dump her here with me, a virtual stranger, and..."

"Fair?" Marsha's dark eyes narrowed. "You want to talk fair? What isn't fair is you sleeping with my sister all summer without a care as to birth control. What wasn't fair was you taking off free as a bird while she was left to raise your daughter all alone and broke most of the time. Get the picture?"

"All right, all right." He wasn't going to get into a verbal match with her.

"Oh, I nearly forgot." Marsh pulled a small animal carrier from the backseat and put it on the ground next to the suitcase. "This is Willie, Emily's cat. She's real attached to him." Marsha scooted behind the wheel and slammed shut the door.

This just kept getting better and better, Devin thought, as he stared at the cat carrier.

Now that she was almost out of there, Marsha mellowed a bit. "I think you should know that Emily's a little...problematic. She's shy, doesn't trust people and...and she wets the bed. But only occasionally." She turned the key in the ignition and slipped into gear. "Good luck." She waved one last time to Emily, then backed out of the drive and drove off.

Feeling more than a little in shock, Devin stood there for long minutes, staring at the little suitcase, the cat carrier, then over at the child. What in the hell was he going to do?

This was one he hadn't figured on, Devin acknowledged as he slowly walked over to where Emily was sitting and watching him with wide, frightened eyes. Poor thing, he couldn't help thinking as he sat down next to her, careful to keep his distance. He searched his mind, wondering what to say, struggling with an unfamiliar panic. It had been years since he'd talked to a six-year-old, except for Molly's niece, Samantha, who seemed so self-assured compared to this sad-faced little girl.

"I guess you've never been to Arizona before, eh?" he began, berating himself for a lame attempt as soon as the words were out of his mouth. What did a six-year-old care about geography?

She shook her head and clutched her rabbit closer.

"Do you like to swim?" he asked, pointing to the fenced pool next door.

She nodded without enthusiasm.

This was going well, he thought darkly. From the corner of his eye, he saw that her clothes looked a little ragged around the edges, her sneakers frayed. He wondered what was in her suitcase, more of the same probably. Marsha had said Sandy hadn't had much money. At the very least, he could do that for her, get her some new things. Little girls, as he remembered from his sisters, all liked pretty new clothes.

But what about right this minute? They couldn't sit out here on the porch until he came up with a plan.

He turned to her, trying to put her at ease. "Are you hungry?" He saw her shake her head again. He was beginning to wonder if the child could talk. Maybe if he asked her a question that couldn't be answered with a nod or a shake of the head. "What's your favorite kind of cookie, Emily? Mine's chocolate chip. I like to have a cold glass of milk with them.'' He noticed a slight spark of interest. He waited her out.

''I like chocolate chip cookies, too,'' she finally said.

At last, a breakthrough. Devin rose. ''How about if we go up to my place and have some cookies and milk?'' Fortunately, Mrs. Bailey had given him a heaping plateful this morning.

''Okay.'' She got up, her rabbit in one hand, the other holding the bulging pillowcase.

''Can I carry that for you?'' he asked, indicating the pillowcase. But she shook her head, so instead, he picked up her suitcase and cat carrier, and led the way around back to his stairs.

King woofed out a welcome, or had he picked up the cat's scent? Devin wondered. He felt the cat stiffen in the case at the same time he saw Emily stop in her tracks, her eyes on the big dog. ''It's all right. King's friendly.'' But she didn't look like she believed him.

Neither did the cat, now hissing madly. Terrific, Devin thought. ''He's fenced in, so don't worry,'' he told Emily. Quickly, before she burst into tears, he hustled her upstairs, both of them dragging her things. Inside, he hooked the screen door before setting down the cat carrier. Carefully, he swung open the cage door. The cat's yellow eyes watched him, but he stayed put. Fine, Devin thought. Just fine.

He supposed he'd have to bed Emily down in his room for tonight while he searched for solutions. He'd sleep on the couch in his office. With Emily following at a safe distance behind him, Devin carried her things into the bedroom, then showed her where the bathroom was, suggesting that she wash up. He hadn't asked how long they'd been waiting on the porch, or how long they'd been on the road, but it was nearly seven and Emily looked tired.

By the time he'd set out a plate of cookies and glass of milk, Emily was back, scooting up onto the kitchen chair. Her hands were still damp so he could tell she'd washed up. She reached for a cookie and ate hungrily, gulping down milk as well.

"Are you sure you don't want something more, like a sandwich?" he asked. Again, she shook her head. Well, what kid would trade cookies for sandwiches? he asked himself. He'd worry about good nutrition another day.

While she ate, Devin glanced through the papers from the manila envelope. There was her birth certificate with his name and Sandy's down as parents, dated February 1st six years ago. Her health report revealed she'd had the required number of shots before starting school last fall and that she'd had the chicken pox at two, but no other problems. The teacher at Fairfax Elementary School where Sandy had enrolled her for kindergarten had written a short note saying that Emily was a bright child, quick to learn, knew her alphabet and could print her name. No report from her more recent teacher.

Setting it all aside, Devin sat back and studied the small person daintily munching on her snack, her eyes roaming around the kitchen, getting familiar with her new surroundings. He had to admit she was handling this disruptive change awfully well for someone so young. Though she'd looked close to tears, she'd managed to push them back. He wasn't sure if that was good for a child.

Perhaps she'd seen a lot of grief in her short life, such as her mother dying. Even a dunce would have noticed that Sandy's coldhearted sister could hardly wait to be gone out of her life, and Emily looked to be a bright child. It would seem she hadn't had many good things happen to her so far.

Yet every indication was that Sandy had loved her daughter. *Their* daughter, Devin corrected himself. He remembered Sandy as a fun person, always smiling, very optimistic. She'd left home at an early age to get away from a stepfather who would surely have molested her had she stayed. She'd wanted to be a marine biologist, Devin recalled now, and had been working as a receptionist for a computer firm and taking night courses. She'd been the least demanding person he'd ever known, never asking a thing of him.

Until now.

Please do right by our daughter, she'd asked of him. But what was the right thing to do for Emily? Surely it wasn't to live the nomadic existence he'd lived so far, leaving town at a whim when the spirit moved him, researching his books in remote locations. Even though he'd decided that possibly he'd settle down in Scottsdale and build a house soon, that didn't mean he'd be there twelve months a year. He hadn't changed that much.

To keep his books new and fresh, Devin felt he needed to meet people who were different than the folks he'd met last month or last year. For that, he needed to travel, to be free, with no encumbrances. His feelings for Molly had mellowed him somewhat, causing him to want to stick around, not wanting to leave her. But he was certain that wouldn't last. It never had.

"I saved some milk for Willie," Emily said in her small, tentative voice.

"Okay." Devin rose to get a saucer and poured the

leftover milk in it, then placed it near the cat's carrier. Still disdainful, Willie didn't move.

"He's just scared," she explained, squatting down on the floor next to the cage, gently coaxing him to come out.

Devin sat back down, still lost in his thoughts. He knew himself to be a practical man. Therefore, he had to consider all his options. Adoption was one possibility. After all, two parents who truly wanted children would be far better for Emily than a father who'd never planned on being one.

There was another choice, to introduce her to his large family and hope that one of his married siblings would take her in. She so resembled the entire Gray clan that there'd be no question as to her bloodline. The best candidate would be his youngest sister, Diane, whose husband couldn't father children so they'd already adopted two. Yes, Emily would thrive in Diane's busy household with two small boys and a husband who was just as nuts about kids as she.

The last option, of course, was to keep her. Devin's green gaze swung to the little girl who now held her yellow tabby on her small lap, talking softly to him. But how could he raise her all alone? Devin asked himself. Oh, he knew the fundamentals. Hadn't his mother pounded them into him for years? But the truth was, he didn't want, didn't *need* the responsibility. Ever since leaving his parents' home, he'd turned from obligations thrust on him by others.

What was this, the gods' cruel joke that he who wanted no encumbrances was suddenly saddled with a live one? To be absolutely honest, he was afraid he couldn't handle such a huge responsibility.

No! It wouldn't be fair to Emily, nor to him. The

best solution would be adoption, two parents instead of one. More attention, more love. Of course, he'd meet his financial obligations with regard to his daughter. But there it would end. Yes, he'd look into adoption agencies tomorrow.

Devin stood and cleared away the snack things, then crouched down alongside Emily. Willie's yellow accusatory gaze stared at him from the safety of her lap, looking most unfriendly. He decided it wouldn't be wise to pet him. The milk, he noticed, was gone from the saucer. "I guess he was hungry, too, eh?"

She stroked a small hand down over his golden fur. "Mmm-hmm."

He took a moment to look her over carefully up close. There were dark smudges of fatigue on the pale skin under her eyes. Now he could see the tracks of tears on her cheeks where she'd been crying, perhaps on the way here. He could hardly blame her for being afraid to face yet another upheaval with a stranger. Her expression was one of sadness. She obviously didn't want to be here with him. However, for now, they were stuck with each other.

She needed a good night's rest, he decided, rising. But first things first. "How about a bath? Or do you like showers better?"

Reluctantly, Emily let go of the cat. "My mom always gave me a bath. I've never had a shower."

"Okay, a bath it is." In the bathroom, he checked the water temperature, then ran the water. From the doorway, Emily watched him shyly. Devin gathered that she could handle bathing alone. After all, despite the fact that he was her father, they'd only just met. He couldn't blame the child for being wary.

"All set," he told her, getting out a fresh towel and washcloth. "I'll get your pajamas from your suitcase."

"I only have a pink nightie."

"Oh, all right, then." He went to the bedroom, opened the worn suitcase on the bed and saw that there was a pitiful assortment of clothes, most as worn as the ones on her back. Tomorrow, he'd get her some new things, Devin decided. Finding the nightie in question, he took it to her. She hadn't moved from the doorway. "Is something wrong?"

She looked up at him hesitantly. "Where are the bubbles?"

The bubbles, of course. He'd given his siblings enough baths to know that bubbles were important. "I'm sorry. I don't have any. But we'll get some tomorrow, okay?"

Emily nodded in that solemn way she had. Finally, she entered the bathroom.

"Want me to leave the door ajar just a little?" he asked, also remembering that kids disliked being closed in.

"Yes, please."

"I'll be in the living room if you need help."

"I can't wash my hair by myself," she admitted.

"Oh. Do you want me to help you?"

She hesitated, torn between an innate modesty and her desire to have her hair washed. "Yes, please," she finally answered.

"Just call out when you're ready for me," he told her.

In the living room in his big leather chair, he pulled on the handle, bringing up the footrest, then leaned back and let out a ragged breath. He'd done some crazy things in his life, Devin recalled. Even some dangerous things, some stunts that had scared him half to death. But never, ever had anything terrified him as much as the thought of fatherhood.

It had been one thing to help take care of his brothers and sisters growing up. First of all, he'd had the arrogant cockiness of youth, sure he could handle nearly any situation. And those he couldn't handle, he had his mother and father to fall back on. But now, here he was with a small person he was suddenly responsible for. Even the thought made his palms sweat.

What if he did the wrong thing, managed to inadvertently hurt her when she'd already been dealt a lousy hand? What if he screwed up her life worse than it already was? What if she grew to hate him? What if she was so unhappy she ran away, got picked up by the wrong people? Damn, but there was so much at stake here.

He checked his watch and saw that Molly wouldn't be home for an hour yet. He badly needed to talk with her. Maybe she could give him some advice. Instant parenthood would be difficult for anyone to handle, but for someone who'd opted to pass on being a father, it shook him to his very core.

Devin was aware that Molly had badly wanted children and was still devastated that she couldn't have her own. But that wouldn't prevent her from instinctively knowing how to treat Emily, he was certain, whereas he was flying by the seat of his pants on this.

He heard a small voice call out. "Mister? I'm ready."

Mister. She didn't know what to call him, though he was certain Marsha had told her he was her father. Feeling vastly inadequate, Devin got up and went into the bathroom.

* * *

Half an hour later, Devin had Emily clean from head to toe and settled in his bed wearing her pink nightie and holding the stuffed rabbit that could also use a good washing. The pillowcase that she hadn't let out of her sight was on the floor next to the bed and her rather large cat was curled up at the foot, his yellow eyes watchful.

It was warm so he covered her only with the top sheet. "If you get cold, you can pull up the blanket," he explained. She only stared up at him, as she had throughout the time he'd washed her hair and helped her dry off. Hoping he wasn't making a mistake, he bent to lightly kiss her cheek. "Sleep well." She didn't answer, but at least she didn't pull away. He walked out, leaving the door ajar, the night light he'd taken from the bathroom casting shadows on the wall.

Drawing in a deep breath, he strolled into his office. Devin had always been able to escape into his writing, to set aside his worries and problems and put himself into the story, forgetting at least temporarily whatever concerned him. He called on that discipline now as he sat down in his comfortable old chair, turning on his computer and bringing up the chapter he'd been working on earlier.

Taking a moment to study his story outline, he positioned his hands over the keyboard and picked up where he'd left off. He stopped to read the paragraph he wrote, then quickly deleted it, knowing it was way off the mark. Perhaps if he scrolled back and reread several pages, he'd be able to jump back in and...what was that?

Angling his head, Devin listened intently to the sound coming from across the hallway. Was that...no, it couldn't be. Yet it sounded like sobbing. He got up and walked over, pausing in the doorway of his bedroom.

Emily was curled into a tight ball, hugging that bedraggled rabbit, the pillowcase of personal items tucked near her feet. Willie watched coolly from his spot on the rumpled blanket. Even in the dim light, Devin could see an endless stream of tears pouring from her big green eyes.

Poor little thing, he couldn't help thinking. In a strange place with a stranger, nothing familiar but a stuffed animal and a haughty cat. Devin was badly shaken up by her arrival, and he was a lot older than six. She had to be thoroughly frightened.

Acting on instinct, not bothering to question if he was doing the right thing, he sat down with his back to the headboard and gathered the slender child into his arms. She stiffened at first, hesitant, but finally gave in and snuggled close.

"I...I'm sorry," she hiccuped out between sobs that shook her.

"Shh. It's all right." He smoothed her soft hair, stroked her thin shoulders, reached for a tissue on the nightstand and dabbed at her cheeks.

"I'm really scared." The admission seemed to be wrenched from her.

"You don't have to be afraid of me. I would never hurt you." He prayed he sounded convincing, reassuring.

Drawing back, she looked at him with swimming eyes. "What's going to happen to me?"

Devin felt his heart twist. He wished he had an answer that would cheer her. "Don't worry, please. Everything will be all right.'' The words, so inadequate to his ears, seemed to allay her fears, at least for now.

Or perhaps she was so tired that it was easier for her to accept his assurances so she could get some rest. In minutes, she fell into an exhausted sleep.

Devin wasn't sure just how long he held her like that, his mind running about in a maze, trying to find answers, a way out for both of them. Finally, he eased himself off the bed, resettled her on the pillows and tucked her rabbit under one small arm before covering her. Quietly, he left the room, walking out onto his back porch to stand gazing up at the stars winking in a cloudless night sky.

What in hell had he gotten himself into? he asked himself.

Molly pulled into her drive shortly after nine and turned off the engine with an audible sigh. She was bone weary, having worked a twelve-hour shift. Her feet were throbbing and her left arm, the one that hot, steaming coffee had been spilled on accidentally by a beefy trucker, ached clear to her elbow. All she wanted was a long shower and twelve hours of oblivion. At least she didn't have to go in tomorrow until noon.

She got out and walked to the back fence to give King a moment's attention, as was her habit. The big dog had become her friend and she tried not to neglect her friends. ''Hey, boy,'' she murmured as he snuggled his head to her. ''How you doing?''

''He's doing a whole lot better than I am,'' Devin's deep voice said from where he was seated on the back porch stairs.

''Men! All they do is complain, right, King?'' She nuzzled him a moment longer, then stepped out, fas-

tening the gate again. Wearily she turned and walked
over to Devin. In the light from the sensor lamp Devin
had installed at the rear of both houses since the rob-
bery at Mrs. Bailey's, she could see that he did look
worried.

"What's wrong?" Molly asked as she leaned against
the stuccoed back wall, finding it still warm from the
day's heat. She was afraid if she sat down she'd never
get up.

Where to begin? Devin wondered. "A problem from
my past showed up today and it's thrown me."

This sounded serious. "Come on in and I'll make
some coffee." It was the last thing she wanted to do
right now, but apparently he needed to talk. Maybe
she'd get her second wind, or would it be third?

Devin sat down at the kitchen table while she fiddled
with the coffee fixings, trying to think of the best way
to explain his situation. When she finally sat down and
looked at him expectantly, he just blurted it out. "I
have a six-year-old daughter and she's upstairs
asleep."

Stunned, Molly's face registered shock. "Whoa!
Maybe you'd better tell me the whole story."

So he did in a nervous, halting fashion, his face a
study in anxiety. "I hadn't seen or heard from Sandy
in years. I swear I didn't know she was pregnant."
Because he badly needed her to believe that, he handed
her Sandy's letter, then watched her while she read it.

Finishing, Molly leaned back. "The poor child, losing her mother at such a tender age, being thrust into
the care of an aunt who can't wait to get rid of her."
She swallowed down a rush of emotion. "How is she
handling things?"

As soft a heart as he knew Molly to have, he should

have guessed her first concern would be the child. Devin told her about the cookies and milk, Willie the cat, the bath and the way he'd found her sobbing. "She's a trouper, but she's scared and I don't blame her."

She looked into his eyes a long moment, trying to see deep inside him. "How do you feel about all this?"

"Honestly?" he asked, needing her to know.

"Yes, honestly."

"I'm terrified. I...I don't know what to do," he admitted. "I'm not equipped to be a father."

Suddenly short on sympathy and long on disappointment in him, she frowned. "That's not that little girl's fault. You should have thought about that when you hopped in bed with her mother."

That got to him. "Look, I *always* use birth control. I make sure because I didn't want to wind up with just this situation. I don't know what went wrong."

Molly had read the note and felt certain that Sandy hadn't intentionally gotten pregnant or she'd have gone after Devin years ago. "Nothing is foolproof, I guess. Besides, it doesn't do any good now to be looking to place blame. The child is here."

Devin rose and began to pace, thrusting a hand through his already rumpled hair. "Yeah, she sure is."

She could see he was overwhelmed and still in shock. She went to him and put a comforting hand on his arm. "I'll help you, if you'd like me to."

He wasn't sure she was offering the help he needed, but he'd take whatever she had in mind for now. "That would be great."

"You'll need to enroll her in school. You said she was in first grade in California?"

Devin frowned. "According to her papers. There's probably only a couple of weeks left in the school year.'' He'd seen a school bus dropping kids off on the corner. ''I don't even know where the nearest school is.''

''I do, and the principal's one of my regular customers. I'm off tomorrow morning. I'll go with you, if you want.'' She saw him nod, but he still seemed shaken. ''I know you're upset, but give it time. You'll do fine.'' How ironic, Molly couldn't help thinking, that a man who had no intention of having children had one he hadn't known of.

Suddenly, she felt her eyes fill. ''Do you have any idea how lucky you are to have that little girl?'' she asked, her voice whisper soft and clogged with emotion.

Shame rolled over him as he realized how this whole scenario must affect Molly since she couldn't have the very thing he'd just discovered he had. Gently, he gathered her in his arms, wiping away the tears that trailed down her cheeks with his thumbs. ''Life sure isn't fair, is it?''

''No, but then, whoever promised us fair, eh?'' She edged back and gazed up at him. ''This will all work out, Devin. You'll see.''

He wished he honestly thought so.

Chapter Eight

Just before seven the next morning, Molly climbed the back stairs to Devin's place, stifling a yawn. She hadn't quite managed twelve hours of oblivion, settling for eight hours of restless tossing instead. Devin's story about his surprise visitor had had her staring at the ceiling for some time. She'd awakened at first light, anxious to meet his daughter.

Peeking in through the screen door, she saw something that brought a smile to her face. The little girl was sitting on top of two phone books on a kitchen chair while Devin brushed her long hair. "Good morning," she called out as Devin waved her in. Joining them, she noticed that he'd begun to braid her hair. "Well, look at you," she said with admiration.

Devin shrugged. "I can't tell you how many braids I did for my sisters through the years." He took a step back. "Emily, this is my downstairs neighbor, Molly Shipman."

Emily's solemn green eyes looked up as Molly moved within range of her vision. "H'lo," she said quietly.

"Hello, Emily." Devin had told her that Emily looked like him and his entire family, but Molly hadn't imagined such a strong resemblance. She couldn't help noticing that he hadn't introduced her as his daughter. He was still getting used to the idea. "You surely couldn't deny her," she commented to Devin.

Frowning as he fastened the end of one braid with a rubber band, Devin didn't comment.

Molly sat down at the table, not wanting to add to the child's unease in this unfamiliar situation. Looking around the kitchen, she saw only a small glass of juice and a cup of coffee on the counter. "What do you usually eat for breakfast, Emily?"

"Cereal," the child answered.

A glance at Devin's pained expression let her know he didn't have cereal in the house. "I have some Cheerios downstairs. After you're finished here, would you like to have some with me?"

Emily nodded, much to Devin's annoyance as he was trying to finish the other braid. Molly saw him grimace, but he didn't scold the child. He was certainly in a grumpy mood, still not adjusted to overnight fatherhood. Or perhaps he hadn't slept well, either. It would take time, but Molly felt sure he'd come around. After all, the child was beautiful, the very picture of her father. How could he not?

Molly felt something rub up against her legs under the table and looked down. "What have we here?"

"He's mine," Emily told her. "His name's Willie."

Molly leaned down to stroke along his soft fur and heard him begin to purr. "He's certainly friendly. I've always liked cats."

"He can't stay," Devin announced as he finished Emily's hair and lifted her down. "King hates cats. With Willie here, he can't come inside. I can't leave my dog in the yard day and night in this heat." Putting away the phone books, he called over his shoulder. "We'll find Willie a good home."

Molly watched Emily's young face cloud up, her big green eyes filling with tears as she sat down on the floor and gathered her cat into her lap. When Devin turned around, she looked up at the father she didn't know, her heart breaking, silently pleading.

Clearing her throat, Molly came to a decision. Emily didn't deserve to lose her pet right after losing her mother, then being uprooted. "How about if Willie comes to live with me?" she suggested. "I'm just downstairs and you can come visit him any time you want."

The child nodded, but when she glanced at Devin, she still looked upset.

"What about your fish?" Devin asked her.

"I've got a lid for my fish bowl." But nothing seemed to lighten his mood.

"This is going to take awhile," she whispered to Devin as she stood up. "Don't make it any harder on her, please." Stooping down to Emily, Molly removed something from her pocket and held it out. "Have you ever seen one of these? It's called a virtual pet and this one happens to be a cat. Someone left it at the place where I work and never came back for it. I'll show you how it works, if you want."

Emily blinked away her tears and reached out for

the small toy. "Thank you," she told Molly and finally smiled.

Watching the two of them, the dark head and the blond, bending together as Molly explained the toy to Emily, Devin felt like an interloper. He hadn't been able to get Emily to smile no matter what he'd done. Maybe he'd lost his touch with kids, if he'd ever really had one. Or maybe Emily was more drawn to Molly because she'd been raised in a fatherless home. At any rate, he welcomed Molly's help. Until he figured out what to do with Emily, he'd need all the assistance she could offer.

"There, you see," Molly finished. "It's not so hard. Maybe your father will get you another one so this cat will have company." Glancing up at Devin, she noticed his scowl. Why was he being so standoffish? she wondered. This child was his daughter, his very own flesh-and-blood daughter. He should be trying to do everything he could to make her feel welcome.

Rising, she decided that he was still in shock. After all, it had been only twelve hours that he'd known he was a father. She'd give him time.

Molly held out her hand to Emily. "Want to go down with me now and have breakfast?" She watched Emily get up and put her small hand in hers. How warm and trusting, she thought. She turned to Devin. "You're invited, too."

With an aggrieved sigh, he followed them down.

Twenty minutes later, they were piling into Molly's Honda for the trip to school. "I think you'd better help her fasten her seat belt," she told Devin.

Devin shoved the passenger seat forward and leaned into the back, annoyed that he hadn't thought to assist

Emily. Lord knows he'd watched enough TV commercials on keeping children safe.

When Molly was settled behind the wheel, she caught his eye. "You know, you're going to have to get something more practical than your Harley. You can't very well drive her all over town on that huge machine." Carefully she backed out of the drive.

Devin sat in sullen silence. He was losing ground, he knew. He'd have to exchange his Harley for a sensible car and disassemble his office so Emily would have her own room. After the night he'd spent on the couch, that was a pretty high priority. Next he had to get her some new clothes, another virtual pet, boxes of cereal and heaven knew what all else kids ate these days. And let's not forget cat food. The list went on and on. His whole life was different, changed, ruined.

He'd never realized it before, Devin thought, but he wasn't terribly adaptable. He liked his life the way it had been before all this disruption, and he didn't want to change one solitary thing.

Then there was the fact that this child—*his* child— scared him to death, which was probably why he was hiding his feelings behind a suddenly gruff exterior. Maybe she'd dislike him and ask to be adopted out. Yeah, and maybe pigs would fly.

"I'm finding out I'm not very good at this," he admitted quietly to Molly.

"You'll do fine. Just give it time."

But he felt stubbornly insistent. "Some people never get the hang of it, you know."

"Oh, come now. Let's remember that in every parent-child relationship, one of them has to be an adult, or at least try to act like one."

Chagrined, Devin saw the school up ahead as Molly

turned the corner. His frown deepening, he braced himself for the next fun-filled parenting experience.

It was ten o'clock before Molly and Devin returned to their duplex after he'd filled out what seemed to be a dozen forms. Had it always been this difficult enrolling a child in school? He doubted if he'd been able to get through it all without Molly's help and encouragement. But she'd been quiet on the ride home.

Strolling with her to the back door, he slipped his arm over her shoulders. "Thanks for everything, Molly. I owe you."

"You don't owe me anything. She's a lovely child. Did you see how close to tears she was walking into the classroom? Poor little lamb."

"Yeah, but kids are adaptable." Much more than adults. "She's probably happily making new friends by now." At the door, he paused, turning her so that she faced him. "Are you okay? You were so quiet on the ride home."

Yes, she had been quiet, a myriad of emotions all but choking her. Molly rarely let herself dwell on the fact that she'd never have a child of her own to care for, but sometimes, the unfairness of it all swept over her and she had the devil's own time shaking it off. Maybe if Devin held her, the pain would ease.

Wordlessly, she leaned into him, hoping he wouldn't question her too much. She was terribly close to breaking down.

Devin stood there on the back porch with her head pressed to his chest and her arms around him, feeling fairly certain he knew why this morning had upset her. The fates could be cruel, not allowing Molly to have a child of her own when she had so much love stored up, yet handing him one when he was ill prepared to be a father. He could think of no words that would comfort her, no way to lessen her pain. So he held her, smoothed her hair, caressed her back.

Molly wasn't the only woman who was barren, she was well aware. And for the most part, she handled it well. But seeing little Emily had broken down her usual reserve. Her arms ached to hold that child, to care for her, to love her. Yet she didn't have the right.

Pulling back, she looked up at Devin, trying to read his thoughts, to see into his heart. Finally, she took his hand and led him into her place, through the kitchen and living room, down the hall to her bedroom. Sunshine poured through the window as she paused alongside the bed.

"Make love with me, Devin, please," she said softly. "I need you."

He couldn't make her pain disappear, but he could do this for her. And for himself. He could make her forget for a short time, could make her feel whole and cared for, could make both their problems disappear for a short while.

Holding both her hands, he leaned down and kissed her, touching only her mouth, a slow, tender kiss. Then he stepped back. "I want to see you."

Anticipation had replaced the sadness in her blue eyes as she slowly unbuttoned her blouse, then shoved off her slacks. When she stepped out of her panties and stood before him, breathlessly beautiful in a beam of sunlight, it took Devin a moment to be able to speak.

"You are so very lovely," he said in a suddenly husky voice.

"No, I'm not. I…"

"Shh." He touched a finger to her lips. "Yes, you

are." He began to undress, unhurriedly, taking his time, his eyes locked on hers. The first time they'd been together in her bedroom, it had been nighttime with only a dim light drifting in, and each time since, it had been in the dark. He wanted to love her in the sunshine, in the daylight. In moments, he stood before her, saw the approval in her eyes and was warmed by it.

His daily laps in the pool kept his body firm and strong, the muscles well defined. Molly reached to run her fingers over his hard chest, then skimmed up to pause at that fascinating dimple in his chin and then around his neck to settle in the thickness of his hair. As he drew her to him, Molly gave herself over to his kiss, emptying her mind, concentrating only on feeling.

And oh, she felt so much as he eased her onto the comforter and followed her down. He seemed to know that today, she needed slow loving, gentle touches, sweet caresses. He kissed her, lingering, lazily brushing her lips with his, then tracing the outline of her mouth with his tongue. His mouth wove a path along one cheek, upward to kiss her eyelids, then trailing back down to settle on the pulse point in her throat, on the inside of her elbow, behind her knees.

Molly lay in a mist of feelings as he slowly trailed hot, moist kisses over her shoulders, down her rib cage, skimming along one slender leg and shimmering up the other, stopping to worship at her breasts, now throbbing for attention. She wanted to whisper his name, but it was all she could do to breathe as his ministrations left her weak and wanting.

Devin's system was straining like an engine traveling up a steep incline, but he was determined to go slowly, to make this something she would remember always. So soft, her skin where sunlight dappled it. So fragrant where bath powder and lotion lingered. So enticing, each curve and cavity; so mysterious, each valley and hollow. When he thought he felt her bones melting, he shifted and captured both her hands, stretching her arms up over her head, holding her captive.

Again, he began a shuddering trail down her body, savoring here, tasting there, teasing everywhere. He thought he could hear her skin humming as he took his mouth on a slow journey of her. Wherever he touched, her muscles tensed and quivered, exciting him beyond rational thought.

"Please, Devin," Molly moaned, restlessly shifting, longing for completion. "I've never wanted like this, needed like this. I can't think when you...oh!" She cried out as his fingers found her.

Devin watched her lovely face in the throes of passion and knew that the seducer had been seduced. No other woman had made him feel so much, feel like this. No one had made him want to be utterly tender, gallantly gentle. He'd always preferred the dark, dizzying thrill of speed and heat. He hadn't known until now that there could be such power in patience.

His senses flooded with emotions he had yet to understand, he slipped inside her and began to move in long, slow strokes. His eyes on her face, her lovely face, he withdrew slowly, then filled her again, watching the pleasure play across her features.

Awash in emotions she'd never known before, not like this, Molly could only go where he took her. She held on, straining to keep up, delighting in the delicious friction, her gaze fastened on his fantastic green eyes.

Then she felt herself hurtling, flying and finally shattering into a million pieces.

Upstairs alone at noon, Devin found himself still smiling. Their lovemaking had left both of them as limp as dishrags. Afterward, they'd showered together and Molly had done her best to rush him, warning him that she'd be late for work if he didn't back off. But in the end, he'd had his way and they'd made love again beneath the warm spray.

It had been quite a morning.

But Molly was back at work and he was back to reality now. And reality was that he had to work out some plan for Emily.

Walking into his bedroom, he took in the disheveled bed clothes. He'd awakened around six, feeling uneasy. The reason why had appeared alongside his office couch, staring at him with her lower lip quivering. Emily had confessed that she'd wet the bed.

He'd been understanding, running a quick bath for her, setting out her clothes, whipping the bedding off and stuffing most of it into the washer. Fortunately, there'd been a thick pad on the mattress so that the mattress itself was barely damp. However, later when he went shopping, he'd have to remember to get a rubber sheet.

He had to get a move on, for there was a lot to do. Taking the steps two at a time, he went down to the laundry room and put the wet things in the dryer and a second load in the washer. Back upstairs, he got out the phone book and sat down at his desk.

The first option for consideration was an adoption agency. More than ever, he felt that Emily would be better off with a young couple, both a mother and father. Once she met them, got to know them, she'd think so, too. And it should be done before she got too attached to him. And to Molly. He decided it would be best not to tell Molly his plan until the arrangements were made. After all, as Emily's father, it was really his decision to make.

He flipped through the yellow pages and found several adoption agencies listed. Hauling over the phone, he started dialing, needing to know just how these things worked.

An hour later, he leaned back in his chair, feeling frustrated. It wasn't as easy as he'd thought. For starters, each agency he'd called had a million questions, some of which he couldn't answer. Second, every person had been less than polite, bordering on rude, after he'd told them about himself. A father who has the means to raise a child, yet offers that child up for adoption is pretty well frowned upon, he'd discovered.

He rubbed his chin, recalling the conversations. He hadn't liked the way the people at the agencies had made him feel. Like a dirty dog deserting his flesh and blood. Nobody seemed to even try to understand that he wasn't father material, that Emily would be much better off elsewhere with a young couple who would love her.

He'd made the colossal mistake of offering a sizeable donation to one agency if they could place Emily. All he'd been trying to do was help out, not buy his way out. That woman had hung up on him in a fit of outrage.

He'd left his name and number with the least offensive person, a Joan Cantrell from Southwest Adoptions, but he had little hope that even she would call him. There went solution number one.

Not one to easily give up, Devin dialed his youngest sister in California. Diane Gray Donnelly was twenty-four, married for five years to Mark Donnelly, an auto mechanic. Diane knew from the get-go that they couldn't have children of their own because Mark had had a bad case of mumps as a child and had been rendered sterile. She'd loved him enough to marry him anyway. And they both loved kids so they'd adopted two boys, Jeff, now four, and Marky, a rambunctious two-year-old.

Leaning back listening to the phone ring, Devin was certain Diane was the answer he was searching for.

Twenty minutes later, he hung up feeling much better. While Diane hadn't wholeheartedly said yes, she'd certainly left him with a great future possibility. Jeff had chicken pox at the moment and she was just waiting for Marky to come down with them. Then they were planning on a family vacation to Disneyland, the first one they'd had since their brief honeymoon.

But in a month or so when things settled down, Diane invited Devin and his daughter to come visit them. If Mark and the boys hit it off with her, they'd certainly consider adopting Emily since they'd been planning on a girl soon anyway. She'd bristled a bit when Devin had told her he'd send support money, then said they'd talk about that at the time.

Devin drew in a deep breath, feeling much better. He couldn't go to California right now anyway. He was writing on a deadline and couldn't leave for a week's trip until the book was finished and mailed in. As it was, with tending to Emily's needs and his own along with trying to spend time with Molly, his writing pace had slowed. But he couldn't neglect Emily and he wasn't about to put Molly on the back burner.

Leaving his office, Devin felt a spurt of hope that things would work out. Meantime, he didn't mind having Emily around, knowing her stay wasn't permanent. She really was a sweet child. He wanted to be able to make her smile the way Molly had so effortlessly. He thought getting her some new clothes might do the trick. He'd check out the things in her suitcase for sizes. After all, she was his flesh and blood and he didn't want her looking like a ragamuffin.

Since Molly was only covering the lunch shift today, he'd asked her to pick Emily up from school this first day, then he'd start her on the school bus tomorrow. He also needed to talk with Mrs. Bailey about watching Emily some days after school so his work wouldn't be interrupted too much. Since he'd tackled the man who'd robbed her, Mrs. Bailey had been awfully nice to Devin, sending over cookies and even whole pies. He knew she sat with several children so Emily would have playmates, getting to know the neighbor kids that way.

Yes, it was going to work out, all of it. By the time his book was done, Emily would trust him enough to know he was acting in her best interest in taking her to California to Diane's home. Grabbing the keys to the Harley, he went down the stairs whistling.

The shopping took him longer than he'd planned, Devin realized as he wheeled his Harley into the drive past Molly's old car. He quickly removed assorted packages from the bike's carrier, anxious to see if Emily would like his choices. Little girls, he remembered, could be fussy.

He found both Molly and Emily in her kitchen busily at work. Emily was kneeling on a chair at the table making cookies with cutters from a flattened chunk of dough spread out on wax paper while Molly supervised, placing the finished products on cookie sheets. Willie, curled up on a padded chair beneath the window, opened one yellow eye, then closed it again. They both heard him come in, responded briefly, then went back to work.

"Press just a little harder there," Molly instructed. "You have to push the cutter all the way through the dough."

Tongue caught between her teeth, Emily bore down on the small star cookie cutter. "Like that?"

"That's perfect." Molly removed the cookie and placed it on the prepared pan before glancing over at Devin as he dumped his packages on the empty chair. "Looks like you bought out the mall."

"Just about." He inhaled the wonderful aroma of baking. "Can I be the official taster, ladies?"

Emily looked up from where she was about to press another cookie, her big eyes serious. "Should I give him his present now?" she asked Molly.

"I think he'd like that," Molly told her.

Carefully, she climbed down off the chair, her dark braids bouncing, and walked over to a small pile of papers. She picked them up and went to her father. She handed him the top one. "We had a test today. We had to make the letter *E* and get it on the line. I only messed up once." Shyly, she watched Devin study the page.

Tests her first day here. First grade wasn't the way he remembered it. He'd met the teacher, a Mrs. Porter, somewhere in her fifties with a round face and rimless glasses. She'd smiled a lot and seemed to like children. He stooped down, studying the page filled with oddly shaped Es. "This is terrific, Emily. I'm very proud of you."

She flashed him a shy smile. "And this is for you." She handed him the second sheet.

Devin studied the crayon drawing. There was a tall stick figure standing next to something that resembled a fence. In the fenced yard was a stick dog with a huge tongue hanging out. There was also a very big sun in the sky and lots of green grass.

"It's you and your dog," Emily explained, worried that he couldn't figure out her picture.

"I see that. It's great." He placed his hand on her dark head, watching for that smile. She didn't give him one, but she'd lost that too-serious look.

"Molly said you could put it up on your refrigerator with magnets. Do you have any magnets?"

Magnets. Something else to get. "No, but we'll get some. Meantime, we'll prop it up in the living room, okay?"

Emily nodded and was about to go back to her cookies when Devin brought her attention to the packages. "I think these might be for you."

Solemnly, she eyed the packages, looked up at him, then at Molly, before her gaze settled back on her father. "For me? Are you sure?"

"Positive."

Molly wiped her hands and went to where Emily was standing so apprehensively. "Come on, honey, let's open them and see what's inside." Her eyes met Devin's over the child's head and she smiled.

Slowly at first, then with more enthusiasm, Emily opened the bags and found shorts and jeans, underwear and T-shirts, a jumper and blouse, socks and new shoes, a couple of nighties, two sweaters and a dress.

Holding one of the soft sweaters in her lap lovingly, she looked up. "It's like Christmas, only better."

"One more thing." Devin reached in his pocket and pulled out a virtual pet. "A dalmation. They didn't have any cats."

"Oh, I love it." Emily's smile was wider than either of them had ever seen. "Thank you so much."

"You're very welcome." Devin noticed that his voice was a little throaty. Poor kid. She'd obviously never had much.

While Emily looked through her clothes again, Molly walked up behind Devin, whispering in his ear. "You done good, Dad."

Dad. Emily didn't feel comfortable enough with him to call him that. She didn't seem to know what to call him. Maybe it was best, Devin thought. He didn't want her getting too attached.

Molly watched the little girl carefully put all her clothes into a pile, her face glowing. She wished that Emily had offered Devin a hug, but she couldn't blame her for being shy. In time, she thought.

"I'd better get upstairs. I've got some groceries yet to put away." Cereal and milk and fruit. "What would you like for dinner tonight, Emily? Chicken or burgers?"

"Could I have a cheeseburger, please?" She held part of her clothes clasped to herself as if not wanting to let go for fear they'd disappear.

"You bet you can." Devin had to admit that Sandy had taught the child some manners. "I can take all these upstairs while you finish your cookies," he suggested.

Reluctantly, Emily handed the pile over to Devin, who gathered everything up.

"We'll take up some cookies when we're all finished," Molly told him.

He paused at the screen door. "I thought you told me you were going to spend the rest of today catching up on your typing?"

She sent him a sheepish look. "That can wait. I'm having too much fun here to stop now."

He should be grateful for her assistance, Devin thought as he went upstairs with his bundles and packages. But in a short time, Molly was already deeply taken by Emily. How would she feel when he took her away to California to his sister's?

Well, he'd just have to worry about that when the time came.

Chapter Nine

The writing was not going well. Again. Devin reread the last three pages he'd just written for the second time, then leaned back in his squeaky chair and frowned. He might as well delete all three since he'd gotten off track again. The problem wasn't with the story, which he'd outlined extensively. It was with his concentration.

Up until recently, with only himself to worry about, Devin had been able to stay focused, to concentrate on his writing exclusively, to shut out the real world for his fantasy world. Both his editor and agent were amazed at how quickly he finished a manuscript once he got going.

No more.

It had been a week since a little bombshell named Emily had appeared on the front porch. And he'd handled things, for the most part, getting her in school, showing interest in the endless array of papers she brought home for his approval, keeping her well dressed and well fed. He'd helped her get past her fear of King so that she was no longer afraid of the big dog but rather often played with him. He'd done things with her, like going swimming together in the pool next door and taking her out for dinner at Molly's café when she worked the late shift.

Yet, although Emily occasionally smiled, he'd never heard her laugh out loud. Undoubtedly this last traumatic year had left her with a sadness that she seemed unable to throw off. One evening before bed, he'd deliberately brought up Sandy, thinking the child needed to talk about her mother. And she had, haltingly at first, then more willingly. She'd cried then and he'd held her close, hoping she'd be able to put the hurtful past to rest.

But there was still that lingering sadness on her face and in her big eyes when she didn't know he was watching her. He could only believe that when Diane and Mark came through and agreed to adopt Emily, she'd at last have a big, loving family surrounding her instead of one inept man who if he'd ever known anything about what little girls liked, had all but forgotten.

Devin placed his hands behind his head and leaned even farther back, testing the limits of his old chair. He wasn't good at doing little girl things, unfortunately. Like nail polish. When Molly was home afternoons, Emily had taken to going down to visit, something Molly encouraged, which allowed Devin to keep working. He'd wandered down late one afternoon and found the two of them on Molly's couch applying nail polish in an unusual shade of green, then gluing on tiny stars and moons. It was hard to say who was having more fun, the little girl or the big one.

In a million years, Devin wouldn't have thought to do that with her. Nor would he have bought a baby doll then proceeded to sew little outfits for it the way Molly had. Although the motley one-eared rabbit was still in Emily's bed, the new doll named Peaches was Emily's current favorite and went with her everywhere.

Molly had introduced Emily to Sam and to Trisha's son, Danny. She'd begun to teach her to play chess and how to take care of Jo-Jo, her fighting fish, the one that oddly enough Willie totally ignored.

Molly had even gotten Emily involved in Sam's Brownie troop. Once a week, this truckload of little girls and their leader would be out in the backyard whooping and laughing and having a high old time. He and King would hide out inside, letting the females have their fun.

Emily had yet to warm up to him the way she seemed to take to Molly so effortlessly. She didn't call him *daddy*. She didn't call him anything, uncertain he supposed what would be the right thing to do. She let him kiss her cheek and hug her occasionally, but she didn't return the hug with spontaneous affection the way he'd seen her embrace Molly. Was it because she'd had so little exposure to men that all men scared her? Had Sandy told her something about him that put her off? Or did he just plain intimidate her because he was so much larger? Hard to say.

Naturally, Devin was pleased that Molly found the time in her busy work and typing schedule to entertain Emily. But he was honest enough with himself to admit that he was a little jealous, for often Molly was so wrapped up in the child that she had little time left over for him. It was temporary, he reminded himself. As soon as he finished the book and Diane and her family were home from their vacation, he'd drive to California with Emily. Afterward things would return to the way they were.

School would be out next week and he'd already made arrangements with Mrs. Bailey to watch Emily on the days he had to work. Now if only he could get a handle on this chapter. Leaning forward, Devin deleted the last three pages and started over.

It was after four when he finally saved his material and turned off his computer. At last, he was back on track; at least he hoped so. He'd be able to tell more tomorrow when he ran off a hard copy and read what he had written so far.

He'd quit now because he heard a howl followed by a childish cry coming from the downstairs back porch where Molly had been outside with Emily. Feeling guilty for having thrust his daughter on her yet again, he hurried down.

"Shh, now, you're all right," Molly murmured as she comforted a tearful Emily sitting on her lap. "Everyone falls once in a while when they're learning to ride a bike."

"What happened?" Devin asked, joining them on the steps.

A towheaded boy of about seven or eight that he'd seen around the neighborhood stood alongside a blue bike, clearly uneasy. "I was trying to help her learn to ride my bike, but she fell. I'm really sorry." His young face looked a little worried.

"It's okay, Jamie," Molly reassured him. "It's just

harder to learn on a boy's bike because of that cross-bar.''

Emily's tears had stopped as she carefully examined her skinned knee.

"We'll put something on that knee," Molly told her. "Thanks for trying to help, Jamie."

"Is your bike all right?" Devin asked.

"Yeah, it's fine." Jamie swung his leg over and got on. "See you later, Emily." He rode off.

Molly helped Emily into her kitchen. "He's a nice boy, isn't he?" she asked the little girl who was limping in, making the most of her injury for sympathy's sake.

"Uh-huh," Emily answered as Molly sat her down and reached into the cupboard for bandages and ointment.

"Does it hurt?" Devin asked, though he could see the wound was slight.

"Not so much," Emily admitted bravely.

As Molly cleaned and bandaged the scrape, she glanced up at Devin. "Your daughter needs a girl's bike, one with training wheels that you can remove once she feels confident enough to ride without them." She saw the quick frown appear on his forehead and felt like popping him. Why was he so reluctant to get her something as simple as a bicycle when she knew he could well afford one? Did he feel overwhelmed with all the needs of one small child?

Now a bicycle, Devin thought. That sounded a lot like long-term commitment. Well, when the time came to take Emily to California, he could take her bike, too. She'd adjust better with some familiar things along. But that led to another problem. He'd have to buy a car and soon. He rubbed his hand over his unshaven face, amazed at how complicated his simple life had become.

But he didn't want Molly to think he was a jerk. He bent down to Emily and brushed a lingering tear from her cheek. "How would it be if you and I go pick out a bike for you as soon as school's out?"

The small face broke out in a big smile. "Do you mean I can really pick it out myself? I...I've never had a bike of my own."

Devin felt his chest tighten, wondering just how bad Sandy's money situation had been. More guilt, even though he hadn't known of Emily's existence then. "You sure can. What's your favorite color?"

"Red."

"I'm sure we can find a red one." He turned to Molly in time to see her smile of approval. "Maybe Molly would like to come with us and help, too."

"Would you, Molly, please?"

Molly slipped an arm around the child. "I'd be happy to go with you." She watched Emily get down and hurry out to play, then turned to Devin. "You're getting a handle on this fathering thing. I'm proud of you."

He turned aside, knowing he didn't deserve her praise.

"You two want to come over for dinner tonight?" Molly asked, wondering why he was retreating. Probably couldn't handle compliments, like most men. "I'm making fried chicken."

Devin put on a smile. "Sounds good to me. What can I bring?"

"Just yourself and your daughter," she answered, putting away the bandages.

His daughter. Devin walked out, a thoughtful look on his face.

Two days later, Molly came home from the café to music drifting out of her screened-in windows. Climbing out of Old Bess, she stopped to listen. Unmistakably Gordon Lightfoot. She recognized one of her favorites, *If You Could Read My Mind.* She'd given Devin a key to her place when he'd given her one to his, mostly because of Emily. So she could go up and help the child change into play clothes when she watched her after school on the occasional day when Devin was away. Apparently, he'd been in her place and left the radio on.

But why?

The back door was locked. She got out her key and went inside to find the blinds drawn though it was not yet two. There was a chunky candle on the kitchen table, its flame softly flickering, and a note next to it. Wondering what kind of game he was playing, Molly picked up the paper and read the short message.

"If you could read my mind, love, where would I be?"

A smile forming, she set down her canvas bag and went into the living room where more candles were burning, tall tapers and smaller squatty ones, their vanilla scent wafting through the still air. Another note taped to her stereo.

"You're tired and achy. Let me soothe you. If you can't read my mind, follow your instincts."

Getting into it now, she turned to the hallway. The bathroom door was ajar, flickering candlelight spilling out the doorway. She peeked in.

He was sitting in her large claw-footed tub which

was all but overflowing with bubbles, at least a dozen candles in every conceivable place glowing a welcome, and on his face a devilish smile. He pointed to another note taped to the mirror.

Smiling, her tired feet forgotten, Molly leaned closer to read the message:

"Come into my web, said the spider to the fly."

She turned to face him. "You're too much."

He hadn't been sure of her reaction, knowing she'd been at work since six, but he could see she was pleased, not angry. "And you're wearing too many clothes. Take it off, take it all off, and come join me."

When she just stood looking at him, her hands on her hips, he decided it was time for drastic measures. "Okay, that request was Phase One. Let's try Phase Two. How fast can you undress? I'll start counting. One, two, three…"

To his pleased amazement, she began stripping, moving ever faster as he continued counting. He was on eleven when she climbed in facing him, the water rising dangerously to flood stage. As the heat enveloped her aching muscles, Molly groaned out loud.

"Glad you made it in time because Phase Three would have meant that I'd climb out, pick you up and dump you in, clothes and all." He trailed a foot along her slender leg, then shifted to give her more room.

"You are a little crazy, but this feels wonderful." She could almost feel fatigue draining out of her. "Even better than a shower." Yet she wondered why he'd gone to so much trouble to romance her when he didn't seem the romantic type.

"Glad you approve. Wait until you see the rest." His hands were stroking along her thighs beneath the cover of bubbles.

"Mmm, there's more? Tell me."

"You'll see," he said mysteriously.

"By the way, where'd you get these bubbles? I'm sure I don't have any at the moment."

Devin pointed to a purple plastic turtle sitting on the counter. "I bought them for Emily. She hates taking a bath without bubbles."

"They are nice." She sank lower in the water, becoming aware of his hands on her skin, his arousing touch. Then abruptly, she sat up, water splashing about. "Emily! She'll be home from school soon."

"That's where Mrs. Bailey comes in," he said slyly. "She's meeting her at the bus stop and baby-sitting all evening. Even taking her upstairs and putting her to bed after a visit to the Golden Arches."

"All evening? Devin, I've got typing to do and..."

"Tomorrow's another day. This day, and evening, belong to us, the two of us." He leaned forward and captured her mouth, swallowing any further protests.

The kiss was so long and thorough that by the time it was over, Molly was putty in his hands. Carefully shifting her in his arms, he turned her so that her back leaned against him and his hands were free to wander over her. "Ever make love in a bubble bath?" he whispered as he rained kisses along her throat.

"No, I think I'd have remembered something like this."

"Good. I like teaching you new things."

"Mmm, you are definitely a good teacher." And she reached for his kiss.

The water had cooled by the time they stepped out. Devin spotted Willie watching from the hallway and shooed him away. He wrapped a large towel around

Molly, picked her up and carried her into her bedroom. Her eyes widened in surprise as she took in the changes.

More candles, of course, but what caught her attention first were the new pale blue sheets on the bed. Awestruck, she stared openmouthed. "Satin. I can't believe you did this."

"I thought they'd be slippery but fun." He set her on her feet, then removed the towel. "Can't wear clothes on satin sheets. Defeats the purpose. You have to feel the softness next to your skin." He urged her onto the inviting sheets and joined her, stretching out, watching her hands caress the soft material. "What do you think?"

"Sinfully delicious. Love in the afternoon and on satin sheets yet." Her eyes trapped his. "Tell me, why are you doing this?" She waved a hand to include the bed, the candles. "All of this?"

"Because I like making you happy. It pleases me." He leaned closer. "Are you happy, Molly?"

Was she? She wasn't unhappy. "Right now I am."

"Then I'm glad."

"I'm just wondering what you'll think of next."

Shifting, he pinned her to the mattress until his mouth was inches from hers. "Oh, I have a feeling you'll be able to guess what's next."

The restaurant wasn't in the best section of town, surrounded as it was by aging homes on one side and a warehouse on the other. But the cars parked in the overflowing lot and along both sides of the street attested to the fine food served. Devin parked Old Bess half a block away and they strolled toward the fenced front yard where a trio was playing hot jazz.

"Maryland Blues," Molly read from the sign. "Best crabs in the nation." She smiled at Devin. "Not just the city or the state, but the entire nation."

"They're right, too. Wait'll you taste 'em." He guided her past the outdoor tables where misters tried to keep the diners somewhat cool and on up the wooden stairs of the weatherbeaten building. A long-legged blonde with a toothy smile led the way to a small table by a window looking out on the parking lot. "Not much atmosphere," Devin said, stating the obvious.

Yet the room was packed, Molly realized. "How'd you hear about this place?"

"A guy at the post office. We got to talking when I was mailing stuff. He asked me if I liked crabs and told me his brother-in-law ran a place with the best crabs ever. So I thought we'd try some." Above the long bar was a sign stating that they carried over a hundred brands of beer. "What's your choice?" he asked, indicating the long list.

"I don't have a preference. You order for me."

"Would you rather have something else to drink?"

"No, beer's fine. It seems to go with shellfish." Molly picked up the menu, studying it. "Did your pal at the post office give a hint as to what's best to order?"

Devin gave the waitress their beer order before answering. "Yeah, he said the sampler platter was great."

The man turned out to be right, Molly thought as she cracked crab legs and forked out the sweet meat, dipping it in spicy sauce, then tasting the crab cakes and shrimp, the red potatoes and coleslaw. Adjusting the bib that covered the front of her, she reached for yet another napkin to wipe her deliciously messy hands. "This is great," she told Devin.

"I knew you'd like it."

"Look over at that far table, the little girl chowing down that plate of shrimp like a pro. She loves the stuff." Smiling, Molly watched the little family, mother, father and the daughter about five. She waited for the familiar rush of envy and it didn't disappoint her. Only something tilted her viewpoint now. "Next time, we'll have to bring Emily. I'll bet she'd love this place."

How quickly she'd begun to think in terms of a threesome, Devin thought, guarding his expression. Busily cracking the main body of the crab, he didn't answer.

"So, have you told your family about Emily? I'm sure they're thrilled." He'd mentioned what a tight-knit group they were, the number of nieces and nephews he had, his parents happy in the role of grandparents.

He kept his eyes downcast, not wanting her to see too much. "I called my youngest sister. She and her husband have two boys. She invited Emily and me to visit next month." He neglected to mention that he'd asked Diane to not tell the rest of the family about Emily just yet.

"That'll be fun." Yet she felt a sudden chill. Suppose Devin decided he and Emily would be better off in California so she'd get to know her extended family? Molly took a swallow of her beer and tasted regret, trying desperately to keep her feelings hidden.

For she'd done the unthinkable: she'd fallen in love with Devin and with his daughter. Knowing full well she shouldn't, that he wanted nothing permanent, no commitments or obligations. Even knowing that he'd likely move on, most especially if he knew how she felt. And now, instead of one, she'd have two people she'd opened her heart to leaving, two to miss, to weep over, to regret that she didn't have what it took to make them want to stay.

She could hardly hope for Devin to concentrate wholeheartedly on their relationship when he had to put all his energies into getting used to instant fatherhood. Still, he'd planned this romantic day. Could he then coolly walk away?

"You're not eating much," Devin commented, noticing that she'd slowed down to a near halt.

"I am, really. It's just a lot of food." She speared a scallop and slowly put it in her mouth. Suddenly, everything was tasteless.

"It is a huge amount." Devin mopped sauce with his roll and stabbed another shrimp, then sat back, taking a wet wipe and cleaning his hands. "They don't skimp on their portions, that's for sure."

Molly put down her fork and busied herself cleaning her hands, wishing she'd never brought up his family. Couldn't she have let things lie for just a while longer? After all, she knew Devin wouldn't leave until his book was completed, which was several weeks off. The intended visit to California was next month. She still had time with them.

She would have to make that time do. Hadn't she learned a long while ago that the road of life took a lot of twists and turns, not all of them good? Those who survived learned to adapt, to adjust. Lord knows she was a survivor.

She wouldn't let herself think of Devin and Emily leaving, of how she'd feel when they were gone. She'd focus on the here and now, one day at a time. With that thought in mind, she put on a smile and reached for his hand. "Thank you for today. It's been wonderful."

Devin squeezed her fingers, wondering what she'd been thinking of the last little while, her eyes clouding up with that underlying sadness she was as prone to as Emily. Whatever it had been, she'd apparently put it aside, so he would do the same. "You're very welcome, but I should be thanking you. You put the fun in the day."

Blinking against a sudden rush of emotion, Molly looked down at their intertwined hands. "What a nice thing to say."

"Haven't you heard, I'm a nice guy." He leaned over and kissed her cheek as the waitress appeared with the check.

It was a beautiful night, Devin thought, driving along the deserted country road. The restaurant south of Phoenix had been worth the drive. He'd rolled Old Bess's windows down since the air-conditioning was broken anyway. The air rushing in was warm but not humid, making for a comfortable ride. And there was a pretty woman seated alongside him, her face kind of dreamy.

What more could a man want?

"Penny for your thoughts," he said, glancing over at Molly whose eyes were half-closed.

With a great deal of determination, she'd relegated all troublesome thoughts to a compartment in her mind marked *For Future Consideration Only*. Lazily, she turned to smile at him. "I was wondering how crickets make that same monotonous sound and why."

That made him smile. "I've heard they rub their back legs together and as to why, I think it's a mating call."

Molly's brows shot up. "Must be a lot of mating going on out there then, 'cause it sounds like there're dozens of the little critters serenading their ladyloves."

"No, you've got it backward. The females serenade the males. Women's lib, cricket style."

"Oh, I see." She reached over the console to take his hand. Such a nice hand. Such a nice man. Feeling contented, she resumed studying the road ahead, letting her mind float along.

"I'm going shopping for a car next week. Care to come along and give a woman's point of view?"

"Depends on what time you're going. I'll have to check my schedule at the café."

"I'll work around your schedule."

"We can take Emily along, maybe get her bike and…" Straight ahead, Molly saw a figure in the road madly waving his arms. "Devin, stop!"

But Devin had seen him, too, and stepped on the brakes hard though he hadn't been traveling fast. In the headlights, he could see that the man was young and seemed greatly upset. A dark car was parked off the side of the road.

"Wait here and I'll check him out." He'd lived in L.A. too long not to be cautious when someone flagged him down on a lonely road after dark. He opened his door.

The young man rushed over, unable to wait any longer. "Thank you for stopping. I…we need help. She's gone into labor and I…I don't know what to do."

Stepping out, Devin could now see that the man was

more a boy, no more than fifteen or sixteen, tall and lanky. "What happened?" he asked, still a bit wary.

"It's my mom. The baby's coming early and my dad's out of town. I was driving her to the hospital when suddenly there was all this liquid and…and I had to stop the car." He thrust a shaky hand through his black hair. "You've got to help, please. I don't want her to die."

Devin motioned to Molly to stay put as he slowly approached the car, following the agitated young man. The back door was ajar and he could see there was a Hispanic woman lying on the seat, her knees bent, the towels under her soaked with a pinkish liquid. She gave a mighty grunt and pushed, then she moaned loudly.

The boy was right, she was definitely in labor and he hadn't the foggiest notion how to help her. Devin motioned to Molly to join them now that he felt there was no danger. The woman was praying in Spanish, her body shifting and straining, while the young man hovered, a worried frown on his face.

"Molly," Devin said as she rushed over, "this woman's in labor. They were on their way to the hospital when her water apparently broke and…"

Molly didn't need further explanation, for she could see for herself. A feeling of *déjà vu* came over her, remembering another time, another woman in labor. There'd been so much blood then, too, Tate's straining face, her cries of pain. Both she and Laura had been scared to death, but Maggie had taken over, directing them to help where they could, to hold Tate's hands, one on each side. If only Maggie were here now, Molly found herself wishing.

"Molly, are you all right?" Devin asked, hoping she wouldn't pass out on him.

Instead of answering him, Molly leaned into the back seat and reached for the woman's hand, realizing that neither Devin nor the boy would be much help. It was up to her. She sent up a fervent prayer before speaking to the woman. "We're going to try to help, okay? Do you speak English?"

"Only a little," the woman's son answered. "But I'll translate."

Molly gave the boy what she hoped was a reassuring smile. "Good. Do you have any more clean towels? And what's your name?"

"Carlo and my mom's name is Rita." The boy ducked into the front seat and grabbed a small handful of towels. "This is all we have."

"That's fine, Carlo." Molly spread a clean towel under the woman. "Devin, we need to call 9-1-1," she told him.

Devin put his hand on the boy's shoulder and guided him toward the front of the car. "Carlo, stay in the road and flag down the next car going either way. Ask if they have a phone. We need someone to call 9-1-1 and get an ambulance out here." Nodding, the boy gladly hurried to do as he'd been asked.

Her hands trembling, Molly spread the woman's legs, afraid she'd see the head crowning, but she wasn't there yet. "We're going to get you some help. Try not to push, okay? Just breathe. Breathe deeply." She demonstrated by drawing in deep breaths. "Yes, that's it." Maybe she could hold the baby off until help arrived.

"*Sí, sí,*" the woman answered.

"Molly," Devin asked quietly, "do you know anything about delivering babies?"

"A little. When I was in college, one of my roommates had a baby in her room and I sort of assisted

Maggie Davis delivering him. You don't forget something like that." She saw a car stop and Carlo lean in, but evidently they had no phone, for they left very quickly. Maybe they'd promised to stop first chance they had.

The woman began huffing and Molly leaned back down. A huge contraction shook her and Molly saw the baby's head crowning. She swallowed hard, torn between being awestruck over the miracle of birth and fear that she wouldn't know how to help. "You're doing fine," she told the woman. "Just fine." Even though she couldn't understand her words, Molly felt her tone might comfort Rita. In less than a minute, another contraction hit, bringing the woman almost upright. There seemed to be no holding the baby back at this point. Molly searched her memory, wondering what Maggie would do.

"Devin," Molly called, "could you open the other door and hold her shoulders firmly. The seat isn't wide enough and she can't get enough leverage to push."

Without a word, he went around, opened the door and fastened his strong arms under the woman's shoulders. "Just lean against me," he told her, his voice gentle, afraid to spook her.

The next contraction was easier to handle, Molly thought, with Devin bracing her. Sweat was pouring down her own face as she watched the woman struggle. "That's it. Just breathe. Almost there," she whispered. The head would be out any minute. Heart pounding, she prayed everything would go well.

In her peripheral vision, Molly saw a second car screech to a stop and then heard the boy explaining the situation. Quickly, the car sped off and Carlo returned. "They had a cell phone. They're calling 9-1-1."

Devin hoped the occupants could explain where they were located out here in the middle of nowhere. He noticed that they didn't bother to stay or offer to help. No matter. Molly seemed to know what she was doing.

They crouched there like that, Devin supporting the woman, Molly at the business end, encouraging, guiding, whispering soothing words to Rita as the woman strained to bring her baby into the world. Then, exhausted, she'd sag back and breathe huffy little breaths before she had to push again. Time seemed to stand still as everyone's attention was centered on the birthing.

Sensing a change, Devin gripped the mother-to-be tightly as she gave another huge push, this one lasting much longer. He glanced up to see Molly catch the infant in a towel, on her face a look of absolute rapture.

"Oh, my, look at you," Molly whispered as she held the tiny, wiggling baby girl, her arms flailing. Using the end of another clean towel, she cleaned the baby's face and mouth the way she remembered Maggie doing, then she wrapped the child and placed her in her mother's waiting arms.

Murmuring in Spanish, the woman had already forgotten all the pain and anguish the moment she looked into her baby's face, Devin realized. Gently, he slipped his hands from her shoulders and settled her more comfortably on the seat. Then he walked over to join Molly as she used one of the larger towels to drape over the woman's legs more modestly.

"Do you carry a knife?" she asked him.

"A knife?"

"Yes. I'd hoped the medics would be here by now, but since they're not, I think it's important to cut the umbilical cord."

Devin dug in his pocket and handed her his Swiss army knife, then watched her cut the umbilical cord with hands that weren't too steady. He couldn't blame her for a case of nerves.

Molly heard a siren in the distance coming closer. Thank heaven she wouldn't have to deal with the afterbirth. She was more than ready to let the medics take over.

Smiling at the woman, she bent to look at mother and child. "How are you doing, Rita?"

"*Sí,* good, *señorita. Muchas gracias.*" Rita beamed a smile.

Straightening, Molly sighed. "It's absolutely miraculous, isn't it?"

Devin stood gazing at the tiny fingers circling her mother's thumb, the small mouth making a sucking sound, the fuzzy dark hair on the round little head. He'd never witnessed anything like it before since his mother had always gotten to the hospital in plenty of time for his siblings to be born. But to see it like that, the incredible strain a woman goes through, yet immediately disregards the moment she sees that child. Amazing. "Yes, I'd say it is."

Carlo stretched out a hand, man to man, to Devin. "I want to thank you for stopping." He turned around to shake Molly's hand. "And you for helping us." He shuffled his feet, embarrassed now that it was over. "I was so scared."

Devin clapped him on the shoulder. "So was I, but not this lady." He slipped an arm around Molly. "She knew exactly what to do, thank goodness."

Wiping her damp face and hands in the last clean towel, Molly just smiled as the ambulance pulled up alongside the car.

In twenty minutes, the mother and baby had been examined and transferred into the ambulance which then took off in the direction of the hospital with a thankful Carlo trailing after. Devin walked Molly back to Old Bess.

''The night's entertainment so far has been surprising,'' he said. ''What are you going to do for an encore?''

Stifling a yawn, Molly folded herself into the passenger seat. ''It has been quite a night, hasn't it?''

''Mmm-hmm,'' Devin answered as he started the car. ''Let's get you home for some well-earned rest.''

But long after he'd taken Molly home, then gone upstairs and paid Mrs. Bailey before checking on a sleeping Emily, Devin lay staring at his ceiling reliving the miracle he'd witnessed tonight. At first, he'd been wary, then uneasy, then a bit scared, then a lot scared. He'd never before realized what an awesome thing a birth was.

What must it feel like to have that tiny bundle placed in your arms and know it's your child? Had Sandy been awake when Emily had been born? Surprising himself, he wished he'd been there to support her through it all. As he finally drifted into a restless sleep, he wondered where that thought had come from.

Chapter Ten

The three of them stood on the Ford lot studying a long lineup of Broncos, trying to come to a decision. Molly had to smile at the way Emily had begun to unconsciously mimic her father. They were even dressed alike in short-sleeved denim shirts and jeans, both with hands on their hips, their faces screwed up in concentration. The only difference from where she stood was that Devin's hair was windblown and Emily's ponytail was tied with a piece of bright-blue yarn.

"What do you think, the black one?" Devin asked, leaning down to Emily.

Her small brow furrowed, she shook her head, then pointed a small finger. "The red one, for sure." She glanced up at Molly. "Red's better, right?"

"Red gets my vote," Molly said.

A man couldn't win against two females. Devin walked over to inspect the red Bronco more thoroughly, opening the door, checking out the dash. This was the first dealership they'd visited. Maybe he should do some comparison shopping. Then again, he kind of liked the salesman who'd moseyed up to them when they'd walked into the showroom. When Devin had stated what he had in mind, Bart merely asked them to follow him out to the lot. Since then, he'd been standing off to the side, lazily watching them, yet listening closely and not missing a thing. Devin had always preferred the soft sell.

"You two want to take a ride?" Devin asked. Molly nodded and Emily jumped right in as Devin waved Bart over. "Can we test-drive this one?"

"Sure thing," Bart drawled. "Just let me make a copy of your driver's license and I'll get you the keys."

By the time Molly had shown Emily how to belt herself in, Bart was back, handing Devin the keys. He smiled his thanks and started the Bronco. The nice low hum of a powerful engine. He liked that. He started out of the lot.

During the last week, while he waited for workaholic Molly to have a day off, he'd boned up on a variety of cars, trying to pick one he'd be comfortable with. The Bronco suited him just fine.

Then, as if things were meant to be, his spring royalty check arrived and he again was slightly staggered at the amount. During his wandering years, he'd barely earned in one year one-tenth of the figure on that check. Hopefully, those lean days were over forever.

The book was coming along better and he was two-thirds of the way finished. Molly had had to work extra hours because Trisha had taken some unexpected time off without pay for personal reasons. But they'd still managed to find time to be together evenings after he'd tucked Emily into bed.

And Emily seemed to be thriving, which filled him with an unforeseen and surprisingly strong sense of pride. At first, he hadn't believed Molly's praise that the child's transformation from a sad and often brooding young girl to a smiling and seemingly happy daughter was due to his influence, for he'd thought Molly had more to do with the changes in Emily than he. But during the last couple of weeks with the hours Molly had been working, she'd scarcely seen Emily. So her care had been left almost entirely to him, although Mrs. Bailey had baby-sat some.

Perhaps Emily had blossomed because Devin had viewed her as something of a challenge. He wanted to see if he could get her to smile, hear her laugh more, make her happy. After all, despite the fact that he still felt she'd be better off with Diane and her family, she was his flesh and blood. If looking just like him wasn't enough, he knew she was his for other reasons. Several times, he'd caught her making some of the same gestures he made, such as scratching his head when he was trying to think of something, being allergic to melons, preferring to sleep with a window open. Small things like that.

Best of all, she'd stopped wetting the bed, something he'd struggled with on and off as a young boy, though he hadn't admitted that to anyone outside the family. Yeah, she was definitely a Gray.

And she had a silly sense of humor that matched his. A couple of times, they'd had giggle sessions that had led to the big spontaneous hugs he'd been craving. Devin didn't consider himself sentimental, yet when those little arms wound around his neck, he melted. So he'd

changed his writing schedule, rising early and working
full speed all morning while Emily slept in or watched
TV or went to Mrs. Bailey's. But he spent most afternoons with her.

They'd go swimming, to the library or sometimes to
a movie. Naturally, he hadn't seen the latest Disney
movies and found he didn't mind sitting through them
because Emily was totally enthralled. She'd pick up the
song lyrics easily, singing off-key around the house,
another trait she'd inherited from him, the inability to
carry a tune.

Perhaps he relished being with her because he knew
their relationship as they knew it would be short-lived.
She was his to enjoy for this short time and then he'd
take her to join Diane's family. For her own good. If
he'd begun to feel a few pangs at the thought of not
seeing her except on occasional trips to California, hol-
idays and family reunions, Devin felt that was perfectly
natural. Because she was so cute, so utterly charming.
All the more reason to do right by her by getting her
the family she deserved, even if it meant he'd miss her.

Devin turned the Bronco onto the open road now
that they were some miles away from the dealership,
wanting to know what it would do on the highway. In
seconds he had her up to fifty, sixty, seventy.

"Tempting fate, are we?" Molly asked. "It'd be
some kind of record, getting a speeding ticket before
you've signed the papers."

Devin eased up on the gas. "Spoilsport," he muttered, but he was grinning. "Not bad, eh?"

"I think it's pretty cool," Emily piped in from the
backseat.

"Sure beats Old Bess," Molly added.

"Okay, then, we're sold." As Emily cheered, Devin

made a U-turn and headed back to where Bart would undoubtedly have the papers on his desk. The easiest sale he's made in a while, Devin thought.

"Oh, not again," Devin moaned. "Can't Hank get someone else to cover? I was planning to take you and Emily to the circus. It was going to be a surprise."

"Did you get the tickets already?" Molly asked, wondering how in the world she could disappoint Hank.

"No, but I called and they said they had plenty of good seats left." His face was as crestfallen as a child's.

"Good, then you two go." She touched his arm, hoping he'd not make this any harder for her. Couldn't he see she'd much rather go with them than go to work? "Look, I'm sorry, Devin. But Hank's stuck. Trisha's having a really rough time. She came in, but she was such a mess he had to send her home."

"She's been off since last weekend. What's wrong? Is she sick? A death in the family?" Although he hadn't heard a word from Mrs. Bailey, who was usually fairly chatty.

"No. It's a personal problem, one she's having trouble dealing with. And I can't say I blame her." Molly was already slipping off her jeans and reaching for her black uniform slacks.

Noticing her expression, Devin thought he could guess Trisha's problem. "Something wrong with her son? Is Danny sick?" He'd met the boy one evening when Molly had agreed to watch him for Trisha. Danny was a cute kid, sharp as a tack. Though he was a bit older, he and Emily seemed to hit it off.

Molly sat down to tie her rubber-soled shoes. "No,

Danny's fine. It's some guy Trisha got involved with a little while back. Jeffrey Midland—tall, dark, handsome and trouble. He seemed head over heels for her, giving her gifts, taking her nice places. I tried to get her to slow down, but she fell for him like a ton of bricks. I swear in less than a month, she was looking through bridal magazines.'' She leaned back, sighing. ''Reality came calling last week. He gave her a key to his apartment, only she arrived on an evening when he'd thought she was working. Just like a bad movie, she caught him in bed with another woman.''

The little Devin had seen of Trisha and from what Molly had said about her, he'd thought she was a little flaky, but she didn't deserve that. ''I guess it's best she found out now instead of later.''

''Yes. It's much harder if you find out after you're married.'' Molly took a clean blouse off the hanger, shrugged into it.

Something about the way she said it alerted him. Was she somehow relating to Trisha's predicament? ''Is that the voice of experience talking? Was Lee unfaithful?''

Her back to him, she buttoned her blouse. ''Maybe not from the start, although I don't know positively. But that last year, when all we did was fight, I had a feeling he wasn't working late all those evenings he didn't come home. When I found out for sure, it was the last straw. Even though he'd already killed any love I had for him, it still hurt like the devil.'' Her movements choppy, she tucked in her blouse.

Devin went to her, turned her in his arms. ''You shouldn't blame yourself anymore than Trisha should shoulder the blame. I've known some guys who couldn't stick to one woman no matter what. It's not in their nature, no matter how beautiful the woman or how good the life he shares with her.''

Hands on his shoulders, she gazed into those dark green eyes. Heart in her throat, she had to ask. ''Are you one of those men, Devin?''

''No. One woman at a time was the way I've always played it. When it was over and time to move on, I was honest and aboveboard. But I didn't cheat while I was with someone.''

Not exactly the words she wanted to hear, but they'd have to do. ''And if a woman cheated on you, what would you do?''

''Walk away and never look back. Fidelity's a two-way street.''

Molly found a smile. ''I agree.'' She kissed him lightly. ''I have to go. Thanks for understanding.''

He didn't really understand, believing that a week for Trisha to nurse her wounds over a broken heart was a bit self-indulgent, especially when Molly had to take up the slack. But he knew her strong loyalty streak, so he kept still.

Walking to Old Bess with her, he took her hand. ''We'll miss you. Emily's going to be disappointed.'' She'd fallen asleep on the ride home in the Bronco, so he'd put her down for a nap since he'd figured she'd be up late at the circus.

''Give her a hug for me and you two enjoy yourselves.'' Molly climbed behind the wheel, thinking her car looked shabbier than ever parked next to the shiny red Bronco. ''See you later.''

''Right. Be careful.'' He watched her drive off, hands wedged into his back pockets.

All he could think was that Lee Summers must really be a fool to cheat on a woman like Molly. Or maybe he'd done it to prove to himself that he was his own man and not under daddy's thumb. Only it turned out he was.

Oh, well, Lee's loss, Devin decided, and his gain. He loved being with Molly, loved seeing her beautiful smile, loved watching her blue eyes turn opaque as he filled her, hearing those soft sighs meant for his ears alone. He loved her thoughtfulness with Emily, the way she'd gotten his daughter to open up. He loved it when the three of them went somewhere together, the admiring looks they'd get.

She was a wonderful woman. What's not to love? He…wait! Just because he loved being with her didn't mean he loved her. There was a big difference between loving a woman and loving to be with her, a mighty big difference. Molly knew how he felt about this; she knew the score. He'd never indicated otherwise, never led her on. Just like with Sandy, he'd warned Molly not to expect too much from him. He wasn't the home-in-the-suburbs, yard-full-of-kids type. She'd accepted that about him.

That settled in his mind, Devin felt better.

Hearing the phone ringing, he raced upstairs before it woke Emily. He answered, sounding only slightly winded.

"Devin? It's Diane. How are you?"

"Fine, thanks." Sitting down in his squeaky chair, he leaned back. "What's new?"

"We're all over the chicken pox, thank goodness. What a messy bout that was. Remember when I came home from kindergarten that year all covered with pox and you caught them? You'd missed them when the others had 'em. You were a freshman in high school and you were so mad at me.'' She laughed, recalling the incident.

Devin smiled. ''Yeah, I remember. Took me two weeks to get rid of those awful red bumps.''

''I hope you've forgiven me for that.''

''Long ago. So, the boys are okay?''

''As if nothing ever happened. A couple of whirling dervishes.'' She paused before going on. ''How's Emily?''

''Doing real well.'' He couldn't resist pridefully recounting the changes in his daughter since his last phone conversation with his sister. ''She's really come a long way.''

''That's great, especially the part about bed-wetting. I've just gotten Marky fully trained and I'd hate to start all over. So listen, the reason I'm calling is that Mark can't take time off from work right now, so we've postponed Disneyland until later. Maybe we can go at the end of summer. I've told Mark all about what you suggested and he's all for it. So you and Emily can come anytime.''

Taken aback, Devin just sat there holding the phone to his ear. How could he take Emily away now when she'd only had one ride in the Bronco? And her new bike wouldn't be available till next week because the store hadn't had a red one in stock. And he'd promised her a trip to Sedona with Molly next week. And...

''Devin? Are you there?''

He cleared his throat. ''Yeah. Listen, this isn't a good time. I...I haven't finished my book yet.'' That was it, the real reason. He couldn't leave until the manuscript was in. He'd almost forgotten. ''I really can't leave just yet.''

''That's all right. I just wanted you to know that

we're ready anytime you want to come. In the meantime, why don't you send us some pictures? I'd love to see your Emily.''

His Emily. ''Yeah, right, I will. You haven't mentioned her to Mom and Dad or anyone else, have you?''

''No, although I don't know why you're keeping this such a big secret. You know how we all love children. Any child of yours is welcome, not just in our home but in the family. Remember how beautifully everyone accepted our adopted boys?''

''I know, but I'd rather be the one to tell them.''

''All right. I've got to run. Send those pictures.''

''Okay.'' Slowly, he hung up the phone and swiveled his chair around to gaze out at the backyard where King was chasing off a bird that had dared land in his territory. Unbidden a picture came into focus in his mind of an evening last week when he'd been watering Molly's garden since she had so little time. Emily had been out there with him and he'd turned around to see her snuggled down in the grass with the big German shepherd. Her arms were around his powerful neck while he gently licked her hand. What a picture that would have made.

He'd turned Diane down because his book wasn't completed. And maybe a little because he didn't want to uproot Emily only weeks after she'd had to leave everything familiar to come here. He needed to make sure she was emotionally strong enough to handle yet another big hurdle. So far, she'd proven to be more adaptable than he, but there was no point in pushing the envelope.

Besides, when he felt the time was right, he'd have to prepare Emily in advance. And Molly. He'd have to explain that she'd be better off with his sister's family rather than living with a preoccupied single father who knew zip about parenting. Oh, he'd managed so far, with Molly's help. But there was so much ahead. Homework and puberty and boys and dating. He wasn't equipped to handle all that alone.

He heard a sound and turned to see Emily padding barefoot into his office looking sleepy-eyed, holding her favorite doll, Peaches. "Did you sleep well, sweetheart?"

"Mmm-hmm. Are we still going to the circus?"

He tugged her onto his lap, inhaling the warm little-girl scent of her. He pressed her head to his chest and held her there, knowing that Emily, like her father, woke up slowly. "You bet we are."

Devin felt her smile and his own slipped a bit. It wasn't going to be as easy as he'd thought, walking away from this child. He had to keep reminding himself that it was in her best interest.

"Can I have whipped cream on top?" Emily asked shyly. "And a cherry?"

Marking on her order pad, Molly smiled. "One chocolate sundae with whipped cream and a cherry on top coming up." She turned to Devin sitting in the booth across from Emily. "And you, sir?"

"Just coffee, thanks."

Molly leaned in closer. "Can I tempt you with carrot cake? Hank buys it from this widow a couple of blocks over, so it's homemade. Your favorite." They'd split a piece one evening when they'd had dinner at the café. That had been over a week ago. She'd been working so many hours lately that she hadn't felt like going out, or even cooking. So Devin had taken to bringing Emily to the café when she was working the dinner shift.

"Mmm, sounds great, but I've got to watch the old calories." He patted his flat stomach, very aware how quickly a guy could get out of shape after thirty. If it weren't for his swimming laps, he'd probably be working on a pot belly.

Molly's warm gaze drifted over him, remembering nights she'd spent in his arms, her hand resting on that hard stomach. "I don't think you have anything to worry about quite yet."

"Really?" he answered, playing along. "Because, you see, I'm dating this chick and she likes her men lean and mean."

"Is that a fact? Lean maybe, but not mean. And who are you calling a chick?" She shifted her attention back to Emily who was wearing her shirt with the tigers, lions and elephants on it that Devin had gotten her last week at the circus. "Your dessert is coming up momentarily, miss." Smiling at both of them, she left to go behind the counter to build Emily's sundae.

She was adding the second scoop when Trisha stopped next to her. "Your face is a dead giveaway, did you know that?" she whispered, her back to Hank who was at the grill.

"What do you mean?" Molly asked, frowning. She was greatly relieved that Trisha was back, seemingly over this last heartache. For some reason Molly couldn't fathom, her friend seemed to attract men who wound up hurting her. Then again, who was she to judge?

Trisha grabbed a milkshake container and bent to scoop ice cream in it. "I think you know. One look at your face and a blind man could see that you're in love with your upstairs neighbor."

Molly straightened, honestly taken aback. She had

no idea she was so transparent. Perhaps if she did a little damage control. "You're seeing things. I'm just glad Devin's adjusting so well to sudden fatherhood." Very few secrets between two women who worked together so closely, Molly thought. "Emily's a little doll."

"Yes, and you're nuts about her, too." Trisha added long squirts of chocolate sauce. "I hope you're not headed for a fall. Didn't you tell me he wasn't into permanence?"

"Nor am I looking for that," Molly told her, reaching for the whipped cream. "But I'm not in love with him, in either case."

Trisha hooked the metal container onto the base, knowing the noise would drown out their words. "I think you are. Don't look so shocked. Loving isn't something we choose to do, honey, nor do we get to choose the object of our affections. Love just happens, despite all our struggling against it. I ought to know. I all but wrote the book on love and stuff."

With a shaky hand, Molly plunked two cherries on top, her expression thoughtful. She could deny it all day to Trisha and others, but down deep, she knew she was in love with Devin. How could she not be when his every touch made her feel like a woman, a very attractive, sensual woman. And, since Emily's arrival, he was gentler, softer, the chip on his shoulder gone. Perhaps his daughter had mellowed the man who'd only a few short weeks ago declared he wanted nothing to do with children.

Was it possible that he'd also changed his mind about marriage?

As Molly grabbed a couple of napkins, Trisha leaned close for one last comment. "Don't worry, Molly. If he stays, wonderful. If he leaves, well, I'm living proof you can survive any number of heartbreaks.''

But she was tired of being a survivor, Molly thought. Tired of having her dreams trashed. All right, so she shouldn't have allowed herself to fall for the guy. She'd been doing fine, goals firmly in mind, on track, when he'd barreled into her life and blown her plans into disarray. Now, here they were. She knew he cared, more than a little. But did he care enough to stay, to build a future with her, including Emily? Why couldn't things work out just once in her favor?

Turning to Trisha, she gave her a determined look. ''It doesn't have to be that way.'' Quickly, she pasted on a smile and walked over to the booth where two people who owned her heart were waiting.

''Okay, I've got one,'' Emily said excitedly. ''Why did the fireman wear red suspenders?''

Pretty sure he knew the answer, Devin played along. ''I give up. Why?''

''To hold up his pants. Why did the fireman wear blue suspenders?''

Behind the wheel of the Bronco, Devin turned the corner and sent her a puzzled look. ''I don't know. Why?''

''Because he couldn't find his red suspenders.'' Strapped in the leather seat behind her father, Emily giggled.

''Pretty good, kid.'' Because it was a warm summer night, they'd gone to Railroad Park after eating dinner at the Pan Handle. They'd toured the authentic old railroad car and ridden the small train filled with parents and kids and grandparents all around the park. After three trips around, Devin had persuaded Emily that it was time to leave. On the ride home, she tried to stump him with riddles. "Where did you learn all these?"

"At school. And some from Jamie. Do you know why bees hum?"

"I'll bite. Why do bees hum?"

"Because they don't know the words." More giggles.

"All right, I've got one. Why did the chicken cross the road?"

"Oh, that's easy. To get to the other side. I've got a better one. Knock, knock."

"Who's there?"

"Wayne."

"Wayne who?"

"Wayne drops keep falling on my head. That's a song, you know." Emily, the expert. "I heard it on Molly's radio when we made cookies last week." She stifled a yawn. "I wish Molly could be with us. I wish she didn't have to work so much."

"Me, too, honey." At the very least, he wished he could get her to give up her second job. Working those long shifts, then typing half the night was crazy. But he dared not suggest that she quit again, remembering the last time he had. And he wished he could think of a way she'd let him buy her a car to replace Old Bessie. The poor decrepit thing had broken down again last week. He'd taken it in for her, but she'd absolutely refused to let him pay for the repairs.

Stubborn. The woman was truly stubborn. He'd tried to tell her that his latest check was a whopper and he could well afford to lend a hand, but she'd stopped him in midsentence, then proceeded to lecture him on pride and independence, and offers that insulted both. He'd had no choice but to back off.

As he turned into their drive, he heard Emily yawn expansively. Checking his watch, he saw that it was past nine, well past her bedtime. He also saw that Molly's car was already home.

He found her sitting on the back porch in an old bentwood rocker sipping iced tea and gazing up at the stars, King lying at her feet. "Hey, glad to see you're home."

Molly wiggled her aching feet. "Mmm, me, too." She smiled at a sleepy little girl. "Where've you two been?" she asked, holding her arms out to Emily.

The child climbed onto Molly's lap with a naturalness Devin wouldn't have believed possible when she'd first arrived. Emily snuggled cozily into Molly and he had a moment where his breath backed up in his throat. The two of them made a picture that all but stopped his heart. To cover his emotions, he bent down to rub King's big head.

"Railroad Park," Emily said, then went on to tell Molly all that they'd done. "I wish you could have been with us."

"Me, too, sweetie. Next time." Molly kissed her hair and continued rocking.

Devin saw Emily yawn yet again. "Come on, sleepyhead. It's time for your bath, then bed. You've had a long day."

"Will you come up with us, Molly?" Emily asked.

"Mmm, not tonight, honey. I'm really beat." She kissed her soft cheek. "See you tomorrow."

Devin turned on the light for the stairs. "I'll be up in a minute to run your bath. Start getting undressed, okay?"

"Good night, Molly." Emily trudged up the steps.

Too tired to get to her feet, Molly touched his hand.

"You, come here." When he leaned down, she took his face in her hands and kissed him slowly, lovingly, thoroughly, then pulled back to look into his eyes.

"What was that for?" he asked.

Molly chose her words carefully. "You're so good with her. Do you know how very special you are?"

Devin dropped his gaze, feeling guilt wash over him. Maybe he should tell her his plans now. But she looked so tired, so in need of rest. She didn't sleep enough or eat right, and he fervently wished he could change that. She was in no condition for a serious discussion. "I'm not special. You're wearing rose-colored glasses. You're the special one."

"A mutual admiration society. I can handle that." She kissed him again, reluctantly removing her hands from his face. "Go bathe your daughter."

"You sure you don't want to come up for a while?"

Molly shook her head. "Honestly, I've just enough energy left to finish this tea before falling facedown on my bed. Rain check?"

"Always." He placed a gentle kiss on the top of her head. "Come on, King. Let's go."

Releasing a soft sigh, Molly watched them leave, then shifted her gaze back to the sky, wondering if wishing on a star would make her dreams come true.

Chapter Eleven

Her small body wrapped in a fluffy white towel, Emily stood still while Devin dried her hair with another towel. Finishing that, he took a wide-toothed comb and gently drew it through her long hair, being careful not to pull on the snarls. "When was your last haircut?" Devin asked her. "Do you remember?" Her hair, especially wet, was halfway down her back.

"I've never had a haircut," Emily answered.

"Do you like it long, or do you want me to get it cut for you?"

"No, please. I like it long."

"Okay, then." Devin set aside the comb. "Do you need help putting on your new nightie?" He'd taken her shopping in the afternoon for a couple of things they needed and she'd spotted the floor-length white nightie, her eyes growing wide. Some sort of soft cotton, it had long sleeves and a high collar with pink lace inserts. How could he not buy it for her? Even though it was quite warm, she'd insisted that she had to wear it tonight.

"I can do it."

Hanging up the towel, Devin smiled. She didn't mind if he helped her bathe or washed her hair, but she insisted on dressing herself. Modesty or independence, he wasn't sure which. That was all he needed, *two* independent females in his life. "I'll be in the living room."

In moments, he was stretched out in his lounge chair, realizing he was sort of tired, too. He'd worked until two, gone shopping with Emily and after that, they'd stopped at the Pan Handle and ended up at Railroad Park. Throughout most of the day, she'd kept up a line of chatter. Kids could wear you out with their questions. Trick questions sometimes so that you had to stay alert or you'd give the wrong answers. But he was proud of how smart Emily was, how he never had to explain anything to her twice. Inherited from her father's side, undoubtedly, he thought with a grin.

He heard her come into the room and glanced up. She looked like an angel as she stopped in front of him holding out the book of fairy tales he'd bought her a while back.

"Will you read me a story, Daddy?" she asked.

Daddy. It was the first time she'd called him that and the feeling that flooded Devin stunned him. Like a fist to the solar plexus. He'd used the word himself in his thoughts, but somehow, hearing it from her made it more real, more special.

Devin opened his arms and Emily climbed up onto his lap, settling her head just under his chin. She smelled like her peach-scented bubble bath from the purple turtle, all warm and fragrant. He gazed into green eyes as familiar as his own. The shadows of fatigue were gone from her cheeks, the sadness had disappeared from her eyes, and she no longer woke during the night crying for her mother. She also had the sweetest smile, he decided as he opened the book. Of course she would. She was his daughter.

Devin swallowed around a clogged throat. "Which story do you want to hear?" He'd read several to her before, but not snuggled together like this.

"I don't like 'Hansel and Gretel.' It's too scary. How about 'The Snow Princess'?"

He flipped through the thick book and found the right page, then began to read. She liked it best when he changed his voice for each character, making the villains sound fierce and the others sound happy or frightened or whatever.

About halfway through, he saw that she could barely keep her eyelids open. "How about if we finish this tomorrow night?"

"Okay."

Devin set the book aside but instead of helping her down, he picked her up and carried her to the fold-out bed he'd opened up in his office. It was certainly large enough for her, yet he wished she had a real bed in a pretty room of her own. Maybe...

He shook his head, wondering where that thought had come from. He settled her under the covers and sat down beside her so he could lean over and kiss her. Winding her small arms around his neck, she whispered into his ear. The simple words "I love you, Daddy" echoed in his head.

"I love you, too, princess," he whispered back, then turned out the light and left the room, his emotions in a jumble. Walking out onto his back porch, Devin stared at a skyful of stars.

That small human being, that tiny little girl was his alone and she'd said she loved him. She'd arrived sad, tossed about, lonely. And by some miracle, he'd managed to change all that for her. He'd replaced her tears with smiles, her nightmares with happy dreams. Imagine having that kind of influence on a child's life. Of course, he hadn't done it alone. Molly had helped a great deal. But he'd played a large part in Emily's transformation.

Maybe fatherhood wasn't such a bad thing after all.

Tonight, when his trusting young daughter had said those three little words to him, something had shifted inside Devin. He stood there struggling with a myriad of strange new feelings: a fierce protectiveness for Emily that he hadn't known he'd possessed, a desire to keep her safe, to be there for her whenever she needed him. Not because her mother was dead and she had no one else, but because he genuinely wanted to. He wanted her to be happy, to grow up to be the beautiful woman he knew she could be.

And love. His heart was flooded with love for her.

Devin watched a shooting star ripple across the night sky and thought it was almost as great a miracle as these brand-new feelings he was just discovering. He wasn't sure how this turnaround had happened or exactly what to do about it now that it had.

For a long time, he just stood there gazing out, searching his mind for answers and his heart for the truth. Finally, he knew what he wanted to do, what he had to do.

Going back inside and locking up, Devin felt he just might sleep better tonight than he had in a long while.

* * *

Molly stood in the pool, squinting up at Emily as she crouched on the edge preparing for an off-the-side slide dive. "Okay, come on, and remember, keep your hands together and your mouth closed."

Her small mouth a study in determination, Emily dived into the water, aiming for the spot where Molly waited. In seconds Molly had the child's hands gripped in hers, helping her surface.

"That was really good." Molly watched as Emily blinked away the excess water.

"Do you mean it? Was I really good?"

"Yes, you were. But that was the last dive. We've been in an hour and it's time to get out now."

"Maybe later we can show Daddy. He doesn't know I've been practicing with you." She swam the short distance to the steps.

Molly stepped out and wrapped a towel around Emily, then grabbed a second one to dry her hair. She couldn't help noticing that Emily had begun calling Devin Daddy. She'd done it earlier when he'd brought her down, and Molly had seen by his expression how much that small change meant to him. After a rocky start, they'd come a long way, these two, and she couldn't be more pleased for them.

Finished drying off, Molly wrapped the damp towel around her waist, stepped into her thongs and opened the pool gate. She followed Emily out, clicked the lock in place and led the way to their back porch. "I'll go upstairs with you while you change, then we'll come back down to my place. You can watch TV while I finish my paperwork, okay?"

"Okay. What time did Daddy say he'd be back?" Emily asked, her chunky legs carrying her up the steps.

She'd filled out, lost that thin look she'd had when she'd arrived, Molly thought. Between her attempts at cooking, Devin's mostly carry-out meals and the food at the café, Emily's appetite had improved.

"He didn't say exactly. Just asked me to watch you for a couple of hours while he ran some errands in town." Molly opened Devin's back door and they stepped into the kitchen. "Do you need any help?"

"No, thanks." Emily scooted off to Devin's office where her clothes had been arranged in the closet.

"Bring your wet suit and towel to me when you're through and we'll hang them up to dry."

Molly reached into the fridge for the bottled water she knew Devin kept in there for her for the times she baby-sat. Sitting down at his kitchen table, she drank the chilled water and wondered what kind of errands he had to do that would take several hours. He usually took Emily with him for shopping and the like. Perhaps he needed to research something for his book in the library. But then, why had he been so mysterious?

Leaning back, Molly decided she didn't really care. She had two whole days off in a row with only a couple of hours of insurance forms typing to do. She had a few errands of her own to run, but she'd get to them later, or possibly tomorrow. She'd asked Devin to pick up some fish they could barbecue for dinner. Maybe, after her typing, she'd make a cake and get Emily to help. The child just loved putzing in the kitchen.

Molly took another swallow of water as the phone rang. She reached to answer it, thinking it might be Devin. "Hello?"

"Yes, is Devin Gray in, please?" a woman asked.

"No, he isn't. May I take a message?"

"Oh, dear. Do you know when he'll be back?"

"No, I don't. Shouldn't be long, though."

"I see. I have to leave for an hour or so, but I'll be in after two. This is Joan Cantrell from Southwest Adoptions." The woman paused a moment, then hurried on. "Would you please tell Mr. Gray that we're ready to take his application to have his daughter adopted if he'll call me to make an appointment?"

Stunned, Molly set down her water bottle. "Let me get this straight," she said to the woman. "You're saying that Mr. Gray has called your office wanting to put his daughter up for adoption?"

The woman hesitated, then finally spoke again. "Yes, that's correct. I believe her name is Emily. Is that right?"

"Emily. Yes, that's right." Molly sat gripping the phone, a score of emotions swirling through her, so shocked she could scarcely think of anything else to say.

"Will you ask him to call me, please?" Joan Cantrell asked somewhat impatiently. She read off her phone number and repeated her name.

"I'll give Mr. Gray your message." Shaken to her core, Molly hung up the phone and sat staring into space.

Adoption agency. Devin had never once mentioned an adoption agency to her, not that he was considering one or that he'd phoned to discuss possibilities with them. Not that he was obligated to talk over his daughter's future with her, but they had become more than a little close lately.

All this time, weeks now, had Devin been merely acting as if he wanted Emily, pretending that he cared for his daughter while quietly making arrangements to give her up? Could he be that devious? Could he be that good an actor, for she'd witnessed countless scenes between father and daughter that had led her to believe he'd come to love the child as much as she herself had?

Emily would be devastated. He'd fooled Molly, too. Despite the fact that she knew Devin was wary of marriage and commitment, she'd begun to hope that his young daughter had softened him, made him want a family and a future with Emily. And possibly Molly herself.

Had he been faking it all? Was he like so many men after all, wanting to turn away from any and all responsibilities? Did he think of women and children as disposable objects to be discarded when they didn't fit the bill, like Lee had? Would Devin honestly hand over his own child for adoption when he could well afford to raise her? If he was capable of that, he must also be capable of playing with her feelings, bedding her to satisfy his own needs, abandoning her when she'd served her purpose and it was time to move on.

Dear God, could she have misjudged him so?

Of course, he'd never said he loved her, never promised her anything. Okay, she'd accept that. But what she couldn't accept was that he'd allowed Emily to live with him for weeks, get used to him, learn to love him, and then scuttle her off to strangers. What kind of man would do that?

Molly became aware of a presence behind her and turned to see Emily standing there in shorts and T-shirt, her little face cloudy, her dimpled chin quivering.

"Is Daddy going to give me away?" she asked, her voice breaking on a sob.

Molly felt a rush of guilt that she'd spoken so frankly with the woman from the agency, not realizing that Emily might overhear. She held her arms out to the child, pulling her close. "Don't worry, honey. Things will work out, you'll see." Molly held her, trying desperately to give her a reassurance she herself didn't feel.

Things will work out, she'd told Emily. But would they? What possible explanation could Devin give them that would take away the pain of that phone call?

Putting on a smile for the little girl's sake, she wiped the tears from her cheeks. "I'm sure your daddy will take care of everything." She stood, needing to get back to her own place, needing to think. "Let's go downstairs. I think Jamie's outside riding his bike. Want to play with him awhile?"

"Okay," Emily said halfheartedly.

Damn you, Devin Gray, Molly thought. *If you hurt this vulnerable child, you'll have me to answer to.*

Devin turned into the driveway and parked his Harley next to the fence near the Bronco. Dismounting, he began whistling. He felt good. Better than good. He felt wonderful.

Securing the Harley's lock, he took a moment to touch King's big head, then headed for the back porch. Emily's bike, the red one that they'd brought home just yesterday, was gone so she was probably off riding with Jamie down the block. Molly's Honda sat in the sunshine looking old and tired. Soon, he'd get rid of that eyesore and get Molly something sporty. Maybe a convertible. Yeah, Arizona had perfect convertible weather.

Patting his pocket where his most recent purchase was carefully entrenched, Devin hurried onto the back porch and gave two knocks on Molly's door, his usual signal. Entering the kitchen, he was about to give her another lecture on keeping the door locked when he noticed her seated at the table, her typing spread out around her. But she sat staring out the window, her chin propped in her hand.

"Hi, there," he began, walking over. The minute she turned to look at him, he knew something wasn't right. "What's wrong?" A sudden thought struck him. "Is it Emily? Is she all right?"

"Emily's fine. She's having lunch at Jamie's. His mother invited her." She studied Devin's face, trying to see beyond the handsome features, past those compelling green eyes. Wanting to look into his heart and see what was there.

Devin stood his ground, wondering what on earth had happened to make her look so coldly angry now when he'd left her smiling and happy just hours ago. "All right, tell me. What happened?"

Molly handed him a note. "I took this phone message for you." She sat back, never taking her eyes from him. As the information about Joan Cantrell and the adoption agency registered, she saw his face turn ashen and guessed the truth.

"I can explain this," Devin began, his voice unsteady.

"I'm listening." Her voice was icy calm.

"I admit I did call about having Emily adopted, but..."

Noisily, Molly slid back her chair as angry tears filled her eyes against her will. "Do you have any idea what I would give for a beautiful child like Emily? And you're ready to give her away like an outfit you'd been given that doesn't quite suit you. You're exactly like Lee who sent me away when I couldn't give him what he wanted. At least I was an adult, but she's just a little girl. How could you even think to send her away when she's come so far, when she thinks of you as her father now?''

Jumping up, no longer able to stay in the same room with him, Molly grabbed her canvas purse and keys and turned toward the door.

He wrapped his fingers around her arm. ''Molly, let me explain. It's not like that.'' He had to make her see, make her understand.

''How could I have been so wrong about you?'' With one twist, she was free of his grip and opening the door.

''Wait! I can explain.''

Molly skipped down the front steps. ''I don't want to hear any more.'' She rushed to the Honda and climbed in, praying Old Bess wouldn't pick this moment to act up. Much to her relief, the engine caught on the first try. Blinking away tears, Molly backed out of the drive and zipped onto the street.

Devin stood in the drive watching her disappear from view. What the hell had happened here? In moments, his happiness had been shattered, all by one stupid phone call.

Angrily, he thrust his hands into his back pockets, debating about whether to try following her or waiting her out. He'd have to check on Emily at Jamie's first and by then, Molly would be long gone. Besides, she'd have to come home sooner or later.

Maybe it would be best to let her cool off. In a way, he couldn't blame Molly for her reaction. Why hadn't he called that woman at Southwest Adoptions and cancelled his request? Because he hadn't seriously thought he'd ever hear from her again. Still, that was no excuse.

Slowly climbing the stairs to his place, Devin knew

that all this was his fault. He shouldn't have taken so long to make up his mind, to wake up and smell the coffee. He should have told Molly this morning where he stood, how he felt, what he wanted. And he should have explained things to his daughter. He had no one to blame but himself.

Dropping into his chair and pushing back, he wondered how long it would take Molly to go from a fast burn to a slow simmer.

Molly sat on Trisha's lumpy couch sipping an iced tea, gripping the glass with shaky hands. "How could I have let myself believe him?" she asked, her voice low.

At the other end of the couch, Trisha lit a Marlboro and blew smoke toward the ceiling. "Because you wanted it to be so. Welcome to the club." She reached for her tea.

"Why are women so trusting? And so dumb?" Molly really wasn't expecting answers; she just needed to vent a bit. She'd driven around for half an hour and found herself on Trisha's street. Remembering that her friend had the afternoon off since she'd been scheduled for the early shift, she'd knocked on her front door and found Trisha watching *General Hospital*. Fortunately, her son Danny had been taken to the movies by a neighbor.

She hadn't been in Trisha's place but one other time and now, looking around, she found the somewhat shabby furniture, the cabbage-rose-patterned wallpaper and the stack of confession magazines piled on the wobbly coffee table even more depressing. Trisha seemed stuck in a financial bind that kept her one jump above the poverty line, which was probably why she seemed so desperate to find a man who'd pull her out.

But Lee Summers had taught Molly that a moneyed man wasn't the answer. The only person she could truly rely on for happiness was herself. How had she forgotten that?

Molly sighed. "I shouldn't be here dumping on you when you have your own problems."

Trisha shrugged. "I'm over Jeffrey, if that's what you mean. He hurt me badly, but I know I have to move on. What do you suppose there is about men that causes them to lie to a woman, to promise her things they know she wants, then when they're through playing house, leave without so much as an I'm sorry?"

"Devin didn't promise me anything. It's not his fault I fell in love with him. And the deeper I fell, the more I forgot that he'd told me early on up front that he didn't want the forever scene. Somehow, I'd convinced myself he'd changed. Because of Emily. I thought I knew him, but I didn't know him at all."

Trisha drew deeply on her Marlboro. "Men are like icebergs, I've come to realize. They let you see ten percent of them while the other ninety's hidden away."

Was her friend right? Molly wondered. She wasn't certain of the percentages, but Devin surely had hidden a side of himself from her. "The worst thing is that that sweet little girl is going to be crushed yet again. She's so young to have to go through so much."

"It seems to me that you care more about Emily than her own father does. Why don't *you* adopt her? Then when Devin moves on, as I guess he's planning on doing soon, you'll at least have his child."

The suggestion wasn't bad. She couldn't give Emily all that her father could, but it wouldn't be long before her financial picture would improve. Maybe Emily would get over losing Devin more easily if she stayed with Molly. The child seemed to care about Molly nearly as much as Devin. And she did love Emily.

Of course, she'd have to look into that little face that would remind her daily of the man who would walk away from both of them. Would she be able to handle that? And would the courts let a single woman with few assets adopt a child?

"I don't know." Molly set down her tea and pushed back her hair with both hands. "Devin would probably prefer that I stay out of it. Knowing I had his daughter would complicate his life, make him feel guilty, even."

Trisha crushed out her cigarette in a large ashtray. "He should feel guilty." She stretched out her long, thin legs and propped her feet onto the coffee table. "I have to say, he's one hell of an actor. The last time he and Emily were in the café, he played the part of the doting daddy to a *T*. He sure had me fooled."

That made two of them. Molly steepled her fingers thoughtfully. "To be fair, perhaps there is an explanation. Something I don't know. In all honesty, I drove off before he could explain." She closed her eyes and leaned her head back. "Maybe I should have at least heard him out."

"What explanation? You said from the beginning that he never wanted kids because of his background. When he found out he had a daughter, he searched for a way out. Only it took longer than he'd thought. Wouldn't you think it would occur to him that the longer Emily was with him, the harder it would be on her to have to leave?" Trisha crossed her arms over her chest, pondering the situation.

When Molly didn't say anything, she went on.

"Maybe the agency couldn't take his application when he first called, for whatever reason. Do you know when he called them?"

Frowning, Molly shook her head. "I should have asked the woman more, but I was just so shocked."

"Don't blame yourself."

Coming to a decision, Molly sat up, drained her iced tea, then stood. "I think I need to go back and talk with Devin. Maybe I was a little hasty to judge him so quickly. He…he just doesn't seem like the type of man who could do this to a child."

Trisha walked to the door with her. "Remember that iceberg comparison I told you about." She hugged her friend. "Whatever happens, I wish you luck."

Molly found a smile. "Thanks, Trisha." Walking slowly, she went out and got behind the wheel. She wasn't sure what Devin would say, but she owed it to him to listen.

Jamie's mother stood on her front porch. "Far as I know, Emily left shortly after lunch, Mr. Gray. She and Jamie watched TV for awhile, then they both went outside. I haven't seen her since."

Devin felt his heart lurch. "Do you know where Jamie is now?" he asked, trying to stay calm. The two kids probably were riding their bikes together. Maybe they'd gone around the block. He didn't think Emily would disobey his strongest rule, that she not cross any streets. But it was a short block and he'd given her permission to ride that, as long as Jamie was with her.

"Let's see, I think he's back by the garage." She leaned over the porch railing. "Yes, there he is, drawing on the cement with chalk."

Jamie was home and his daughter wasn't with him.

Not good. Nerves rattling, Devin thanked the woman and walked to the back. "Hey, Jamie, do you know where Emily is?"

Turning, the boy straightened. "Hi, Mr. Gray. I haven't seen her for awhile."

"I see. Do you know where she was going when she left here?"

The boy dropped his eyes to the cement, regarding his work. "Not really."

Devin crouched down. "Look, this is important. Do you have any idea where she might have gone? She didn't come home. Was she upset in any way?" Emily had never strayed before, never gone where she'd been told not to go.

Reluctantly, Jamie looked up. "Yeah, she was upset."

"About what?"

Jamie's canvas shoe kicked at a stray stone. "About the adoption agency."

Fear settled on Devin like a heavy weight. How had she found out about that? Surely Molly wouldn't have said anything. "What did she say?"

"She said you were going to give her away, that this lady from this adoption agency called and talked to Molly. Emily heard her on the phone." Innocent blue eyes met his. "Are you sending her away?"

Devin stood, balling his hands into fists. "No, Jamie. There's been a mixup. I'm not sending her away."

His young face brightened. "Good. She'll be glad to hear that 'cause she was crying when she left here."

Damn! "Did you see which direction she went?"

The boy pointed toward Devin's place half a dozen houses up the street. "That way. I thought she was going home."

''Thanks, Jamie. You've been a big help.'' Leaving the yard, he headed back, wondering where to begin looking.

Was she holed up in Molly's place, hiding? Had she gone to visit Mrs. Bailey, her baby-sitter, to pour out her little heart to someone who'd understand? Had she taken off, run away, thinking her father didn't want her?

Hurrying now, Devin felt emotions clog his throat. She was so young, so small. She'd lost her mother, her aunt hadn't wanted her and today she'd overheard that her father had called an adoption agency. The poor kid had to be feeling terrible, hurting, devastated.

Almost running, he looked up the street and down, then began calling her name, trying not to panic.

Where was Emily?

Chapter Twelve

"This is Tim, Mr. Gray," Jamie said, introducing his tall towheaded friend. "He's ten and he's allowed to go all the way to the park. I told him Emily's missing and we both want to help."

Touched, Devin nodded, not trusting his voice. For half an hour now, he'd driven around the neighborhood and even several blocks beyond, shouting his daughter's name. He'd stopped to ask every child he'd spotted, every cluster of kids, to ask if they'd seen a little girl, six years old, with black hair riding a red bike, but no one had seen Emily. How could that be? She couldn't have simply vanished in the middle of a bright summer day.

Finally, Devin spoke to the two boys. "Thanks, guys. I appreciate your help. Jamie, you keep circling our block. If you know some of the kids around here, stop and ask if they've seen her. Tim, you go as far as your mom lets you and do the same.''

"What was she wearing?" Tim asked. "I'm not sure I know what she looks like.''

Undoubtedly a kid in the fifth grade wouldn't pay much attention to a first grader, Devin thought. "I'm not sure." He'd looked through her things, found her wet bathing suit on the porch railing drying, and knew she'd gone swimming with Molly. "Probably shorts and a T-shirt.''

"Okay," the older boy said. "Don't worry. We'll find her.''

Out of the mouths of babes, Devin thought, wishing he was as confident as Tim. He heard his name called and turned to see Mrs. Bailey walking toward the fence between the two properties. He went to meet her. "Did you remember something?''

"No, dear, I didn't. I was coming to ask if you'd made any headway.''

Devin ran a hand through his already mussed hair. "Not so far. I just can't imagine where she's gone.''

"I saw her in the pool with Molly earlier. They were laughing and having a great time. What could have happened to cause the child to want to run away?''

More guilt piled on top of what was already weighing him down, but he didn't want to go into it with Mrs. Bailey just now. "If you hear anything, please let me know." He started walking away, wondering if he should call the police. How long does a child have to be missing before they'd get involved?

"Does she know your phone number?" Mrs. Bailey called out.

Devin berated himself for not teaching it to her. Why hadn't he? Maybe Molly had. "I don't know.''

Suppose, hurt by what she'd overheard, Emily had ridden off on her bike and gone too far. Now she was lost, confused. Would she stop somewhere and try to call him? No, he was the one who'd hurt her. Maybe she'd call Molly. Did she know that number? But he couldn't just sit by either phone in the hopes she'd call.

Pacing the driveway, wondering what else he could do, he heard a car approach and recognized Old Bessie's wheezing engine. Molly got out as soon as she'd pulled to a stop. He rushed over.

"Devin," she began quickly, "I shouldn't have rushed off like that. I..."

"Never mind that. Emily's missing."

"Missing? What do you mean, missing?"

"I mean after you left, I went upstairs for about ten minutes, then I decided to walk down to Jamie's house to get her since you'd said she'd gone there for lunch. His mother said she'd left awhile ago and Jamie didn't know where she went." Restlessly, he paced the length of the car and back.

"Oh, no." Molly's face went pale as she leaned against her car. "It's my fault."

Devin halted in front of her. "What do you mean, your fault?"

She told him that Emily had overheard her talking with the woman from the adoption agency, that she'd asked Molly if her daddy was going to give her away. She watched his already anguished face, saw him struggle for control, and she wanted to take him in her arms. But he held himself stiff and unapproachable, as if, should someone touch him, he might crumble. "I'm so sorry," she whispered. "I didn't realize she could hear me."

Devin shook his head. "It's not your fault. It's mine.

I shouldn't have taken so long to acknowledge my feelings, to realize how much I love that little girl. I should have told her the minute I did, but no! I wanted to surprise her. And you. Now, look at the mess I've made." Agitated, he resumed his pacing.

Molly followed after him. "Surprise us? How?"

"Never mind now. The important thing is to find Emily."

She had to agree. "All right, how long has she been missing?"

Devin shrugged. "Altogether about an hour since she left Jamie's house, I'd guess. Jamie and a friend of his are riding their bikes throughout the neighborhood, calling her name and asking other kids if they've seen her. I've driven around in every direction calling for her. Mrs. Bailey hasn't seen her." Thrusting his hands in his pockets, he gazed up at the sky. "She can't have disappeared into thin air."

"No, of course not. I read an article not long ago that said that children under the age of ten don't usually run away from home. What most of them do is hide out somewhere if they're hurt or confused. I have a feeling she's somewhere around here. Did you search your place and mine? Maybe she's hiding in a closet or even that long cupboard in your office."

Anything was better than standing here worrying. "All right. You check your place and I'll go up and check mine."

Both rushed off, but ten minutes later, they were back down, faces registering another dead end.

"How long before I get the police in on this?" Devin finally asked, voicing his worst fear. He had to face the unthinkable. "What if...if she was snatched on her way home from Jamie's, some guy reaching over and grabbing her off her bike and..."

"And then after stuffing her into his car, he stopped to put her bike in his trunk? I don't think so." Yet the thought had occurred to Molly, too. But they had to keep a cool head.

"Can you think of any place else she'd hide?" he asked. He felt even worse realizing that he probably didn't know his daughter as well as Molly did. "Did she ever confide in you about a place she'd like to go?"

"Only Disneyland because a schoolmate had been there. Did Mrs. Bailey check out her house?"

Devin nodded just as Jamie came rolling in on his bike. "Find anyone who's seen her?"

"No." Jamie parked his bike. "Tim's gone to the park. Maybe he'll find someone." He wandered back to visit King who'd been pacing along the fence line, aware that something was happening.

"I don't suppose King has any bloodhound in him so you could let him pick up Emily's scent and he'd track her?" Molly asked hopefully.

"No, that wouldn't work. Do I have to wait until she's been gone twenty-four hours before the police will get involved?" The very thought had his palms sweating.

"No, not with children." But Molly had another idea. "Maybe I should walk the neighborhood and call for her since it's you she's upset with right now." She hated wording it that way, but this was no time to spare his feelings. The important thing was to find Emily.

"Sure, go ahead. I'm open to any and all suggestions."

"Uh, Molly," Jamie called out as he walked over to

where they were standing, "Can I talk with you a minute? Privately?"

Molly glanced at Devin before turning back to the boy. "Sure, Jamie." She walked to meet him and they strolled toward the back yard together.

He nodded toward the storage shed that was at the far side of the lot along one fence line. "Emily's in there, but she doesn't want to come out."

Relief flooded Molly. Thank God she was safe. The rest they would handle somehow. She slipped her arm around the boy's shoulders. "Good work, Jamie. How'd you think to look in there?"

"I heard a cat meowing so I pushed open the door. Emily's sitting on this old chair holding her cat. Her bike's in there, too. I went in to talk to her."

"So, why doesn't she want to come out?" Although Molly thought she knew the answer to her own question.

"Because she thinks Mr. Gray's going to give her away. She says she's not coming out because no one wants her." He looked up at Molly, his young face questioning. "Mr. Gray said he wasn't going to send her away, but I'm not so sure."

"No one's sending her away. I know for a fact that one someone wants her." She glanced over her shoulder at Devin, noticed his agitated pacing. "Maybe two someones. Do you think she'd talk with me?"

"Maybe. I could ask her."

"Wait here one minute, okay?" Molly walked over to where Devin was standing, hands on his hips, his expression a mixture of fear and frustration.

"What'd the boy want?" Devin asked, heading her off.

"I'm going to tell you, but I want you to promise

me you'll stay calm." She watched his dark-green eyes narrow, but finally he nodded. She told him the situation and saw the elation on his face when he heard that his daughter was in the shed.

Devin drew in a shaky breath. "Thank God, she's safe."

"But you're not home free yet. She doesn't want to come out, doesn't want to talk to you. Jamie's going to ask if I can go in. I'll do my best to coax her out. The rest, the explanation and reassurance she needs, is up to you. Can you handle it from there?"

"Yes, absolutely." Devin gripped her arm. "I do want her, Molly. I think I did almost immediately, but the responsibility of fatherhood scared me so much that I convinced myself she'd be better off somewhere else."

"Tell Emily that. I'll be back. You understand that physically you can force her out, of course. But what is needed here is to convince her there's a good reason to come out voluntarily, that you care about her."

"I do care." Devin let out another relieved breath. "Bring her to me, Molly, please."

Maybe there was hope here yet. Molly walked over to Jamie and told him to go in and ask Emily if she'd talk to her. Moments later, the boy came out of the dim shed and beckoned to her. Bracing herself, Molly went in.

Devin walked back and hugged Jamie. "Thanks. I owe you."

Embarrassed, the boy just nodded and got on his bike, then rode off.

Devin sat down on the back steps, feeling weary yet elated. The last couple of hours had drained him emotionally. And he knew he still had a ways to go. But

Emily was safe and that was the best news of all. The hideous mental pictures he'd been struggling with he could now banish.

Elbows propped on his knees, hands steepled by his chin, he sat waiting, planning his words carefully. He didn't want to blow this, for he might not get another chance.

It was several long minutes later when Molly stepped through the door of the shed carrying Willie in one arm and holding Emily's hand. Slowly, they walked over to where Devin was sitting. Shyly, Emily sat down next to her father while Molly put the cat safely inside her place, then joined them on the steps, slipping one arm around the little girl reassuringly.

It hadn't been easy to talk her into listening to what her dad had to say. But Molly had finally convinced Emily that grownups made mistakes, too, just like kids, and that they deserved to tell their stories. There was a lesson in there somewhere for her as well, Molly realized, for she, too, had run off too quickly.

"Devin, you've got the floor," Molly began.

He could see the tracks on his daughter's face where her tears had dried, and it hurt him to know he'd caused those tears. Knowing that this little talk, with the two females who'd come to mean the world to him, was one of the hardest he'd ever had to have, he began.

"Emily, I know you heard Molly talking with a woman from an adoption agency. I have to confess that I did call her to discuss the possibility of having you adopted. But that was on the very first day you arrived here." He took a deep breath, noticing how her big sad eyes watched him solemnly. "At that time, I didn't think I could give you what I felt you needed, both a father and a mother. I thought I was lousy father material, a man living alone. I wanted you to have more.''

Molly hadn't jumped in to help him, not that he'd expected she would, so he went on. ''But since then, I've come to realize that although I still have a lot to learn, I believe I've come a long way. I've tried to be a good dad, to be there for you. But the most important thing that happened was that I realized that I love you very much, that I don't want anyone else raising you. That inexperienced as I might be, I want to be the one.''

Devin saw Emily's lower lip quiver at that, but he needed to say the rest. He looked to Molly this time. ''Last night, Emily called me daddy for the first time and told me she loved me. I have to tell you that it was like a bolt out of the blue, the way she made me feel. Everything shifted and changed. Things fell into place and I realized I've been running away from the very things I always wanted.''

He saw Molly blink back tears, so he hurried to finish. ''In the past, I thought the word love, the very idea, came with a noose that would forever stifle me. Instead, hearing Emily say those words, I discovered that her love was a gift I hadn't known I wanted or needed until then. It's the same as my feelings for you, Molly. I've loved you almost from the very beginning, but I was afraid to admit it.''

Now he reached up to touch Molly's face, her lovely face. ''You're beautiful and giving and everything I've ever wanted. And, oddly enough, it was this little girl who showed me the way, who taught me not to be afraid.'' His hand drifted to Emily's dark head where his fingers lingered lovingly.

''There it is in a nutshell, ladies. Can you forgive

me for taking so long to wake up? Can we start over and be a family?'' Feeling uncharacteristically nervous, he waited.

It seemed forever before someone spoke.

''Would that mean Molly would be my new mom?'' Emily asked hesitantly.

Devin's eyes sought Molly's over the child's head. ''It would if she loves us, too. If she'll marry me. It's asking a lot, I know, because Emily and I come as a package deal.''

Engulfed by emotions, Molly blinked rapidly through tears that she wasn't sure how long she could hold back. ''Are you sure, Devin? Because more than you and I are involved here. Emily can't handle another upheaval. And then there's the problem of no more additions to our family,'' she added, reminding him of her barren state.

''That's not a problem,'' he told her emphatically. ''We have Emily and I love both of you with all my heart. If we want more children, we can adopt.'' Leaning back, he pulled a velvet jeweler's box from his pocket and held it out to Molly. ''This was the errand I had to run today. I wanted to get something just right.'' He flipped open the lid to reveal a beautiful diamond flanked by a smaller emerald on each side. ''To remind you of two people with green eyes who want to be a part of your life. Will you marry us?''

Molly searched his face, those wondrous green eyes, and finally saw there what she'd been hoping to find. ''I love you, too.'' Her arm around Emily tightened. ''What do you think? Should we do it?''

''Yes!'' Emily answered as happy tears fell. She hugged each of them in turn, then looked up at her father. ''We'll really be a family?''

"You bet we will." He kissed the top of her head, grateful that kids were resilient. He'd been given a second chance here to try to make up for Emily's rocky start in life. And perhaps he could convince Molly that she hadn't made a mistake this time in loving him.

Emily spotted Jamie circling around the driveway on his bike. "Can I go tell Jamie, please?"

"Sure." Devin watched her run off, then reached over to pull Molly closer. "Say it again," he whispered.

Pressed to his side, she looked up at him. "I love you."

"Mmm, I like the sound of that."

"However, I think there's something you should know."

"What's that?" Now that Emily was safe and Molly loved him, he didn't think too much could upset him.

"I held Willie for some time in the shed and, by the feel of things, we need to think up a new name because Willie's going to be a mother real soon. I imagine that the father's somewhere in California since we never let him, rather her, outside until today."

Devin smiled, thinking all his problems should be as simple. "The more the merrier," he said, holding her close.

This from a man who hadn't wanted a child or her cat, to say nothing of a wife. How sweet it was, Molly thought as she reached for his kiss.

Epilogue

It was warm for the last day of December, Devin thought as he crammed the last piece of luggage in the Bronco and closed the tailgate. They'd celebrated Christmas in California in the midst of all the Grays, large and small, and had just flown back home to Scottsdale. He was still amazed at how easily Molly had taken to his big family.

He walked around to where Emily was trying to fasten her seat belt and watched with a look of amusement as she struggled to secure the buckle. "You want Daddy to help you?"

"I can do it myself," she answered. "But it's twisted, see?"

Indeed it was. Patiently, Devin untangled the belt, then handed it back to her. Quickly, she buckled it, then gave him a triumphant smile. At nearly eight, Emily was just as independent as her mother ever was.

At that thought, he glanced across the back seat to where Molly was carefully placing their sleeping three-month-old son in his car seat alongside his sister. Devin Gray, Jr. with his black hair, green eyes and dimpled chin was their miracle child, the one Molly had been certain she'd never have.

But she'd gotten pregnant anyhow, only a few months after their autumn wedding last year. Molly had been more than a little shocked, though enormously pleased. The doctor had explained that quite possibly she'd been chemically incompatible with her first husband. What had pleased her almost as much was the knowledge that her inability to have children with Lee hadn't been her fault entirely.

No baby had been more greatly anticipated than Devin, Jr. As if he knew from the start how much he was wanted, he was a good baby, eating well, sleeping through the night in short order and hardly ever fussing. And he was the apple of his sister's eye.

"Mommy, where's Tammy?" Emily asked, looking around somewhat frantically as her parents settled themselves in the front seat. The doll her grandparents had given her had become her constant companion.

"She's right here, sweetie," Molly answered, handing Tammy over into the back seat, then watching Emily snuggle the doll close. Just as she herself had as a child, her daughter preferred dolls that were babies rather than dress-up Barbies. Molly sighed. "It was a good visit, but I'm glad to be home."

"Me, too," Devin answered as he started the car. His family was terrific, taking Molly and the children to their hearts, but the constant round of dinners and parties had him longing for his quiet life. "I'm ready for our own bed."

"I'm looking forward to that, too," Molly said, smiling. She'd always wanted a big family and now she had one, but there'd been a distinct lack of privacy during their week-long visit.

Still, Molly knew she was happier than she'd ever been. She'd finished her courses and passed her CPA exam, but she'd put the rest of her dream on hold. Because another bigger and better dream had replaced it.

Maybe one day she'd open an office, but right now, she was too busy. They were building a much bigger house for their extended family up in North Scottsdale, and she had to supervise that. Plus Devin's latest book was such a hit that the publisher wanted him to go on tour to promote it and, since he refused to go without his family, they were making plans for that for next summer. Yes, she was far too involved right now for more work. Her family was her full-time job.

"I sure hope Aunt Lucy and Sam took good care of King and Willie and Muffin," Emily said.

They'd given away the other kittens, but Muffin, Emily's favorite, had stayed. But she still refused to call the mother cat anything but Willie. Stubborn, Devin thought, not for the first time. Like her father.

"I'm sure they're fine," he told her.

The ride home was short but by the time they pulled into the familiar drive on Cactus Lane, Emily was dozing, worn out by the holiday activities.

"You carry the little guy and I'll take Emily in," Devin told Molly as he turned off the motor. From inside his fenced yard, King barked a welcome just as Lucy and Sam came out onto the porch.

The next hour was busy as Molly and Devin thanked

her sister and niece for taking care of the animals, and told them they'd talk more after everyone rested up.

After settling the children in their beds and unpacking, Molly wandered over to their telephone answering machine and hit the play button. Minutes later, that's where Devin found her, a frown on her face.

"Bad news?" he asked.

"Just annoying, I think." She walked to the couch, sat down and waited for him to join her. "You remember I told you about Tate's son, Josh, and his father?"

"Sure, the mystery man whose identity only you and Laura know. Did he call here?"

"No, but his aide did. Actually, from what Tate's told me, Rafe Collins is more of a bodyguard than an aide."

Devin placed one arm along the couchback and stretched out his long legs. "What does this guy do that he needs a bodyguard?"

Molly sighed. "I can't go into what he does without revealing who he is, and I promised Tate I wouldn't do that. Let me just say that he's an important man, quite wealthy and hasn't many scruples."

"Sounds like a nice guy. So why is this Rafe Collins calling you?"

"He says his boss wants to know where Tate is. No, actually, he *demanded* to know where Tate is." Her expression, though thoughtful, was also worried.

Devin caught the look and leaned closer to his wife. "What makes him think you would know where your friend is?"

"Probably because Tate and I and Laura have been as close as sisters for over ten years." Molly decided to give him a little background so he'd understand. "This mystery man walked out on Tate and married someone else before she could tell him she was pregnant with his child.''

"The child you and Maggie and Laura helped deliver?"

"Right. So, as I've probably mentioned, she decided that Josh was hers and to hell with the father. Only he came into town one day when Josh was about four and spotted her with him. Of course he noticed the resemblance to himself because the boy looks much more like him than Tate, and told her in no uncertain terms that he wants his son. It seems his wife can't have children. Naturally, Tate wouldn't let him take Josh. So she left town and has more or less been on the run ever since. You remember she'd promised to come to our wedding, then backed out at the last minute? I'm sure she was afraid he'd find her somehow.''

Now Devin was frowning. "That's a hell of a way to live. Why doesn't she go to the police?"

"Because the mystery man is rich and powerful and she's just a small-town woman with limited funds. She's certain she'd never win against such odds." Molly sighed. "And she's probably right."

"Is this the first time Rafe Collins has called you?"

Molly let out a sigh. "He's called once or twice before, and Laura told me he's phoned her, too. But he's never been this insistent. He wants me to meet with him and tell him where they can find Tate."

"The hell you will." Devin got up and went to play the message. His face tightened in anger as he listened. Returning to her, he took her hand. "I don't want you to worry about this, Molly. He left a number. I'll call him back tomorrow. He won't bother us again."

Used to handling everything on her own before her marriage to this man, Molly was nevertheless glad to turn this one over to him. Squeezing his hand, she smiled up at him. "Thank you. You know, the funny thing is, that I really don't know where Tate is, but this big jerk won't believe me."

"I'll take care of it. Is there any way you can get a message to Tate?"

"I can try leaving one with Maggie in Tucson. Tate checks in with her occasionally. Why?"

"I think she ought to know what's going on. Maybe she'll rethink things and decide to quit running, to ask for help. This can't be good for the boy, moving around, changing schools."

The man who'd once said he didn't care much for children was concerned about a boy he'd never met. How far he'd come, Molly thought. "I should have known you'd come through."

"Transparent, am I?"

"*Wonderful* is what you are." She kissed him then, long and lovingly, grateful for her newfound happiness. If only Laura and Tate could be as happy and contented as she. Perhaps one day.

* * * * *

That day might come sooner than anyone thinks! Watch Laura find love, as Tate fears her time is running out, in DOCTOR AND THE DEBUTANTE, coming in July 2000 from Silhouette Special Edition.

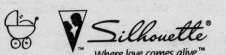

If you enjoyed what you just read,
then we've got an offer you can't resist!

Take 2 bestselling love stories FREE!

Plus get a FREE surprise gift!

///////////////////////////////////

Clip this page and mail it to Silhouette Reader Service™

IN U.S.A.	**IN CANADA**
3010 Walden Ave.	P.O. Box 609
P.O. Box 1867	Fort Erie, Ontario
Buffalo, N.Y. 14240-1867	L2A 5X3

YES! Please send me 2 free Silhouette Special Edition® novels and my free surprise gift. Then send me 6 brand-new novels every month, which I will receive months before they're available in stores. In the U.S.A., bill me at the bargain price of $3.57 plus 25¢ delivery per book and applicable sales tax, if any*. In Canada, bill me at the bargain price of $3.96 plus 25¢ delivery per book and applicable taxes**. That's the complete price and a savings of over 10% off the cover prices—what a great deal! I understand that accepting the 2 free books and gift places me under no obligation ever to buy any books. I can always return a shipment and cancel at any time. Even if I never buy another book from Silhouette, the 2 free books and gift are mine to keep forever. So why not take us up on our invitation. You'll be glad you did!

235 SEN CNFD
335 SEN CNFE

Name	(PLEASE PRINT)	
Address	Apt.#	
City	State/Prov.	Zip/Postal Code

* Terms and prices subject to change without notice. Sales tax applicable in N.Y.
** Canadian residents will be charged applicable provincial taxes and GST.
All orders subject to approval. Offer limited to one per household.
® are registered trademarks of Harlequin Enterprises Limited.

SPED99   ©1998 Harlequin Enterprises Limited

THE FORTUNES OF TEXAS

Membership in this family has its privileges...and its price. But what a fortune can't buy, a true-bred Texas love is sure to bring!

On sale in February 2000...

The Sheikh's Secret Son
by
KASEY MICHAELS

When Sheikh Ben Ramir chose his country over her love, Eden Fortune tried to forget him. But that was impossible—she had borne his secret son. Now the handsome lord of the desert had returned, demanding a place in his child's life—and tempting Eden's long-hidden desires....

THE FORTUNES OF TEXAS continues with
THE HEIRESS AND THE SHERIFF
by Stella Bagwell, available in March
from Silhouette Books.

Where love comes alive™

Available at your favorite retail outlet.

Visit us at www.romance.net

PSFOT7

ENTER FOR
A CHANCE TO WIN*

Silhouette's 20th Anniversary Contest

Tell Us Where in the World
You Would Like *Your* Love To Come Alive...
And We'll Send the Lucky Winner There!

Silhouette wants to take you wherever
your happy ending can come true.

Here's how to enter: Tell us, in 100 words or less,
where you want to go to make your love come alive!

In addition to the grand prize, there will be 200
runner-up prizes, collector's-edition book sets
autographed by one of the Silhouette anniversary
authors: **Nora Roberts, Diana Palmer,
Linda Howard** or **Annette Broadrick**.

DON'T MISS YOUR CHANCE TO WIN!
ENTER NOW! No Purchase Necessary

Silhouette®
TM   *Where love comes alive*™

Name:

Address:

City: State/Province:

Zip/Postal Code:

Mail to Harlequin Books: **In the U.S.**: P.O. Box 9069, Buffalo, NY
14269-9069; **In Canada**: P.O. Box 637, Fort Erie, Ontario, L4A 5X3

*No purchase necessary—for contest details send a self-addressed stamped envelope to:
Silhouette's 20th Anniversary Contest, P.O. Box 9069, Buffalo, NY, 14269-9069 (include
contest name on self-addressed envelope). Residents of Washington and Vermont may
omit postage. Open to Cdn. (excluding Quebec) and U.S. residents who are 18 or over.
Void where prohibited. Contest ends August 31, 2000.

PS20CON_R

Silhouette®

SPECIAL EDITION™

COMING NEXT MONTH

#1303 MAN...MERCENARY...MONARCH—Joan Elliott Pickart
Royally Wed

In the blink of an eye, John Colton discovered he was a Crown Prince, a brand-new father...and a man on the verge of falling for a woman in *his* royal family's employ. Yet trust—and love—didn't come easily to this one-time mercenary who desperately wanted to be son, brother, father...husband?

#1304 DR. MOM AND THE MILLIONAIRE—Christine Flynn
Prescription: Marriage

No woman had been able to get the powerful Chase Harrington anywhere near an altar. Then again, this confirmed bachelor had never met someone like the charmingly fascinating Dr. Alexandra Larson, a woman whose tender loving care promised to heal him, body, heart...and soul.

#1305 WHO'S THAT BABY?—Diana Whitney
So Many Babies

Johnny Winterhawk did what any red-blooded male would when he found a baby on his doorstep—he panicked. Pediatrician Claire Davis rescued him by offering her hand in a marriage of convenience...and then showed him just how real a family they could be.

#1306 CATTLEMAN'S COURTSHIP—Lois Faye Dyer

Experience made Quinn Bowdrie a tough man of the land who didn't need anybody. That is, until he met the sweetly tempting Victoria Denning, the only woman who could teach this stubborn rancher the pleasures of courtship.

#1307 THE MARRIAGE BASKET—Sharon De Vita
The Blackwell Brothers

Rina Roberts had her heart set on adopting her orphaned nephew. But the boy's godfather, Hunter Blackwell, stood in her way. Their love for the child drew them together and Rina knew that not only did the handsome doctor hold the key to Billy's future—but also to her own heart.

#1308 FALLING FOR AN OLDER MAN—Trisha Alexander
Callahans & Kin

Sheila Callahan dreamed of picket fences and wedding rings, but Jack Kinsella, the man of her dreams, wasn't the slightest bit interested in commitment, especially not to his best friend's younger sister. But one night together created more than just passion....